Against the Fading of the Light

Against the Fading of the Light

STU JONES

ISBN-13: 9781514880395
ISBN-10: 1514880393
Library of Congress Control Number: 2015910967
Createspace Independent Publishing Platform
North Charleston, South Carolina

Author's Note

THOUGH THIS STORY can be enjoyed without prior knowledge of previous events or characters, it is the author's intention that this book be read after finishing the first two books in the *Action of Purpose* series, *Through the Fury to the Dawn* and *Into the Dark of the Day*.

It should be noted that certain locations, terrain features, roads, and railways had to be altered or transplanted entirely in order to coincide with events in the story.

This is a work of fiction in the strictest sense of the word. All characters, locations, cultures, tribes, organizations, and events are either products of the author's imagination or are used fictitiously. This greatly pertains to the Native American Comanche Indian Nation. Customs, religious beliefs, practices, and some languages have been altered for continuity within this series. I have done my best to preserve the historical and cultural elements, and any misrepresentation is my doing alone. In no way is this interpretation meant to show anything other than profound respect for these proud people and their vast, rich heritage.

To Kara:
God knew the fears of my heart when he blessed me with you.
As long as you will have me, I will be found by your side.
I love you.

Prologue

 L ONG AGO, IN **a time beyond recorded history, a mighty kingdom trembled on the brink of war...**

Raziel, the high keeper of secrets, took the ancient stone blocks two at a time as he ascended the long twisting staircase. As he went, the heavy cloak he wore shifted against his muscular legs, his sandaled feet powering him upward into the fortress crowned with heavenly lights. He was built like a mountain man and had the wild, unkempt hair and beard of a hermit. His strong, worn brow bent in consternation as he worked the situation over in his mind. No matter how he tried to make sense of it, something was wrong. He was never summoned to the royal court like this without some advance warning. Not ever. He knew the entire kingdom had been thrust into turmoil. It was because one of their own, one of his brothers, had challenged the supremacy of the king. There were whispers that war was coming.

Moving with urgency, Raziel passed between two mighty celestial sentries as he crossed beneath the massive archway of the royal court, the sentries' armor glinting by the low, flickering flame of the white-fire sconces that lined the walls. He gave them a nod and continued on across the open expanse of the outer court, where the high, vaulted stained-glass ceilings gave the breathtaking arena a violet glow. Ducking through the scarlet drape that hung as a crimson partition between the outer court and the inner court, he stepped inside and dropped to one knee, bowing his head low. For a long, quiet moment, he held this posture as if frozen in space and time. With a lowered tone, full of care and reverence, he spoke.

"It is I, Raziel, high keeper of secrets, guardian of the way, and humble servant of the most high king. I have responded here in light of your urgent summons. What is it you desire of me, my king?"

Before him, as he continued to kneel low, a form materialized out of the darkened corners of the room. As it moved, it separated into three distinct shapes, their figures tall and powerful, adorned in glowing armor. "Please stand, old friend. Your king is not present, though his spirit still presides over us, as always."

Raziel scarcely tried to conceal his surprise as he raised his head and stood, looking into the wizened eyes of his oldest friend. "Michael?" he whispered, glancing at the two who flanked the archangel: his standard-bearers and personal guard, Zadkiel and Jophiel, two of the kingdom's most notorious warriors. He turned back to his commander, speaking now with urgency and confusion. "But I was summoned by our great father. Why are you here—and in this sacred place no less?"

"I know this is all highly unusual, but we have all been thrust into perilous times. The heavens are embroiled in a turmoil the likes of which none of us have ever known before. The Dragon has made his move, and his spies are everywhere. We must act with the utmost secrecy."

"The Dragon…" Raziel paused, tasting the words. "Is that what they're calling Lucifer now?"

"It is."

The keeper of secrets hung his head. "He and I came along together, you know. He was once a brother to us, Michael."

— x —

The archangel nodded. "They all were until they began to believe that equality with our great father was something they deserved. Now they are our enemies."

"How many have gone with him?"

"At least a third of our number—maybe more."

"How could they do this? How could they betray us?" Raziel said.

"We don't have time to concern ourselves with that now. War is upon us. The high king has tasked me with leading our forces against Lucifer. We will drive him and his followers from this, our holy realm, and we will extinguish this unforgivable act of treason."

Raziel nodded his head resolutely. "Very well then. I will take up arms with you against these defilers of the throne."

Michael smiled and laid a powerful hand upon the shoulder of his friend. "I admire your devotion, brother, but you have been called here for another reason. This order comes down from the very top, and the task is one of utmost importance."

"Go on."

"You are familiar with the Machine—the secret device our great father has entrusted to your care?"

Raziel froze, unsure if he should answer.

"Raziel," Michael said and smiled, "I know of it. I know you were sworn not to speak of it. And until very recently, you were one of only a very few who knew of its existence."

"How could I be unfamiliar with it?" Raziel shrugged. "It's the most sacred of all the great secrets that have been entrusted to me: the Machine, a device that has the power to create worlds—or destroy them."

"Yes, the very same device our great father created to assist him in *speaking* this universe into existence."

"But you said we were the only ones who knew until recently—how has that changed?"

"Lucifer and his fallen are now aware of the device. Our great father knows the Dragon will make an attempt to seize it in hopes that it will provide him an advantage against our armies in the battle to come."

"No…" Raziel whispered.

"I'm afraid so, my friend. He desires to remake the universe, and everything in it, in his own terrifying image. Time is short, and by now he knows that you possess the most intimate knowledge of its whereabouts. In fact, he may already be making a play for the device as we speak."

"Then there's no time to waste. Follow me," Raziel said, turning and disappearing through the heavy crimson curtain as Michael and the others followed suit.

Across the outer court, they raced, passing the celestial sentries who only managed a brief acknowledgment of their commander as the four blew past. Down the stairs they continued at a breathless pace, their royal garments swishing beneath their glinting, mirrorlike armor. Reaching the bottom of the steps, Raziel took two strides and launched over the open balcony and into the precipice below. As he fell, the others fell with him, their backs arching as immense, light-filled eagles' wings flapped open from under their garments. Soaring across the starry expanse of the heavens at the speed of light, they arrived in moments at Raziel's secret archive nestled in the side of an enormous spire-like mountain.

Landing at the entrance with a few flaps of their brilliant wings, Raziel began toward the door, but his companions remained where they stood, rooted in place behind him.

"What is it?" Raziel said.

But Michael did not reply as he continued to stare forward at the entrance of the archive. There in the darkness of the shadow, several figures stepped forward.

"I knew you would come to try to claim the Machine, Lucifer," the massive shadow before them said as it stepped forward from the mouth of the archive. "You're not as clever as you think."

Raziel's eyes widened as he took in the massive form. Standing there before him was Michael the archangel—the *real* Michael.

The archangel drew his glistening heavenly blade and was flanked by the very imposing and very real Zadkiel and Jophiel. "Stand with us, Raziel! The Dragon is behind you. He has deceived you!"

"What is this trickery?" Raziel gasped as he turned to his companions saw something wicked flicker under the facade of the false images they bore. Without missing a step, Raziel spun, releasing the Blaze from its scabbard on his side as he swung his fiery blade in a rearward arc. "Traitorous devils!" he snarled as he lunged toward the imposters behind him, the white-hot spirit fire of his weapon clashing against the dripping, dark blade of his foe.

Behind the weapon stood the Dragon, his physical beauty already replaced by a rotting, disfigured appearance, the corrupt result of a new existence forged in the absence of God.

"I don't fear you, Raziel, even though you bear a weapon forged by the king himself. You were too easy to bend to my will, you feeble-minded pawn!" the fallen angel hissed. "If it weren't for Michael, our father's lapdog, you would have led me straight to it. But that's of no consequence now. You all may have been created immortal, but you are not invulnerable. I will shed your pure blood upon this stone and seize what belongs to me!"

"You shall not have it!" Raziel growled as he pressed the fight and felt Michael, Zadkiel, and Jophiel join in it beside him. They were moving fast, fighting faster than the speed of sight and sound, heavenly armaments forged in the fires of heaven clashing against each other with blinding flashes of light and smoke. The battle raged as heaven's warriors appeared to get the better of Lucifer and his followers. But then the other fallen began to arrive, first just a few at a time but then in droves. It was only moments before Michael, Raziel, and the others were cut off from the mouth of the archive.

Moving as one, Michael and his standard-bearers came together to form a wedge like the point of a spear. "Raziel, get between us!" Michael shouted. Raziel needed no explanation. While he was highly trained and created of the warrior class, he was not as skilled in frontline combat as Michael and his standards. He was the high keeper of secrets, and the king had seen fit to bestow upon him other strengths. As he slid between them, Michael's voice bellowed again, "Zadkiel, Jophiel, carve your way through these bottom-feeders; they are no longer our brethren. We must make it to the archive!"

The din of battle grew almost unbearable as the three forged ahead, their glistening heavenly weapons cutting down their fallen brothers, as sword and war hammer slammed against armor and shield.

"Forward!" Michael screamed into the chaos.

"Stop these slaves! The Machine will be ours!" Lucifer howled to his faithful.

With an earsplitting crack, several blinding bolts of light struck down upon the cliff at the entrance to the archive, the light swelling and encapsulating the goliath forms nestled within. The battle seemed to slow as all eyes watched the glowing, whirring suits of armor as they came to life, rising, towering above the group.

"That's…" Raziel began.

"Yes," Michael called, "the king's seraphim!"

Raziel watched as true fear slid its way across the faces of the fallen. Before them, the blinding, mechanical hulks come to life with a hiss—the seraphim, the high king's elite guard. Nothing in the heavens, or below, could stand against them. With a titanic boom, the armored giants thrust forward, slamming into the lines of the fallen, whose dismembered bodies flew into the air like scores of shattered mannequins.

"Move!" Michael called to Raziel. "Get to the Machine! Spirit it from this place!"

"Where am I to take it?" Raziel shouted.

"As far from here as possible."

As the group closed on the entrance, Raziel separated from them and stepped into the fray. Dodging left and then stooping low, he leaped high into the air. Swinging the Blaze down into the skull of one of the fallen, he saw the fiery blade cleave the evil creature below him in two. With a parry and counterstrike, he dove for the entrance, rolling and rising, swiping his blade upward to the torn screams of another demon.

Slipping through the warring lines, he made it inside, moving with uncanny speed through the vaults and stores and reliquaries. He only had a small window to act before all was lost. More than anything, he wanted to stay and fight, to stand with his brothers in the heat of righteous battle, the sting of Lucifer's near-successful scheme still fresh in his mind.

But no, his task was why they were fighting. He had to see the Machine safely away. Ducking into a secret alcove, Raziel moved his hand in a practiced manner down the length of the wall. With the sound of grinding stone, the thing was revealed, shrouded in light, an orb no larger than one's fist. Draping a heavy cloth over it, Raziel wrapped it tight and covered it with his hand. The device gave off a slight hum and even slighter warmth. Raziel hesitated. He knew he could not hold it in his bare hand for long. With a final resolution, he plucked it from its place and turned to run—but was stopped mid-step. There, beyond the darkness of the alcove, something stirred.

"Michael?" Raziel called out. "Zadkiel? Jophiel? Is that you?"

"You should be so lucky," a terrible voice intoned from the darkness, deadly fangs just visible beneath black, lifeless eyes.

"Abaddon," Raziel growled. "How could you do this? You…How could you side with the Dragon?"

"Because I like to win. And win we shall."

"You're delusional. Look at you—what you've become. When did this poison begin to eat you from the inside? You used to be like a brother to me; you were my mentor."

"That I was. I suppose you could say I taught you everything you know."

"Not everything. I still know something about loyalty."

The dark shape laughed a menacing sound. "Enough of this squabbling. Give me the Machine. You cannot hope to defeat me; you never could."

"Listen to yourself. Listen to your vanity. Do you really believe that the power of the most high is yours to share?" Raziel spoke with conviction. He sidestepped, jockeying for a better position as he continued to stall. He knew his adversary was right. He did not stand a chance in single combat with this monster. Flight was his only option—flight and deception.

"Why should the power of heaven belong only to one? It is ours to share, and the Machine is our path to redemption! Join us, Raziel. Join us, that you may enjoy the power for yourself."

"Never. I would rather die than abuse the charge the high king has bestowed upon me."

Abaddon laughed mirthlessly. "You are but a sheep awaiting the slaughter. I certainly will oblige you the death you so long for—but it will not be swift. Give me the Machine. Lucifer has commanded me to seize it from you—dead or alive. I will not stop until I have completed this task."

Raziel paused and appeared to labor significantly before looking back up. "Very well. Come and have it then. I am not yet ready to breathe my last," he stated plainly.

Caught off guard by this response, Abaddon was stepping forward when Raziel made his move. In a stunning flash of fire, Raziel swept Blaze from its scabbard and lashed the fiery blade across the eyes of his tormentor. Abaddon howled in pain and clutched at his face as Raziel lunged past him and leaped from the balcony, sailing out into nothingness. As he fell, he arched his back and felt his wings pull free of his garments. But as they did, a crushing force slammed into him from behind as Abaddon clamped down upon his body and with a roar brought his dark blade down across Raziel's back. Raziel screamed like he never had before—the pain tearing a jagged hole in his mind.

"You cowardly fool!" Abaddon raged as he raised his sword again. "You do not deserve the wings of heaven!"

With a shriek of pain, Raziel felt the blade strike down again as his beautiful golden wings cleaved free from his body. He and Abaddon spun, twisting like broken marionettes as they fell down, further into the earth's atmosphere.

"You will not stop me from seizing it!" Abaddon grabbed Raziel by the throat and raised his dark blade one final time. "You will die knowing that you have failed! The Machine is mine!"

Spinning, catching his foe by surprise, Raziel drew the Blaze and pivoted upward, sinking it to the hilt into the chest of the fearsome beast. Enraged, the monster struck Raziel across the neck with a crushing blow from the back of his arm, knocking him away and sending the Machine flying into the dark.

They dropped through the earth's atmosphere, their bodies catching fire and streaking across the night sky like falling stars. Raziel gasped, his strength draining from him as he watched the Machine and Abaddon fall with him down into the earthly realm. He knew his chances of surviving the fall without his wings were nonexistent. All he could do now was pray; his final whispered hymn was one he knew well, the words spilling out as his consciousness faded from him. "Holy father, guard your secrets against the wicked—for it is you alone who can protect them."

Part I

Ashes and Dust

The light shines through the darkness, and the
darkness can never extinguish it.

—John 1:5

When a lion or a bear came and carried off a sheep
from the flock, I went after it, struck it, and rescued
the sheep from its mouth. When it turned on me,
I seized it by its hair, struck it and killed it. The
Lord delivered me from the paw of the lion and the
paw of the bear.

—1 Samuel 17:34–35, 37

1

*U*NDER A DESOLATE charcoal sky, the motley caravan of dust-covered vehicles led by the fuel tanker truck with *American Oil Products* in faded script along its length slowed and shuddered to a halt along a deserted and dusty stretch of South Carolina's Highway 45. Before them, a small army of bandits blocked the road, some with bloodthirsty smiles on their faces. Behind the convoy lay the remains of the Francis Marion National Forest, blackened by fire, the trees but burned stalks stretching upward toward the cloud-covered sky.

With a long squeal of hydraulic pressure releasing, the large tanker truck loaded with precious unleaded fuel rocked from side to side and became still. A time passed, and it became unclear whether the occupants, due to some fear or uncertainty, planned to exit the vehicles at all.

"Well?" Malak, the leader of the Coyotes, stepped forward from the barricade, his huge muscular body quivering with powerful, dark energy. "Looks like you want to make me wait all fucking day."

As the driver of the tanker exited, a gusty coastal wind whipped up the sand and dust at his feet with bits of trash and created a scene, not unlike a long-forgotten western showdown. With a hesitant push, the man clicked the cab of the truck shut and stepped to the ground. Following his lead, the doors to the vehicles behind him opened, their occupants emerging into the dark day. As he reached the ground, the truck driver brought his hands together and began to rub them. "We ran into a few snags, boss…"

"Is that supposed to mean something to me?"

The man swallowed hard. "Uh…we assaulted the radio station according to plan, and…uh…we did pretty good. Got the tanker like you wanted." The man motioned at the full tanker of unleaded fuel behind him.

"And?" Malak questioned.

"Raith took that woman he had his eye on. Tied her up. We burned the rest of them inside the station. Children too, just like you sa—"

"Where are the rest of my men?" Malak growled.

The man wrung his hands together. "They…uh…That giant hit our group just as we left with the tanker. The guys that were still there—they tried to fight him, but he tore them apart. Some of the guys say he's invincible. That he's sent from God—"

Without warning, Malak launched through the air with a snarl, his body crashing through the sound barrier and crossing the space in a flash. The unsuspecting man didn't get a chance to scream before the ferocious bandit leader slammed into him. In an instant, his body was eviscerated, muscle separated from bone, fluid from vessel, as his corpse came apart in a pink mist under the force of the cloaked man. The explosive sound of a thunderclap followed.

The men behind the obliterated truck driver fell on their faces, moaning in dismay as chunks of meat and clothing rained down around them. The goons stationed at the roadblock let fly a wild, slur-filled cheer. The cloaked man stood motionless as bits of blood and bone continued to drip from his garments.

"Beg me for mercy," he intoned.

A myriad of voices called out from the shuddering, bowed figures before him: "Please! Please! You are a god! We worship you!"

"Let it be known," Malak yelled, as the men behind him fell silent, "that the next one of you that mentions the name of God will share the fate of this worm. God is dead. His warrior Kane and the others are dead. I killed them. There is nothing left but this wasteland and the darkness of despair that inhabits it. Do I make myself clear?"

The bandits behind him, his Coyotes, gave a resounding "Yes, my lord!"

Malak gazed upon the men prostrate before him. "You," he said, pointing a heavy finger toward one of the closest bowed men, "continue the narrative."

The man tried to stand, his legs wobbling beneath him like a newborn fawn. He knelt back down, mumbling something about being sorry. The goons along the barricade laughed and made lewd gestures. Malak motioned to his second, a rough man with a painted blue face and a long, braided ponytail.

"Saxon, stand this gutless piece of shit up."

Saxon stepped forward and seized the man by his collar. "Stand and give account to your lord!"

With great effort, the man stood, the front of his pants blossoming with a dark stain as he began to urinate.

The bandits laughed again. Saxon swore, "You nasty son of a bitch, give your account or lose your life!"

"Www..." the man stuttered and licked his dry lips, "We thought we were good, my lord. We burned the radio station to the ground. Did it with everyone inside. Even the children."

"And?" Malak brooded.

"Raith took the woman he wanted. Had her tied up and everything. But as we were leaving out of there, the giant returned. He was pissed about what we had done. Killed a bunch of our guys."

For the first time, Malak raised his head and allowed the bloodied hood to fall away from his bald head. Breathing in deep through his nose, he surveyed the darkened sky. He had known the giant would be a problem again. A constant thorn in his side, he was the only member of this pitiful resistance that had a chance of standing against him and his Coyotes.

His day will come soon enough.

"Continue," Malak growled.

"We left outa there. Raith and some guys were behind us, but we lost them." The man gave an involuntary shudder, expecting the violence that didn't come.

Malak stared on, his eyes, formless black holes in his face.

"We doubled back," the man continued, "found the truck… found Raith and the others—they were all dead. The woman was gone too. Looked like an ambush."

Malak paused, mulling this information over. Raith had gotten himself killed over that woman. Fucking idiot. He had been an obsessed, incompetent loner—something Malak didn't need. It was just as well.

Turning to survey his gang of murderous bandits, he worked it over in his mind. Could it have been some other outlaw group? Mutants? No. Something was wrong here. It was one of the Christians, the giant or another one of them who had survived. He took another deep breath and allowed the darkness to soothe him.

Like a miserable rash, they just won't go away.

"What about the woman I sent against Kane's group? She was captured from their group. Shana, was it?"

The man shook his head. "I don't know of her, boss. We came straight back here."

Malak curled his lip in disgust.

"Please spare us, Lord Malak! We are forever loyal!" the bandit moaned.

The thought of partial success irritated Malak beyond belief. Most of the Christians he'd encounter wouldn't or couldn't fight. They would be slain as they clung to the hopes they placed in an unsympathetic and vain God. But this group was different. They had been willing to test his claim to power, and they demonstrated this by a significant show of force. Just a handful of these insignificant Christians had been capable of untold damage to his cause. It had been an expensive lesson for him—now only to find out that two, maybe three, had survived his retaliation. He had intended to wipe out this stubborn enclave once and for all, but it would seem fate had different plans.

"Lord Malak," Saxon said, "is this going to be a problem?"

"No." The brutish warlord rolled his shoulders. "I will proceed as planned. This changes nothing. Kane and the other Christians are dead. He died knowing that his children, his legacy, have been taken as my slaves." He motioned to the two children, Michael and Rachael, who sat in the back of a nearby truck tied to each other with deepening looks of terror written across their little faces. "My only real opposition—those stubborn fools at the radio station—has been wiped out. This is what's important. The fact that the giant and the woman live is inconsequential. Alone they are nothing. They can't stop me now."

"And them?" Saxon motioned toward the cowering group of men who had failed to succeed in their mission.

Malak gave a deep sigh, as though decisions of this kind were below him. "The men need an example, and I cannot abide weakness. Cut out the eyes and tongue of the pathetic worm who gave his account. Leave him along the road with some symbol of our passing."

Stu Jones

Saxon nodded with a smile and gave a flick of his wrist. The man began to moan as he was dragged away by two murderous goons.

"Reinstate the other men. Until my plan is complete, I will need as many soldiers as I can get."

"Yes, my lord, and where are we headed?"

"Up to I-40. We'll head West from there."

"And may I ask what's West, Lord Malak?"

Malak's lips spread into a wicked smiled as he turned away from Saxon and moved toward the convoy. "Blasphemy," he whispered, the word slipping away into the whipping of a dusty wind.

▲ ▲ ▲

In the darkened room, cluttered and ransacked, a man stirred, a soft moan escaping his lips as he lay alone on a single cot. As he moved, his bandages and the sutures beneath them began to pull. A fresh grimace flashed across his face, and a cold sweat beaded across his brow as he wrestled with the pain and anguish that now plagued his dreams.

In the shade of a nearby corner, the great form of Courtland Thompson raised his face from his hands. Below him, the chair creaked in protest under the weight of his massive bulk. Every inch of the aging former professional athlete's eight-foot, five-hundred-pound frame sat unnaturally still. His earnest brown eyes surveyed the man from where he sat enveloped in troubled thoughts and the quiet that filled the space between them.

So much had happened. The world as they knew it had ended. It had been fast and furious, drowning the planet in plague and fire. Few had survived. And yet still, God had been there, preserving Kane and Courtland and uniting them with the others that God had

— 8 —

chosen. They had felt the presence of God, as it directed them, but none of them had known the magnitude of what they were starting when this all began—what it would do to them. From the beginning he had known it wasn't going to be easy, but this had truly tested his faith.

Courtland had done everything he could. He'd fought for the lives of the innocent and tried to protect his friends. For what? For the enemies of God to come in and destroy the people he now knew as family anyway? So many had been lost, and now only he and a few others remained. It was almost too much. He knew he shouldn't allow the thought in, but he just couldn't stop it.

How could a just God allow this?

He rubbed at his face and eyed the still form on the table for a moment longer. Rising, he moved to his friend's side and pulled an old wool blanket up over the shivering body of Kane Lorusso as he began to whisper a few ancient words to his friend.

"I have many enemies, Lord. Many fight against me and say, 'The Lord will not rescue you!' But you are my shield, and you give me victory and great honor. Though ten thousand enemies attack from every side, I am not afraid."

Kane stirred, his face twisting in agony.

"Yes, that's right, brother. You fight it. You have to fight. We need you."

"Any changes, Courtland?" Jenna whispered as she pushed halfway through the doors of the examination room. "I heard someone talking."

"It's just me, Jenna. I felt like he should hear my voice."

She turned her gaze upon the unconscious, defeated form of Kane Lorusso, lying on the dingy cot. "What happened? How did this happen, Courtland?"

Courtland took a moment to collect his thoughts; there was so much. "The Coyotes happened. Malak happened. You know first-hand what that man is capable of. All he's ever wanted was to ruin Kane—to ruin all of us. All that we went through in the past few weeks—every bit of it was done to divide us. They used Kane's family to bait him."

"Oh…"

"They made him choose, Jenna." Courtland looked up at her, his deep brown eyes full of sorrow. "He had to let his wife die so he could try to save his children, only for them to be enslaved by the Coyotes. They took everything from him, and then, they meant to murder him."

"I…I didn't realize…" Jenna lowered her head.

"Whatever his previous shortcomings, whatever our personal divisions, we have to stand together now."

Jenna gave an earnest bob of her head. "Of course."

Courtland looked his friend over. "He's shaking pretty bad." The giant glanced at her with genuine concern. "Is that normal?"

"For a man who came as close to death as he did…yes. His body is trying to fight off the infection." She stepped into the room and crossed to the side of the beaten, disheveled-looking man, who lay shivering on the cot. "He's going to have to ride it out. Hopefully he's strong enough to beat it."

"How bad are his wounds?"

"They look worse than they are, though that's not to say his injuries aren't bad. The vest he was wearing stopped two rounds to the chest. The third hit the edge of the Kevlar and only had about an inch of penetration into his abdomen. That's the main infection site. The head wound looks bad but is just a flesh wound. To take a bullet in the skull at point-blank range and for it to not penetrate…he's hardheaded."

"We've known that," Courtland said and smirked good-naturedly.

"That's about it. Add in a couple of decent lacerations and contusions due to fighting and his fall from the cliff."

"Need anything from me?" Courtland said.

She shook her head and pushed her hair out of her face. "Supplies—more clean or bottled water for hydration and wound irrigation. I need more to cover him at least for the next few days. That makeshift IV has worked well enough." She motioned to a suspended, overturned plastic liter-size water bottle with a length of rubber hose running from it to the needle in his arm. "I've been able to introduce some fluids and a solid initial dose of Keflex to help him fight the infection. I could use more though. I don't know if it will be enough. Either way, it's going to be a struggle for him."

The giant smiled and patted the quaking body of his friend. "If there's anything Kane knows how to do, it's struggle. The rest is up to God."

Jenna turned her attention toward the giant, her thin frame almost childlike before his great athletic bulk. "What about you?" she said, touching his arm. "Have you slept at all?"

"I'm alright."

"Courtland," she said, giving him a scolding look, "you need to rest. You don't do us any favors if you're exhausted too."

"I know, but I can't leave him, Jenna. I left him once. I won't do it again. He's lost so much…I want him to know he's not alone."

"He knows."

They stood in the silence of the dim, cluttered room for a moment before Courtland spoke. "We'd be lost without you to patch everyone up, Jenna."

"Thank God, instead. It was sheer providence that you found this clinic. Even though it's been picked over and ransacked, I still found enough usable stuff to stabilize him."

"And you? How are you holding up?"

"I'm fine. A little sore and banged up from the past few weeks of fighting mutants and getting kidnapped—again. But you know, it's no big deal." She flashed a small smile at Courtland.

"And Dagen?"

Her countenance darkened. "He'll be alright. Surprisingly, the stab wound in his leg is clean."

Courtland shook his head. "I have no idea how he did what he did, coming after you and all."

Jenna nodded. "Well, that makes two of us."

"I believe God is working in him, Jenna. You're a big part of that."

"Look, Courtland, I've been thinking," Jenna changed the subject. "I'd really like to go back to the sta—"

"Jenna, we talked about this," Courtland interrupted, his demeanor growing serious. "I don't think you should go back there. There's nothing left of the radio station. No one would have survived what I saw. Going there is just going to break your heart. The children are gone, Jenna. Everyone that wasn't killed in the mutant siege was burned alive when the Coyotes raided. I don't know what we have to gain by going back."

"I have to go. I have to see for myself."

Courtland pursed his lips. Jenna was a strong-willed person, and he already knew he wasn't going to win this fight. "Okay, but do me a favor. Stay with us for now. We can't take any more chances with you. If something happens to you out there, then who's going to take care of us?"

Jenna looked up at the giant and smiled, nodding her agreement as he touched a meaty hand to her arm.

"One step at a time, my dear Jenna, and when Kane is stable, we'll all go, together."

Jenna gave a knowing look. "And then what? After all we've been through, what are we supposed to do now?"

"At all costs, we must pursue the will of the Lord." Courtland's eyes seemed to drift far away as he spoke the words with stone conviction. "And the heart of our God burns for justice."

▲ ▲ ▲

Kane strained his eyes but saw nothing in the unyielding tomb of black. His senses seemed to be functioning, except for his eyes. He could hear the muffled sound of anguished cries somewhere in the distance and smell the smell of something pungent burning, the rotten stench of it stinging his nostrils. And his mouth—what was in his mouth? It was filled with smoky leaves and dry twigs that made a rustling sound when he tried to work his jaw.

Think. Remember where you are.

The strange filling in his mouth, dry and uncomfortable, swarmed backward toward his throat. He panicked. The thought of choking was overwhelming, suffocating here in the warm dark of this place. He gagged, his stomach heaving upward inside him.

Remember you. Remember who you are, and the rest will return.

He stretched his legs outward, reaching down, reaching for the ground, reaching for anything beneath him. He touched nothing. He thrust his arms outward, reaching slow for any solid thing, then madly as he began to flail. He was suspended in the unyielding, oppressive inky black. Spinning and whirling in the darkness, he felt the twiggy bundle in his throat push farther back as it began to gag him.

"Agh!" The sound of his own garbled screams slipped away into the nothingness.

This must be hell. The agonizing torment that occurs in the void left by the complete absence of God.

As this dooming realization lay down upon his spirit, he felt the weight of it begin to crush him.

Oh, God. I have forsaken you.

Nothing moved in the black.

I deserve this, forever.

Still nothing remained—nothing but sadness and despair hanging inside him.

Stop! Think. This can't be hell. Remember who you are.

Choking, spinning in the black, he began to calm his mind.

Calm. Think. My name...My name is Kane Lorusso, and I'm not dead...yet.

In a flash of light, Kane found himself on a seaside cliff as the wind whipped at his clothes, the smell of the garbage-filled sea pushing its way into his nose. It was beautiful. But something in his vision changed, a distortion, like looking through a rain-soaked windshield. The clarity of the dream took hold and became real. His heart dropped in his chest. He knew this place.

No. Not again. I can't.

Before him on the edge of the seaside bluff sat his fierce, determined wife and his innocent children. His wife alone and his twins together—they were tied up with rope. The children were crying.

Please. No. I can't go through this again.

As if his mind were in fast-forward, the scenes flashed before him. The thugs sneering, his family crying, and then as clear as day, Malak was there, inches from his face, his scarred mug plastered with a wicked grin.

"Tell them it's going to be okay. Lie to them."

Dear God. I can't do this again.

"I want you to know…This is the dark future you and your God could not prevent."

No, Susan, please.

"Save our children, Kane."

Jesus, save us! Please, save my family!

"Choose!" Malak raged, the thugs kicking everything he loved over the edge of that cliff as he screamed and threw himself forward. Everything was moving faster now—the flashes of memory coming at blistering speed. He was crying, the tears blurring his vision, the rope searing its way through the fleshy meat of his hands. He'd tried to save all of them. He'd tried so hard.

"When you see your whore of a wife," Saxon said, sneering, through the fog of his dream, "tell her I've got her kids now." Gunshots. Silence.

Frozen before him, the terrible scene sat emblazoned in his memory. His wife had been murdered and his children enslaved by a man possessed by a living demon. Kane had been unable to stop them on his own. He'd thought he didn't need God's help. He was wrong. These evil bandits, the Coyotes, had then tried to kill him too when they'd shot him and flung him from a seaside cliff—but he wasn't dead. He had survived survived for a reason. He always did. The words of his dear wife clanged like a million iron church bells inside his head.

"Save our children, Kane. Save them. Promise me."

"Susan, don't leave me…"

"Save them, Kane. Everything I've done has been to spare them. Don't let it be for nothing."

As he heard his own voice speak the words, they sounded lifeless, broken—just a frail oath hanging by the thinnest thread.

I promise.

2

TYNUK SAT ON the dusty desert turf with a heavy rope lashed around his midsection. The evening was growing long as night crept in, gliding into existence beyond the faceless, shrouded clouds. This was not where he wanted to be. Not like this. These Comanche were supposed to be his people, and he had expected a far different reception than the one he had received.

He was now their prisoner, and they had stripped him naked, an act intended to humiliate him. The older boy with the broken nose, Neraquassi, made a point to humiliate him further every chance he got. Tunuk had now been spit on, slapped, and Neraquassi had even gone so far as to urinate on Tynuk's head and face. It was clear the warrior was still enraged that Tynuk had gotten the best of him during their first encounter.

In a moment where Tynuk was forced to defend himself, he had done so effectively—as Neraquassi's flattened nose attested to. There have always been bullies. In every time, in every culture, they've existed. And the only thing a bully understands is force—the force they apply against others and the force applied against them to make them stop. But Tynuk's mind was far from the present, shameful condition he now found himself in as he sat naked on the barren ground.

He closed his eyes, the crisp wind of the Palo Duro mixing with the granulated particles of the canyon rock that stung his skin. He needed guidance. He thought he had done what Grandfather wanted. Why had his own people, true-blood Comanche Indians, greeted him with such hostility? Had he made some mistake? Was there some customary or ritualistic gesture he had omitted? Or had he simply misjudged the character of his people and how they would receive him?

Sitting there, his mind drifted back to how it all had begun—back to the origins of everything. He had been a nobody, a trailer-park kid named Reno Yakeschi, whose full-blood Comanche father walked out on him and his mother when he was a very young boy. His life had fallen apart; the only reprieve from the school bullies and the excesses of his abusive mother came in the form of a quiet old man, his father's uncle, Nuk'Chala. The old man, whom he had always called Grandfather, saw the boy's needs and agreed to take him in under his wing. He taught him the ancient ways—what their people referred to as *tsumukikatu*, the quiet spirit, as well as the coveted *narohparu*, or *naro* for short, the name of the Comanche's ancient, mythical style of close-quarters combat and weapons training.

It had taken years for him to master these disciplines, to calm the angry tempest in his mind, temper the flame of his spirit, and harden the fibers of his body. But when he had emerged, he was no longer Reno Yakeschi. He had become something else—something fierce and fearless. He had become Tynuk, the warrior.

His fearless nature was emboldened by the constant companionship of a fearsome, wolfish beast. A creature of truly fantastic appearance and proportions, like the fabled shape-shifting lycanthrope, conjured into this world from one much more ancient. Tynuk had stumbled upon and befriended the strange, wolfish pup back when all this begun. For the creature, he had chosen the name Azolja, or *vigilant one* in the ancient tongue of his people. To date, it had been most appropriate. The beast followed his every move like a loyal dog, always there, always regarding him with those majestic silver eyes.

Where the beast came from, he didn't know, but they belonged to each other now, truest of friends in the darkest of times.

Tynuk squinted and scanned the nearby rock outcroppings for any sign of his friend. He was sure his dark companion was watching from some distant ridge. Always watching and waiting, the beast would bear witness to the entire ordeal—and it would be difficult for Tynuk not to call upon him for aid in this upcoming trials. But he could not. This was his burden to bear, and he refused to accept any help in proving himself in what was to come. He would rather die.

There was a purpose in this. Everything happened for a reason, and even in this dark place, some hidden purpose still remained. He could feel the Great Spirit moving as it spoke to him. The winds of change were blowing, and there would be no stopping the events that would now unfold.

What the boy did know was that he was a prisoner of these warrior people—these survivors whom he shared blood with and who had one foot in the old world and one foot in the new. He also knew that because of his claims, because of his training, and because of Grandfather's belt that he'd carried, he would have to prove himself. He feared the uncertainty of this more than anything. Grandfather had prepared him well, but this trial would take something more— something he didn't possess.

Tynuk leaned his head back against the cold, dust-covered boulder behind him as his eyes searched the sky for some break in the oppressive, black cloud cover. His mind began to wander, reaching back to his friends at the radio station; to Courtland, Kane, and Jenna. He hoped they were alright, though, like some terrible premonition, he sensed that they were not. He didn't know how he knew, but he did. Something had happened. Something terrible. All that was left for him now was to trust. He had to believe that this was all a part of their destiny and that it had been put in motion long before they had each chosen to follow this path. He had to trust. It was all that remained.

"Great Spirit, guide us," the boy whispered as he felt a dark cloud of uncertainty encircle the shallow warmth of his heart.

His name was Dagen. That was it. Dagen, the former US marine. Dagen, the career criminal. Dagen, the one-time lieutenant of Malak's wasteland gang of bandits, the Coyotes. But all of that was in the past. Now he was just Dagen—a broken man with a sordid past and a complicated future, a man desperate for true purpose and real redemption.

He rotated the small, blackened twig between his fingers as a putrid, garbage-tainted ocean breeze blew inland, ruffling his hair. He tossed the twig to the ground and pulled his thick military-surplus jacket tighter around him. He didn't know what to believe anymore. Didn't know who he was supposed to be or what he was supposed to do. All this business of God and purpose swirling around inside him made him feel crazy. Why would God want anything to do with a man like him? He had murdered innocent children. He wanted to believe Jenna. He wanted to believe more than anything that there was such a thing as redemption for a man like him, and recent events had almost convinced him. He couldn't have done what he had without outside help, without the protection and empowerment of something greater. The way his broken body had been so emboldened, so filled with strength. It now seemed dreamlike to him as he recalled the moment, dashing in to rescue Jenna from the clutches of those sadists. It felt good, really good, to protect her—to do something good for her. Jenna. The lingering thought of her caused his skin to tingle.

She'd pulled him back from the brink. For some inexplicable reason, she had shown him mercy on him. Mercy, even after he had murdered her husband and infant child. After he held her hostage, then stood by as the Coyotes raped her and abused her. What kind of person could forgive that? Jenna could. She'd told him that God had spared him for a reason. That Jesus had died for him—that even *his* life could still have value. It was almost too much for him to believe. When he hit the very bottom, she was there with, gentle, consistent guidance toward the truth. And even though he hated himself for it, he knew without question that, because of her devotion, he loved her. He loved her with unbridled desperation, and he knew there was no distance he wouldn't travel, no battle he wouldn't enter, to secure her safety. He would never be able to do enough to atone for his injustices against her.

"Ugh," Dagen sighed with exasperation as he pushed at the twig with the tip of his boot. It was enough to make a man lose his mind.

The door to the clinic squealed open as the subject of his thoughts emerged, pulling her jacket on. Dagen looked over to catch her glance. He cleared his throat.

"How's he looking?"

Jenna gave him a strange look. "You're concerned?"

Dagen held up his hands. "I can't ask how the man is doing?"

"You can ask. I just didn't think you cared."

The words stung, but she wasn't wrong. To say he and Kane had never gotten along was putting it mildly. Dagen was sure it had something to do with Kane's disposition as a former police officer and the fact that their first encounter involved a fight where Kane knocked Dagen over a third-story balcony, a fall that cost Dagen the use of his legs.

"Okay, I'll concede to that. What I'm saying is I just think he has been through enough. I mean, aren't we all supposed to be playing for the same team now?"

"Yeah," Jenna nodded and shoved her hands into the pockets of her jacket.

"I…" Dagen paused, considering his words. "I think something has been started here. I don't know exactly what it is, but I think Kane is at the heart of it. And he's going to have to be there to finish it—that's all. Everyone deserves a second chance."

"Yeah, they do." Jenna nodded. "And sometimes a third and a fourth." She paused, a strange little smile on her lips. "You've come a long way, Dagen."

Dagen ducked his head and grabbed his crutches to avoid having to acknowledge this praise. "So, what are we doing then?"

"We're in limbo for now. We've got to wait and see how Kane does. Then, regardless, it looks like we're headed West. Like you said, something has been started, and it might be up to us to finish it."

"That will mean confronting Malak, again."

Jenna nodded, a grave look on her face.

"Nothing good ever comes of that," Dagen said as he used the crutches to help himself to his feet. "So what do we need?" he asked.

"We need to scavenge more supplies before it gets dark. Courtland will stay with Kane. We'll take the Jeep."

"Yes, ma'am," Dagen said with a mock salute.

Jenna playfully rolled her eyes. "Just get in the Jeep. I'm driving."

"What? You don't trust me?" Dagen gave a false gasp as he hobbled along.

Jenna moved to the Jeep's door and opened it, dropping a backpack and an AR-15 rifle in the back. "Let's just say my experience with you and vehicles tends to make me feel a little out of control."

"I can live with that." Dagen pursed his lips as he pulled himself into the passenger seat and loaded his crutches. "Where you wanna go?"

Jenna turned to him with a spirited look of defiance in her eyes as she cranked the Jeep and it roared to life. "We're not supposed to, but we're going back to the radio station."

Dagen drew a 1911-style handgun from its holster on his hip and racked a round into the chamber. "Let's do it then," he said, snapping on the safety and jamming the weapon back down into the leather holster.

▲ ▲ ▲

In the semi-darkness of the murky operating room of the small, disheveled doc-in-the-box clinic, Kane Lorusso's eyes flashed open. Wild with fear and panic, they jerked back and forth. His body spasmed, his legs flailing across the tabletop as all manner of bottles and instruments were sent clattering across the floor of the small room.

"Nnnnnnnnn...Sssstop!" he moaned in pitiful desperation as he clawed at his surroundings and rolled from the table, falling to the hard floor with a thump. "You can't! You can't!" he shrieked at the top of his lungs as he bucked and rolled across the trash-strewn floor.

Behind him, the door burst open as Courtland's huge frame pushed into the room. Dropping to his knees with a wince, he scooped Kane up off the floor and pulled him against his massive barrel chest. "It's alright, brother; I've got you. You're safe now."

"No!" Kane clawed at the giant. "You can't have them! I won't let you take them from me!"

"Shh..." Courtland whispered, "it's over, brother. You're safe. You're alive. It's me, Courtland. I will protect you."

Kane became rigid, his body freezing in place amid the thick arms that encircled him as the words began to soak in. A trickle of blood dripped from just below the crease of his elbow where the IV had been yanked from his arm. "Courtland?" Kane whispered.

"Yes, brother, I'm here."

Kane's posture drooped, sagging with the weight of his failures. "Courtland," he moaned, "don't let them hurt my family anymore. It's not their fault. *Please.*" He cried, the tears dribbling from beneath his swollen eyes.

Courtland shook his head as his own tears splashed down across the body of his friend. "I'm sorry, Kane. I'm so sorry I wasn't there to stop it."

"My Susan. She's alright? It was a bad fall, but she's alright?"

Courtland clinched his jaw. "No, Kane. She's gone. She's with the Lord now."

Kane began to quake, his body shuddering with the tremors as he gasped. "Oh, Susan, I'm so sorry. I was all wrong. If I had just…If I could've just held on to you a little longer…" He said, sobbing.

"You did everything you could, brother. There's nothing to be ashamed of."

"If I had just listened to you, Court. You were right. I killed my Susan. I killed her just like I killed Molly."

"Stop."

"Just like I killed Jacob. Let me die, Courtland."

"Stop it, Kane."

"Let me die, please. I'm no good to God. I'm no good for anyone."

"No, it's not true. We all fail. We all fall short."

"Just let me die, man. Everything I love has been taken from me again. I was so selfish. I caused this to happen, and my family paid the price of my arrogance. What is left for me to go on with?"

"Listen to my words, brother," Courtland said, composing himself. "Listen to me and hear my words. Your children are alive."

Kane grew still. "They can't be. They were taken…" His voice cracked. "They were taken by that monster. I can't bear the thought of what's happened to them."

"They're alive."

"Why do you keep saying that? Don't fill me with false hope."

"It is not false. They are far from safe, but they are still alive."

"You can't possibly know that."

"Just trust me. Your children are alive, but they are held captive by Malak and his Coyotes."

"Courtland," Kane mumbled, "and if they are? If that's true… what am I supposed to do? How do we fight against such an evil?"

"We fight it with the power of the almighty God."

"God has left me to my own devices."

"No, he never left you. But he did let you suffer the consequences of your choices—your sin."

Kane lowered his head.

"But that's in the past now. Now it's time for you to decide where you're going to go from here. Are you going to let this destroy you? Are you going to go to your grave beaten and ruined? Or are you going to allow yourself to be redeemed? To take up this mantle and be the man God created you to be? I told you once that God will always take you back, no matter the score. That he'll never hide his face from you. But the question is—do you believe it?"

Kane nodded.

"No, sir," Courtland grunted. "I want to hear you say it."

"I…believe it."

"Say it with conviction!" Courtland shook Kane.

"I believe it!" Kane cried.

"As well you should. Look how far we've come—what we've accomplished so far. Our God has saved us from this world, from our very hearts, and this—our story—is not fully written yet. It is far from finished."

"So, what are you trying to tell me? That we can still save my children? That we can somehow stop Malak?" Kane faltered. "Courtland, you didn't see…I shot him in the face and then watched the hole mend right before my eyes. How does a flesh-and-blood man destroy something like that?"

"We destroy it with the power of heaven. That is the only weapon that will devour this demon."

"You seem so sure."

"Because I *am* sure. Our God has pursued the darkest corners of our hearts, and he has prevailed there. He has saved us from monsters and demons before, and he will *not* fail to win the day now. Let's not forget that you were shot in the face as well—and here you are." The giant smiled.

Kane touched at his scalp and winced.

"You, Kane, are here to bear this burden. It is you who must see it through. This is your purpose, as it is mine. And together, with the power of the Lord at our backs, we will see this thing through to the end."

Kane gave a deep sigh and rested his hand on Courtland's heavy forearm. His swollen features seemed to relax just a little.

"Thank you for being here with me. I need you, brother."

"I won't leave you again, my friend. Not until this is done. Because now, it's time for you to come back home. Now it's time for us, all of us, to believe again that anything is possible."

"I believe it." Kane nodded as one last tear slipped from the corners of his bruised eyes. He sniffed and gave a firm nod of assurance.

"I believe."

3

MALAK'S FATE HAD been sealed from an early age. There was life, and there was death. And then there was this place, this strange existence between worlds. It was not a place of comfort or security, as evidenced by the dull aching that rippled across every inch of his huge muscular body. It was a pain that grew with each passing day. Though uncomfortable, this place was also a place of power. What he'd given up in the human quest for comfort and pleasure he received tenfold in power—unbridled, vicious, life-consuming power. And since comfort and pleasure had always been foreign concepts to him anyway, he had accepted this toxic gift with open arms. All he'd ever wanted for as long as he could remember was power. As much power as he could possibly entertain—he wanted it all. He wanted to rule and conquer and enslave. He wanted to forget the weakness of the past, the days before the Voice. He wanted to be God.

Malak lowered his head and considered it, this faint memory of the past, and how he'd come into the knowledge of the Voice. It had been anything but a pleasant experience. But it was one, nevertheless, that he would remember forever.

It was a Friday night, and he was strapped to the modified recliner, as usual. It had always been like this, ever since his mom left them when he was just a small boy. His father, a twisted psychopath of a man, had somehow maintained custody of him in the absence of his mother. As a result, Malak lived more like a prisoner than a child, trapped in his own version of hell by a cruel twist of fate. He did not attend school. He did not have friends. He did not play or have hobbies. Chained or strapped to something almost twenty-four hours a day, his existence was little more than that of an animal, a slave forced to wordlessly grunt and grovel for scraps under his father's table, eating them off the floor like a dog when a few bits fell. He was a doomed person, a child who lived in constant fear of retribution and the activities that his father made him watch.

It was summertime. He was eleven years old. The humid south Texas night drenched him in a fine mist as he sat and watched his father work. The woman struggled, gagging as his father choked her against the hardwood floor of their living room.

Malak shifted his eyes down and pulled against the leather, buckled straps his father had fashioned to the chair to hold him there.

God help me.

It was no use. He groaned as he pulled against his prison. The sound stopped his father. The cruel man released the woman and turned toward him, the dim light of a single bulb in the ceiling behind him lighting his back and the black-and-blue face of the gasping woman on the floor.

"You were trying to get out," the shadowed face said to him.

"I wasn't."

"You were, and now you must be punished."

"No, I was just uncomfortable. Please—" Malak cried.

His father lunged forward and slapped him hard across the face, grabbing him by the throat and choking him against the soft cushion of the chair. It was always choking. His father loved the dominating power it gave him over others—the gasping, the eyes wild with fear, spittle frothing across the lips as the body fought against the suffocating, panic-inducing position.

His father laughed and released him, giving Malak's hair a jerk backward as he leaned in toward the boy's face. The smell of the man's stale body odor covered him as his father bared his teeth, hissing through them. "Stop being such a weak fucking coward. You're pathetic. Watch and learn how a man behaves."

The woman was moving again, rolling onto her stomach and trying to push onto all fours. How many women had it been now? There were so many Malak had lost count. With this one, just like the others, his father had used him, his son, to charm her and make himself seem safe at the local grocery store. Malak's father had offered to carry her groceries home. She'd seemed unsure. When he insisted, she accepted. On the way there, he stated that he needed to grab a rain jacket for his boy—just in case. She had been courteous and agreed to make a quick stop with them by their house—inadvertently sealing her fate. The young lady had been nice to Malak, inserting a quarter into one of the dusty machines at the front of the store. He had gotten a green gumball just like he wanted. His father faked a smile and allowed him to chew it, though he could tell by the look in the man's eyes that the idea of the boy having anything he enjoyed irritated him. A green piece of sugar you could chew now seemed like such a stupid thing to get excited about.

"No. No. Please don't—" The half-naked woman was drooling blood and mumbling when the man forced her back to the floor by the back of her neck.

"Would you like to go home?" his father asked with a syrupy tone.

"Yes, yes, sir. Please. I just want to go. I won't say anything to anyone. I swear." The look of terror in her eyes was tangible. She was so young, only ten years older than Malak. A young woman who would have had her whole life to look forward to had she not met them. Had she not been so polite. But Malak didn't care about her. He wanted out; he was tired of being controlled, tired of the power this man he called Father exerted over him. He wanted to be free. He wanted the power for himself.

God help me. Get me out of here!

"You're lying," his father growled. "You'd go straight to the police, and I can't have those sons of bitches sniffing around here—not now."

"I wouldn't. I wouldn't lie to you," the young woman babbled.

"But you already have," the man said as he began to choke the woman again, her feet swimming small flutter kicks against the dark hardwood of the floor.

God, please, I'll do anything—

It was then that the Voice spoke to Malak for the very first time.

He doesn't love you. He's not listening.

"What?" the boy whispered to himself.

God—he doesn't love you, but you love you, and I want to help you take the power for yourself.

"Who are you?"

I am your ally, your savior. I am the power that you crave. I can free you from this place, but you must first do one thing for me.

"I'll do anything."

Kill him.

Malak shook his head, wincing at the pain in his mind. He looked to the left, pulling his eyes from the woman groaning on the floor as she clawed at the darkened form of his father. The room was empty except for the three of them. Strange—it had sounded so real. Then it spoke again.

Kill him or remain his slave here forever.

Malak swallowed hard and squinted against the stinging of the Voice. "How?" he whispered, so his father wouldn't hear.

I'll set you free. You'll be free to do as you wish. Kill him, and the power is yours for the taking, boy. That's what you want, isn't it?

"Yes."

Then stand, and kill him.

Malak looked down: the leather straps across his arms lay open before him like a strange magic trick. The woman was still now as he stood from the chair and took two quick steps to retrieve the cleaver from the kitchen counter nearby. Malak approached from behind his father, who was still kneeling over the woman. The man turned, a snarl upon his lips as he saw the boy.

"How the *fuck* did you get loose? Sit your weak ass down in that chair right now, or I'll beat you fuckin' stupider than you already are."

Malak smiled, something dark now hiding behind his eyes as he raised the cleaver.

"What do you think you're gonna do with that? You don't have the balls, you stupid bastard kid! You'll never be anything! You're—"

Malak brought the cleaver down fast as his father raised his hand to try to stop it. The blade cleaved the man's hand in half between the fingers and continued through the meat of the forearm. With a sharp gasp, his father stopped, his mouth hanging open as a spray of blood jetted onto the floor. "You cut me, you little bastard! Put that down and help me! Help me!" he shrieked.

Malak raised the cleaver again.

"No, stop! Don't!"

"How does it feel to be powerless?" the boy said with evil glee. With a chunking sound, Malak brought the cleaver down again and again into the skull of his father, the warm blood, and bits of bone spraying across his face as the boy began to laugh.

▲ ▲ ▲

Malak inhaled the smell of charred flesh, a smell that wouldn't be that different from a roasted pig if it weren't for the aroma of burning human hair. He was very pleased with himself, and though the

Voice did sometimes chastise him, he could feel that now it was pleased with him as well. He was the crucial piece of the puzzle, the true coming of the Voice. He alone had the power to make it real on this new earth.

For a moment Malak considered his bleak past. Murdering his father had only been the beginning. Untouched by the justice system over the incident that was pitched as a terrified child defending himself against a serial killer, he had come away from it more or less free. Well, not exactly free, but free enough. For years he bounced from foster home to foster home, caught between the system and abusive or neglectful foster parents. This had not been a good experience by any stretch, but the reign of terror his father had subjected him to was over.

It was his turn to be the monster. Over the years, the Voice inside him grew and matured. It worked behind the scenes, affecting every decision and influencing every move he made as he grew from boy to man. When the Voice told him to strangle the neighbor's harmless cat, he did it. When it told him to rape and beat a cheerleader at school so badly that she was comatose, he did that too. There was nothing he wouldn't do for the Voice and for the power he could feel cultivating inside him.

For Malak, falling in with a gang early on was a no-brainer, and committing himself to a life of crime seemed like the obvious choice since there was no question that he was suited to the nature of criminal efforts. On top of that, the Voice protected him from the law. Evidence ceased to exist, witnesses turned up dead, and a majority of his cases were dismissed. Somehow, out of all the evil shit he did, he was convicted only once, in a silly misdemeanor case over a public disturbance. It was laughable. The Voice chided him, telling him that there was greatness in store for him if he would only heed its words and guidance. Greatness indeed. He had no idea that the events marking the end of civilization would take place the way they did. What he did know was that the Voice had a plan, and he was the focal point of it. Malak knew that, because of the Voice, he had come a long way from those early days of powerlessness—and he would now go much further.

The pungent odor of cooking flesh was beautifully unmistakable as it wafted across the encampment toward him. His men were hungry, and he had encouraged them to indulge the darkest corners of their depraved natures. This small settlement was a scattering of desperate, dirty, makeshift tents filled with desperate, dirty, makeshift people. They had screamed and cried and begged for their lives. Only a few that tried to fight were slaughtered. His Coyotes had ransacked the area, pillaging and murdering as they went. Then the raping of all who had surrendered began—women, children, and even the surviving men and a few dead bodies. His soldiers had urges, and he intended that they fulfill their basest needs and darkest desires. It's what the voice wanted when it had told him, *God is dead. Nothing is sacred. Everything is yours if you will only seize it.*

No longer did foolish notions of chivalry, honor, or morality fit into the equation. The world was now a depraved place: the law of the land, manifest destiny. If one had the means to seize something, then one was obligated to seize it and do what one wished with it. It was that simple. There were no longer any laws. No more rules. Only the survival of the fittest—it was chaotic and horrific and perfect. It was his world. Nothing could stop him now in his journey West—his quest to find and unite with the final thing the Voice needed to begin the coming of the Master's reign.

"Lord Malak."

The large, cloaked man stirred from his moment of contemplation and spoke with a slight twinge of irritation in his voice. "What?"

"These fucking kids won't stop crying. Saxon wants permission to do his thing with them an' then shut 'em up, for good."

"No. He's not to touch them. I need them pure. Innocent."

"But, Lord—"

"What the fuck did I just say to you?" Malak growled, standing, towering over the man.

"You said not to touch them," the man almost whimpered.

"That's right. I need their innocence. It must be palpable enough for me to consume when the time is right. You can scream at them; you can beat them; you can deprive them of food if you wish. But you will not rape them, or injure them until they have served their purpose. After that, I couldn't care less what you do with them. But until then, you all will show some restraint. If you or Saxon or anyone else has a problem with that, then I can have the rest of the men slaughter and eat you as well." He gestured to the nearby fire where a thug was rotating a metal spit with a large chunk of meat on it.

"No, Lord, no, I understand. It's just…"

"What?"

"They won't stop praying."

"Grow the fuck up. They're children. Gag them and then beat it out of them. But show some restraint. My wrath knows no limit."

"Yes, Lord."

"Praying." Malak huffed and made a disgusted face as he spat out the word. "They'll give that up as soon as they realize it'll only bring them more suffering."

The thug hurried away, and it wasn't long before the shrill screams of the five-year-old fraternal twins rose in the humid night air. It was a singularly beautiful sound, the screams of Kane's children. It sounded like subjugation and hopelessness and victory. Malak let a broad smile creep across his face as he settled in beside the fire and allowed the children's cries of terror to soothe him to sleep.

4

WITH A SWIPE, Tynuk's restraints came free. The warrior boy wasted no time leaping to his feet and bringing his hands up in front of him in a defensive fighting posture. The encircling crowd laughed, jeering as he stood there naked, bruised, and covered in canyon dust. His thin, muscled form, stronger than it should be for a boy his age, was just visible in the early morning darkness of the canyon as the light of dawn grew behind him.

"Look at him!" one of the young warriors mocked, waving a torch forward. "This hairless creature has yet to become a man."

The crowd laughed. Tynuk flushed, the blossoming of a terrible rage growing inside his chest. He closed his eyes and slowed his breathing. Anger would only serve to distort the path he must now try to find amid this mess.

"Yes, he is just a boy," Neraquassi said. "A lying thief who thinks he's a great warrior. A child who carries around a stolen Comanche war belt so that he may try to steal the honor tied to it as well."

That's it.

Tynuk stooped low, snagging a handful of red dirt from the ground, and flung it in the direction of Neraquassi, who quickly sidestepped the thrown debris and yanked a knife from his belt. Immediately several warriors stepped forward with their weapons at the ready.

"I bested you," Tynuk said, pointing at Neraquassi's flattened, broken nose. This released a few chuckles from the crowd. Neraquassi scowled.

"You aren't afraid of an outsider, are you?" Tynuk called out. "Surely a *boy*, naked and unarmed, is no threat to you? Ahh, but what if he is?" Tynuk said, his eyes wild. "What if I am that dangerous?" He pointed at the young warrior, their eyes locking for a long, tension-filled moment. "You'll regret not having killed me when you had the chance."

"That's enough of that," war chief Queenashano, said as he stepped to the front of the crowd. He shot a cutting glance at Neraquassi, who was huffing like an angry bull. "Remove yourself and go make ready for the trials."

The young warrior reluctantly ducked his head and turned away, the crowd parting as he went.

"You have a fire within you," Queenashano said, turning his attention back to Tynuk. "Something guides your actions, but it is unclear to me what or why." He paused and seemed to consider his own words. "It is for this reason that I have decided to spare your life, for the moment, and instead let fate tell us what it will of you through the trials of the ancients."

The crowd grew hushed, as though the mere mention of the trials demanded a show of respect. Tynuk looked around trying to gain any new knowledge of what these trials might have in store for him. But the faces of the crowd were like a still pool of water, where nothing could be seen. Tynuk blew out an exasperated puff of air.

"Okay, I'll bite. What is it you expect me to do?"

Queenashano, who seemed pleased with himself for baiting the question, just smiled. "We expect you to die."

The battered, bullet-hole-riddled Jeep eased to a stop along the access road in front of the emergency radio control station. Beyond the charred façade, a few isolated fires produced tiny wisps of smoke that seeped from the doors and windows, pulled from the blackened building by the garbage-tainted ocean breeze.

Jenna sat back in her seat and pulled her hands from the wheel. She sniffed, wiping a single tear from her eye as it fell. Dagen glanced over at her, noting her emotion as he looked back toward the burnt husk that had been their home for most of the previous year.

"I didn't think it was going to be this hard to see," Jenna said, wiping her face again.

Dagen nodded. "A lot went down here—good and bad. But I guess Courtland may be right. What good does it do to come back here? This isn't our home anymore."

"I know. I just wanted to see for myself. Besides, we stored a lot of supplies here, and the Coyotes couldn't have taken everything. It's worth a look."

Dagen pursed his lips. "Guess I can live with that."

Jenna took her foot off the brake, and the Jeep began to roll toward the main gate. As they went, the scenery before them evoked a wash of memories: the perimeter fence, twisted and ruined like some hellish roller coaster; the piles of rotting, half-charred corpses, both human and mutant; the heavy doors to the outer cellar, where the children had hidden, standing wide open. Jenna clenched her jaw and pulled the Jeep into the center of the courtyard, where she brought it to a stop.

Exiting the vehicle, Jenna grabbed her rifle, and Dagen swung his feet out, helping himself up with his crutches. He looked at her for a moment as she surveyed the building. "Go where you want, but I'm gonna be behind you. We're not splitting up. There's no telling who's taken up here since we left."

Jenna simply nodded, her mind far away as she walked toward the front of the building and stepped around the eviscerated bodies of several wasteland bandits. She motioned with her head. "Courtland was here."

"Yeah. I can see that."

"Let's make this quick, Dagen; with all these bodies, this place is a biohazard."

"Yeah."

Taking careful steps to avoid the masses of bodies, friend and foe alike, they made their way through the first floor of the station. Stopping before the burned double doors of what had been the make-shift medical clinic Jenna had helped run, she raised her hand to touch the door.

With a squeal, the brittle door pushed open on blackened hinges. Jenna gasped and pulled her hands to her mouth. She shut the door back. "I can't go in there. I can't do it."

Dagen said nothing as he moved around her and slowly shouldered the door open. In the center of the room was a large grouping of charred skeletal remains. Many of the forms were quite small. They'd found the children.

"Damn," Dagen said as he furrowed his brow and regarded the sad scene. The small, charred forms huddled together en masse with a few adult ones, most of them with hands clasped, no doubt praying in their last moments.

"Come on, Jenna; let's grab what we can and get out of here."

"It's my fault." Jenna whimpered, trying to be strong. "I couldn't stop them when they came for us."

Dagen stopped her with a hand on her shoulder. "Hey," he said and paused, uncomfortable with all the emotion. "Look, you did the best you could. Nobody thinks differently."

"I should be on the floor in there with them."

"Then who would take care of us?" Dagen gave a sincere smile and urged her forward. "Come on. Let's go."

Jenna nodded, but just as they turned to go, something moved at the other end of the darkened hallway. Immediately Jenna's rifle and Dagen's 1911 flew up, locked in the same direction down the desolate corridor.

"You're surrounded," a voice called out from the darkness.

"Says who?" Dagen shouted.

"Put down your weapons and leave this place, and we won't shoot you where you stand."

"I recognize that voice." Jenna screwed up her face.

"Put down your weapons and leave now!"

"Put it down and let's go, Jenna." Dagen motioned. "It's not worth it."

"No, wait," Jenna whispered. She paused, listening. "Winston?"

Silence.

"Winston, is that you? It's Jenna."

"Jenna?" came the sheepish reply.

A huge smile broke out over Jenna's face. "Winston!"

"The radio-room guy?" Dagen murmured.

Out of the shadows, the pudgy figure emerged holding a bolt-action rifle. "I...I can't believe it. Jenna, Dagen, you guys are alive! I was sure we were on our own for good."

"We?" Jenna asked.

"Yeah." Winston sheepishly opened the basement door to reveal a handful of dirty, hungry little faces crowded on the steps; behind them, a few of the adults from the medical bay stood, staring up at them with expectant faces.

"Jenna!" the children called out as Jenna gave a cry and dropped to her knees to hug them.

"Man, it's great to see you guys." The old gentleman named Sam sighed with relief from behind the children.

Jenna hugged the kids close as they all cried, and she whispered a few words of comfort to them. After a moment she stood, gave a hug to Sam, and turned to Winston.

"What happened, Winston? How did you—"

"I couldn't rescue everyone…" Winston hung his head. "When those bad guys came, I just did my best to get as many kids and injured folks as I could. I got them down into the radio room without anyone seeing us. They never even looked down there. It was a real good thing too, 'cause I'm not sure I even know how to use this thing." He motioned to the rifle. "I made up that bit about you being surrounded to try to scare you off."

Jenna grabbed Winston by the shoulders. "Winston, you are so incredible and clever and brave!" She gushed as she grabbed his face and kissed him on his cheek.

Dagen smirked from behind her, and the children giggled.

The shock and awe on the pudgy young man's face were replaced by a crimson-red blush that was visible even through the dirt and grime. Winston couldn't help himself as he unleashed a big, goofy, gap-toothed smile. Everyone laughed as they all put their arms around each other and took a moment to revel in the warmth of simple companionship, and even the smallest of victories.

5

KANE OPENED HIS eyes, his body still, his hands folded across his chest as he lay in the quiet of the ruined clinic. The thin sheet that covered him rose and fell with the rhythmic cycle of his breathing.

His fever was gone, but it hadn't been for long; the sheet over him still clung to him, damp with his sweat. How had he survived this? He slowly moved his body, and though painful and stiff, he felt alive. His eyes tracked across the makeshift IV. He wouldn't be recovering like this without Jenna's constant care and the healthy dose of antibiotics she'd recovered. He owed her another apology. Actually, he owed everyone an apology.

Exhaling, Kane brought his hands up and rubbed at his eyes. So, God wanted him to live after all. But how could a wounded, conflicted man like him possibly make this right? How could he go on, after everything he'd done—after everyone he'd lost? Kane pulled his hands down his face and rested the backs of them across his mouth, his eyes roaming in restless arcs around the room. He couldn't sit here anymore watching the minutes tick by, knowing the fate of his children might still hang in the balance. It was time to get back on the horse. Time to start down that road less traveled. Courtland was going to be so pissed at him.

Before he had time to reconsider, Kane rolled on his right shoulder and off the narrow cot, where he flopped against the ground, gasping like a fish out of water. He was sure the impact pulled some of his stitches free. Summoning all his strength, he began to execute slow, smooth push-ups, his arms flexing and contracting as he raised and lowered himself to the floor.

"One, two, three, four," he mumbled to himself in pained cadence. It was a struggle in his weakened state, but he forced himself to make it to fifty before resting. Lying flat on his stomach, he rolled onto his back and began to do sit-ups, groaning out the count as he executed each movement.

"What do you think you are doing?" The deep voice came from the doorway behind him.

"Mind your own business," Kane mumbled.

"I heard a crash, and you *are* my business."

Kane didn't miss a beat as he continued to sit up and lie back again against the cold, dirty laminate tile floor. "I'm doing sit-ups."

"I can see that. You're supposed to be resting," Courtland grumbled.

"What are you, my mother now?" Kane continued to work as he rolled back onto his stomach and began pushing again. Though he looked at the floor, he could feel the penetrating gaze of his friend from across the room. He lowered himself to the floor and rested as he looked up at his massive old friend. "What?"

The crow's feet in the corners of the old giant's eyes deepened as a smile formed across his broad face. "Stubborn as a mule. Always have been."

"You call it stubborn. I call it determined."

"Very well, my friend. I'm just happy to see the Kane Lorusso I know and love is returning. Just don't overdo the push-ups, alright? We've got a long road ahead of us—and we need you well."

"Yes, mother," Kane said as he pushed up and pulled his knees under him, wincing at the pain.

"Easy, that's what I'm talking about." Courtland stepped over and pressed a clean dressing against the wound in Kane's abdomen, which was weeping again. "Let me help you."

"That's fine, man. I just can't stay in this room anymore."

"Good, because I have something to show you outside."

Courtland helped Kane to his feet and supported him as he hobbled across the room and out into the interior hall of the ransacked clinic. Taking easy steps, Kane gritted his teeth at the effort as they navigated the cluttered hallway.

"We've traveled some bad road recently, but that time is over. As the good book says, 'The light shines through the darkness, and the darkness can never extinguish it.'"

"What are you talking about, Court?"

"I can feel it in my bones. We're back on track."

Kane let out a loaded sigh. "And how do you know that?"

"Because," Courtland said, smiling and pushing open the front door of the clinic to reveal Dagen, Jenna, Winston, and the other men, women, and children who had been recovered from the radio station, all gathered before them, "God still chooses to bless our efforts."

"Oh..." Kane faltered, as Courtland supported him further. "It's not possible."

"You're not the only stubborn one around here." Courtland tossed his head at Jenna and Dagen. "They found these survivors at the radio station. I suppose that justifies the fact that it was stupid to go alone." The giant looked sideways at Jenna, who nodded in silent agreement. "But as you can see," Courtland said, opening his arms and gesturing to the others, "we're not yet finished."

The others approached and put their hands on Kane, some grabbing and shaking, others patting him on the back or arm, as a host of voices greeted him.

"Thank God you made it!"

"Good to see you, Kane!"

"Glad to see you on your feet!"

"Praise God for you, Kane."

The praise was almost too much for him as Kane lowered his head and fought back the tears. *What did I do to deserve this? I abandoned these people to die.*

"I, um," Kane shook his head as he looked up at those gathered around him, his eyes bleary. "I don't know what to say. I don't deserve this kind of loyalty from you."

"We understand, Kane." Jenna put her hand on his chest. "We understand, okay? There's nothing you need to atone for."

Kane composed himself. "How did you guys survive?"

Jenna smiled. "Well, Courtland is…Courtland." She shrugged playfully. "Dagen rescued me from the Coyotes, who captured me… again." Kane looked up to see Dagen standing at the back of the group, his eyes averted as though he hadn't heard the accolade. "And Winston here," she motioned for the pudgy man to step forward, "single-handedly saved everyone else, including these children."

Kane swallowed and wiped at his face. He looked up at the group. "I owe you all an apology. I abandoned you."

"It was your family, man." Winston piped up. "Which of us wouldn't have gone after our own?"

"Winston," Kane said and turning toward the pudgy man, "during that whole thing with the Sicks, I treated you like you were a coward. You aren't. You did good, man. You did real good."

Winston beamed, his chest puffed outward.

"Jenna, I'm sorry—"

"Stop, Kane. You don't need to apologize anymore. I'm serious. We understand."

Sam piped up from the rear. "We're with you, Kane. We always have been."

"We've talked about it." Jenna looked him in the eyes. "What else are we going to do? We have to help you get your kids back."

Courtland turned to Kane. "We're all behind you, Kane. Until it's finished." The group before him responded in agreement.

Kane paused to consider it. He had a handful of people, a few of whom were still wounded, a few children, a reformed criminal thug with broken legs, an angelic caregiver, and a giant filled with the power of heaven. There were no more than twenty-three to their group—and that included the children. If rescuing his kids was even remotely possible, he was going to have to trust again. Just like Courtland said, he was going to have to trust that anything was possible.

▲ ▲ ▲

A dry, dusty wind rose hundreds of feet out of the Palo Duro Canyon, whipping Tynuk's long, dark hair against the unshielded nakedness of his lithe frame. He stood near the edge of the canyon, flanked on either side by warriors much older than him and twice his size. Their unmistakable iron grip encircling his biceps remained a clear reminder that he was without question their prisoner. And though surrounded by so many of his own people, many of whom had come to see the spectacle, he felt completely and utterly alone.

He knew it was foolish to believe that he could survive this, that he had any chance of overcoming the trials of the ancients. But deep in his chest, there was a spark. The tiniest glimmer of hope that the ultimate path of the spirit was somehow greater than his current situation. He remembered something his grandfather had told him years ago. He said that belief without trust was nothing more than fantasy, but belief bound to trust required a personal investment, a showing that you truly had faith that your belief would sustain you. His grandfather had likened the description to a chair. One could believe that it would sustain one's weight, but it wasn't until a person trusted in it by sitting that they discovered that what they believed was real. It was time to trust.

Queenashano stepped forward as the crowd parted to make way for the Comanche war chief. As he walked, he wore a confident smile upon his face that betrayed his true intentions. He knew Tynuk was as good as dead. Queenashano stopped before Tynuk, raised his hands to the small crowd, and spoke in Comanche. Tynuk struggled to make out the entire meaning.

"We are but a small war party, encamped here on the mighty Palo Duro, and soon we will again move westward to rejoin with our brothers who now move under the guidance of Penateka. I have sent a rider to inform him of our situation and how our return shall be delayed by the running of these trials."

The crowd of short, round-faced people murmured their approval, as warriors in light battle dressings held their weapons close in the morning half-light. Tynuk surveyed the group. No more than 150 people, and that included the women and children—none of whom were warriors. The old patriarchal culture was still strong in this New Comanche Nation.

"This boy," Queenashano said again, "claims to be a great warrior. He claims that Nuk'Chala instructed him in our ways, and he believes he has a right to carry a sacred Comanche war belt that he himself did not earn. He is at best a liar and at worst a murderer and a thief. Our ways demand that he be put to death if he is guilty of these things. But there is still some part of the story missing, and I will not make a rash decision in this matter just yet. Instead he will be forced to endure the trials of the ancients—the sacred ritual that our ancestors created for separating those of pure purpose and unmatched skill from the rest. It is in these trials that his fate will be determined.

Though it is possible to succeed, one false move, one misstep, will mean his end."

This solicited another murmur of acknowledgment from the crowd. Queenashano turned to the group. "Who will answer this call and test the boy?"

"Nu suana takwainitu!" Neraquassi stated as he stepped forward, his eyes and the bridge of his nose now black and blue.

"Nu suana takwainitu," stated another proudly dressed warrior.

"Nu suana," called another as he stepped forward and placed a fist over his chest.

This continued until eight warriors in total had stepped forward to accept the challenge of administering the trials.

"Good." Queenashano took a step toward Tynuk. "Are you ready to begin, young Tynuk?"

"Yes," the boy stated, his face betraying no emotion.

"Very well, then. The trials have begun. Now I will ask you three very important questions that you must answer quick without contemplation. Should you pass this test, you will carry them with you in your heart on this journey."

Tynuk remained motionless.

"Whom do you love the most in this life?"

Tynuk did not hesitate. "My mother."

Queenashano continued. "What do you value most in this life?"

"The teachings I have received from Grandfather Nuk'Chala."

A few warriors in the crowd snickered, but Queenashano silenced them with an outstreatched hand. "And what is your purpose in this life?"

"To serve the Great Spirit with everything that I am."

Queenashano looked long and hard at the boy, his steely gaze attempting to penetrate through the boy's emotionless visage. He motioned at the sky. "Taahpu, Big Father, cares not for us. He has left us to our own devices. You are a fool for answering this way."

Tynuk clenched his jaw. "Those are my answers. You don't have to like them."

After what seemed like an eternity, the clan leader straightened and waved his hands toward the naked boy as he spoke to the crowd. "He has failed the trials already." Queenashano turned to the men flanking Tynuk. "Kill this bastard child and throw him into the canyon."

Tynuk felt the men on either side of him tense and shift as one drew a knife from his belt, and knew he only had milliseconds to react. As the warrior on his right came across, thrusting the knife into where Tynuk's chest had been just moments earlier, the boy dropped his weight and yanked to the right on the arm of the man to his left. The bloodcurdling shriek that followed told him everything he needed to know. The man on his left fell to the ground with the knife buried deep in his chest as the man on his right lunged toward him.

It was in this moment, as he calculated his next movement, that something flew into his face. At first, he thought the wind of the canyon had blown dust into his eyes, but as they began to burn and his vision distorted, he knew it was something far more sinister. The boy cried out and tried to clear the chalky, white cloud away from him as the burning powder seared its way into his eyes and up his nostrils and crawled its way into the back of this throat. He was so preoccupied with the imminent feeling of suffocation that he hardly realized the other man had grabbed him again. Before he could think, he dropped his weight again, this time twisting and pinning the man's hand to his shoulder as he spun. Tynuk felt his toes curl and grip what had to be the edge of the canyon as he hip tossed the man over the edge and into the abyss. The man never made a sound as he pinwheeled into the dark void of the canyon below.

"Wunu hupiitu!" Queenashano threw his hands in the air, his warriors stopping short, their short spears aimed at the blinded boy.

"What did you do to me?" Tynuk gasped.

Queenashano laughed. "You are skilled, boy, but you have failed the trials before they have even begun. You failed to answer correctly. You have shown us the weakness of your true heart. Now it is time for you to die."

"You didn't even give me a chance! What did you do to me!"

"Since entering the spirit realm is part of the trials, I brought with me the ground powder of the datura plant. In medicinal doses it allows a warrior to walk in the realm unseen, to know the spiritual. But since you have already failed the initial test, I have instead given you a lethal dose. There is no cure for what will happen now. Even with all your skill, you cannot fight it. It is known as 'the devil's snare' for good reason."

"You poisoned me..." Tynuk tried to calm his mind as he repossessed himself. He was trapped against the cliff face, and time was running out. There was only one thing left for him to do.

"Wait for him to weaken and fall; then sever his head and throw the rest of him over the edge." Queenashano spoke to his warriors with utter confidence.

Only one thing left.

Queenashano and the rest of the Comanche war party watched with visible astonishment as Tynuk turned and flung himself from the canyon rim, his body soaring out into open space, falling, tumbling like a discarded doll into the mists below.

6

THE MENACING CLOUD cover that had rolled and churned like the open sea above them for the last year and a half, was finally showing weaknesses. Whether Mother Nature was actually ridding herself of the filth in her atmosphere was still questionable, but the breaks in the oppressive cloud cover were unmistakable, tiny cracks of light shining through the oppressive barrier of soot and storm.

"The light shines through the darkness, and the darkness can never extinguish it," Kane said to himself as he watched the slits of light open and close, shifting against the blackened ceiling of the world. He went over everything again in his mind. Ice-skating uphill was the analogy that came to mind when he considered what was to come next.

Courtland told him that he'd recovered Susan's body and buried it next to Molly at the radio station. Kane had all but demanded that they stop one last time at the radio station, so he could say good-bye before they departed and headed west. Courtland had of course agreed and set the others to scavenging the area of the station while they waited for him.

Kane arrived at a sloping sand hill and touched his hands to the tops of two short rebar crosses that jutted out of the sand at the foot of a few short mounds.

"Well…" Kane paused, his eyes drifting past the waste-tainted ocean to the horizon beyond. "I'm still here." He offered a weak smile. "Guess that's my curse. I get to stay while everyone I love slips through my fingers." He looked to the somewhat-fresh grave and lowered his head. "Hey, baby." Kane paused, struggling to find the right words. "I'm going to get our kids back. I don't know how, but I made a promise to you, and I'll die before I stop trying. That means I've got to go West. I have to try to catch up to the bad guys before they get too far—before they get away from me." Kane struggled to fight back the emotional tidal wave that gathered in the depths of his heart. Strange, the way old failures always had a way of threatening to steal his resolve. He swallowed and ran a hand over his beard. "I just wanted to say good-bye, since I may not get another chance. You were the best part of me, and…I miss you, baby." A tremor shook through his body, and Kane thought for a moment that he might lose his composure. "I couldn't save you. I couldn't even save myself. I did my best, sweetie, but I tried to do it on my own—I suppose that's the whole point. I'm not big enough to save us. I won't cut God out of this anymore. I won't make that mistake again with our babies. I promise." He ducked his head. "You and the kids are my heart. I love you so much. Always will."

Kane took a breath, composed himself, and turned his focus on the second, well-worn grave. "Molly, this is Susan, whom I told you so much about. I'm glad you guys get to rest here together. At least that makes me feel a little better." He paused, searching for the right thing to say. "We're going on an adventure, Molly. I know how much you loved a good adventure. Wish you could go with us…" Kane patted the cross one final time. "Take care, kiddo. I'll never forget."

Kane turned and did not look back as he moved with as much speed as he could muster toward the front of the station. As he went, his mind swirled with mixed memories of the past, horrific tokens of his ultimate failures.

He rounded the corner, wincing with the effort, to find everyone in motion, carrying items, gathering their few supplies and weapons and loading everything up into the caravan of old vehicles. It was time to put the past behind him. He needed his mind right for what was to come next.

Kane took a moment to inventory their resources one last time. In addition to whatever they'd found here, they had twenty-six people, five vehicles, eight rifles and handguns, a handful of various ammunition types, and just enough scavenged food, water, and fuel to get this journey started. They would need more resources soon, or they wouldn't make it far.

Kane huffed and rubbed his forehead. And where exactly were they going? Courtland told him that Malak was headed to some as-yet-unknown location in New Mexico or Arizona. All they could do was go up to catch Interstate 40 and head West. About the only thing they had going for them was the fact that Malak and his savage group were anything but subtle. He wouldn't know yet that they were being followed, and it was more than likely that they'd be carving a trail of death and destruction across the heartland as they went—a trail that would be all too easy to follow.

Kane took a shallow breath and eyed the group, who now appeared to be slowing. He winced and leaned back against the outer brick of the clinic. The wound in his abdomen had stopped weeping and started itching. He supposed it was a good sign, though the change didn't do anything for his comfort. As long as no further complications arose, he should be on his way to a full recovery. How long that would be, however, was a whole other question.

Courtland motioned from across the way, questioning if he was ready to depart. Kane nodded.

"Hang on, Kane," Jenna said as she approached and slipped under his arm to help him to one of the vehicles.

"I'm fine," he managed to say as he made a painful grimace.

Jenna nodded. "I know, but that doesn't mean I can't help," she said as she helped him toward the caravan of vehicles. "Get to say good-bye?"

"Yeah," Kane muttered.

"I never got to meet Molly or Susan, you know. I think the three of us would have been friends."

"They would have loved you. I have no doubt."

Jenna smiled, opening the door to an older-model Chevy truck and helping Kane into the passenger seat. She produced a full-size GLOCK handgun and pressed it into his hand. "Here. It's one of the few. I know you feel vulnerable without one." Jenna smiled again.

Kane bobbed his head sincerely. "Thank you, Jenna. Really. Thanks for everything."

"Don't thank me, Kane. Everything happens for a reason. After all this, I have to believe that."

Kane winced with morbid thoughts. "I just can't stop thinking about my kids. What they must be going through…"

"Don't do that." Jenna shook her head. "Don't do that to yourself. We're going to find them and we're going to bring them home."

Kane nodded and lowered his head.

"You ready for this?" she said, her question reaching much deeper into his heart than he anticipated.

Kane took a minute as his eyes wandered up the lonely stretch of ruined highway before them, to the unknown fate that awaited each of them. He turned to Jenna with a weariness that seemed to know no end.

"I guess it's time to find out," Kane said and shrugged as he pulled the door to the truck shut.

As the small entourage of vehicles pulled away, a woman watched with great interest from inside the shadow of the blackened radio station. Kane was alive, and she had just found her ace in the hole. She turned and limped away from the cover of the building, toward a hidden vehicle that was awaiting her return. It was time to finish these cowards. She had waited far too long already.

▲ ▲ ▲

"We're going to follow them."

"Follow them?" the ugly man snapped at the woman, who was acting like she was in charge.

"You're actually too stupid to live, aren't you? Kane is alive. Malak wanted him dead. What that means is Malak *thinks* Kane is dead, or he wouldn't have left him alive! He's going to want to know this."

"So what are you saying we do?"

"Take Kane a fucking bouquet of flowers and a get-well card," Shana quipped. "What do you think, you idiot!"

"Call me an idiot again, and I swear—"

"You'll do what? Idiot," Shana snapped, raising her AK-47 rifle and staring a hole in the ugly bandit who looked on with disdain.

He glanced at the other two dim-witted Coyotes they had gathered in their search for Kane's group. Neither of the men flinched at her openly threatening him. He dropped his head. So, she was going to be in charge after all. The dirty man gave an exasperated sigh. "What are you proposing, woman? Get to the point."

"The name is Shana. And the point is, ass clown, that we can't return to Malak empty-handed." She dropped her rifle and let it hang from a sling on her shoulder. "Do you want to go back like that? Would you want to face *him* empty-handed—a failure?"

"What kind of question is that?" the man mumbled.

"Exactly. You don't. And neither do I, which means we have to make ourselves useful again."

"And?"

"We're going to follow Kane's group and exploit them. We're going to find out what their plan is and return to Malak with news of his pursuers."

"You know where Malak was headed? How we can find him?"

"I know where we can find out." Shana winked and tapped the side of her head. "You gotta use your noodle, dipshit. Because when we take this group to him on a silver platter, he'll have no choice but to draw us back into the fold, maybe even make us generals in his army."

"Yeah," the bandit greedily rubbed his hands. "That sounds alright."

"Besides," Shana boasted, getting into the blackened, dust-covered Datsun pickup with her rifle, "I've got a job to finish."

The bandit appeared puzzled. "Which means?"

Shana rolled her eyes and put her feet on the dash. "It means Kane and his people have to die. Is that clear enough? Now get in the truck and step on it."

7

CRAMBLING ON ALL fours for the rifle that always lay next to her when she slept, Ari tried to get her bearings. The fires throughout the small camp were spreading, and the gunfire and screams that had torn her from the clutches of her slumber were getting closer. She had to find her brother.

"Aviel!" She hissed his name into the darkness. No reply. Her hands touched the rifle, and she pulled it to her chest. Moving fast in a low crouch, she crossed the gap and entered under the tarp that her brother set up as his shelter. In the darkness, she mashed her hands down against the blanket and felt them touch the cold, hard earth.

Where is he?

More sporadic gunfire filled the smoky night air, followed by a woman shrieking. She peeked around the canvas and saw a group of men stabbing another man to death as they taunted him. Farther down the way, the shrieking woman was being raped by a group of half-naked thugs.

"Shit," Ari hissed. "Highway bandits."

She had to do something. If she could just find Aviel, then they could at least provide a unified resistance. Highway bandits were often small, unorganized, untrained groups of idiots. With a solid show of force, they could be defeated or routed fairly easy. But a sizable show of force was something she didn't have.

Alone she felt isolated, hobbled, and vulnerable. She had to find a way to turn the tide in her favor. She had to find Aviel. Ari scanned a few nearby bedrolls; the people occupying them wore masks of fear, unable to do anything but wait for the terror to end, one way or another.

"Have you seen Aviel? Have you seen my brother?"

One woman managed to shake her head.

"Get your people and go. If you stay here, you will be raped, tortured, and murdered—the children too."

The woman remained frozen.

"Go! Make your way into the hills and hide. They will not spare you if they find you."

The woman managed a nod before pulling a few adults and children together with hurried whispers and disappearing into the dark beyond.

Ari gave a quick 360-degree scan of her surroundings. How had it come to this? How were they now living in fear and squalor like animals? It hadn't always been this way. Back before, she had lived her life with nobility and purpose. Never before had she lived in fear, not even when the Palestinian missiles rained down upon her hometown of Sderot when she was a child. She and her brother and her mother and father would take to the shelter each time, hoping to survive the blasts. *Shh...shh...Ariella,* her father had soothed her as he stroked her long, dark hair. *God will protect us.* Her father was right. God had protected them. They survived. They persevered. It was what Jews had done for thousands of years. Surrounded by enemies on all sides, not only had they survived—they'd flourished and, in the process, become a proud nation, a people of indomitable strength.

It had been her privilege to serve her nation for three years in the Israel Defense Forces as a part of the famed Caracal Battalion. And served with distinction she had. Highly decorated and with extensive training in desert warfare, hand-to-hand combat, and special weapons, she had been willing and capable of dealing with any terrorist threat. This fact ensured that she saw multiple deployments along Israel's southern border with Egypt and other dangerous sectors of her home country. It also ensured that she was later noticed and recruited by Mossad, one of the most respected intelligence agencies in the world.

Her father had not been in favor of her service, but that didn't much concern her. It was all she had ever wanted—to serve her country, to serve her God, to fight against the evil in the world.

Now here she was—half a world away from her family, trapped in the wasteland that used to be America. She longed for home, for an Israel she might never see again. How could she have known that she would never return from her vacation visiting her brother in the States?

Snapping back to the present, Ari rubbed her face. It was the hand they'd been dealt, and now they would have to play it. Clearing her head, she stayed low, moving to the outside of the camp and up into the hillside beyond. Staying low she navigated the hillside, picking her way around a few large rocks to where she would have the best vantage point.

Crouching down on one knee, Ari unslung her AR-15 and looked through the stubby, four-power tactical scope. She hissed through her teeth. It was a sizable force. No, not sizable—downright large. Maybe several hundred bandits total. Looking up the road, she could see their caravan headed by a large fuel tanker stopped further up the road. That tanker was a grand prize in its own right. They had likely stopped to raid and pillage on their way through to somewhere else. Ari thought it through for a moment. These were no ordinary highway bandits. They seemed more empowered, more driven. There was no way for her to fight them off, not a group this big.

If she could just spot her brother, reconnect with him, and get the hell out of this place, everything would be fine. Ari scanned the small camp, a group of people she and her brother had allied with out of sheer necessity. That was where the allegiances stopped. The only person she cared about was Aviel.

The bandits were now bringing their spoils out into the open. Torches were lit as the area became covered in the orange glow of firelight. Men, women and a few children were crying and moaning as they were dragged out into the open and tossed upon the ground like trash. A couple of thugs were fighting over who got to keep a found rifle. She watched this infantile squabbling for a few moments before resuming her visual search for her brother. It was then that she saw him. She gasped as the men dragged him across the light of the fire and threw him to the ground. He had already been beaten. Her baby brother. Ari gritted her teeth and aimed through the scope to assess her shots.

They weren't going to murder her baby brother. They wouldn't get the chance. That much she was sure of.

God help me. Elohim guide my hand.

She had one full magazine and a half full one in her left cargo pocket. Nowhere near enough rounds to take on a force this size, even from an elevated position of advantage. She bit her lip.

Come on, Ari; you can do this. God will protect us.

The crack of a gun snapped her focus back on her brother, who was now raising himself off the ground. They had shot another man who had been struggling with them. Now the bandits, led by one with blue face paint, began to taunt and murder the captives, stabbing or shooting some and sinking their knives into others as they screamed and wailed against their captors.

Barbarians.

She had witnessed the same barbarism years before. Whether it was Hamas, Hezbollah, or wasteland bandits—the visage of true evil manifesting itself in a person was always the same. She huffed out a breath and brass checked the action of the rifle. There was no good way to do this, and they were working their way down toward her brother. A child squalled and threw itself upon its mother, who now lay facedown on the ground in a puddle of gore. With another cruel swipe of the bandit's knife, the child rolled over, unmoving atop its mother.

She couldn't stand by and watch this madness anymore. She had to do something—even if it meant a death sentence for her. As Ari raised her rifle, she watched in horror as her brother spat upon a nearby thug, damning him in Hebrew. In response, the thug lunged forward and buried his jagged blade in Aviel's side under his ribs, twisting it as he yanked Aviel's hair back. Aviel cried something out, and though they were a distance away, she knew with a distinct dread exactly what he was screaming. Her name.

Ari gasped and took aim on the thug as he pulled his knife and drew it back to stab her brother again.

Her rifle cracked across the open expanse, the sound freezing time in its wake. The bandit's head popped open, launching a stream of red into the air as he fell, dropping the knife. Shots rang out, maddened screams in the darkness, as rounds began to strike the hillside around her. She was pinned down. Rising just beyond cover, she began firing on each new target, watching them spin and pirouette like the pop-ups at a shooting gallery as they charged the short hill.

They were holding her brother down now.

No! Please, no! God protect us!

Her weapon ran dry as she fumbled with the magazine in her cargo pocket and instinctively tried to insert it behind the trigger guard as she would have with her IDF-issued Tavor rifle. She slammed the new magazine in and slapped the bolt catch. She didn't have enough rounds to stop them. Tears dumped from her eyes as the thug with the blue face began to saw at her brother's neck with his rusty knife. Her baby brother was still screaming her name when the man cut his throat with a wet gurgle.

"Hear, O Israel, God is our Lord," Ari bawled, centering her crosshairs on her brother's forehead, tears dripping from her chin as she chanted the words with true conviction.

She would not have him suffer. Not like this.

▲ ▲ ▲

The world burned, the screams of the lost echoing into the darkness, the moon boiling and turning to blood. This part of the vision was always the same. Tynuk watched, awestruck, as the stars in the sky died, one by one, their eternal lights winking out against the backdrop of an everlasting darkness. Below, the fires raged, the world consumed, the people in it gone mad without the light of the Great Spirit to guide them. On the horizon, the dark ones waited for their moment to finish the war that had been started so long ago. It was a place without hope, the blood of the innocent crying out to a sky that now held nothing but endless, inky black. Like a cancer, it would devour every last spark of light until there was nothing left of those who'd served the Great Spirit.

This is how it ends when you allow the light to die.

Tynuk awoke with a start, his face pressed into the dry sand of the canyon bed, his head swimming with the toxin that still circulated through his system. Was he dead? Had he transitioned into the spirit realm? His head floated, woozy, separated from the crushing weight of his body. He couldn't be alive. Not after a fall like that.

The warrior boy groaned and rolled to his side, his dilated pupils scanning the strange, drug-induced blurring of earth and sky. His heart pounding in his chest, Tynuk swallowed the dryness in his mouth and rolled to his stomach, pushing himself to all fours as his world reeled around him. He struggled to maintain his balance even on all fours, his limbs trembling under the strain.

"I...I can't...move," Tynuk mumbled to himself. His lungs worked to supply his body with oxygen, pulling with it the earthen scent of decay in the shadow of the canyon floor. How had he gotten here? He had leaped from the cliff. He shouldn't have survived that. Tynuk looked down at his chest again, the thick, black animal hair sticking to the naked sweat of his body.

Azolja.

Tynuk scanned the rocky outcroppings that surrounded him and located the darkened form of his companion nearby, peering at him from a ledge above. The lights from the sky swirled with the rock, the clouds, and the sand as the colors forced their way through his eyes, causing him to feel overwhelmed at the sensory overload. Tynuk fluctuated between lightness and heaviness, a painful undulation between floating and sinking followed by a wave of nausea.

"Az!" Tynuk called to the black beast that watched over him, majestic and fearsome, like something out of a fairytale. "Az..."

The beast flicked his head, a gesture the boy understood as an acknowledgment. His vision distorted, the skin of the world pulling back to reveal the underside, the things unseen. Tynuk flinched and gasped as eyes, yellow and seeing, penetrated the darkness beyond, watching him, waiting for him to expire or continue, they did not seem to have a preference. He was the source of some hidden entertainment in this place, the whispers of the eyes scratching at the back of his consciousness. He looked at the beast again but this time saw something else; a two-legged creature, not unlike a man, but different—and much, much larger. The man stood above him, his posture straight and noble. The worn and tattered black-and-purple robe fashioned tight around him scarcely concealed the massive musculature beneath.

"Who are you?" Tynuk managed. "What did you do with Az?"

The figure did not reply, only stretching out its hand, motioning for the boy to come forward.

"You want me to follow?"

The figure nodded.

"Are you one of my ancestors?"

The figure motioned again for him to follow again.

Tynuk raised himself up. Unsteady like a newly birthed foal, he wobbled and fell against the cliff to support himself. The many probing eyes continued to watch from the darkness as Tynuk looked again at the figure. There was something about this powerful creature. Tynuk could feel it. Something noble and full of righteous purpose, and though he had no real reason to do so, he felt that he could trust it. Ignoring the many whispered laughs of the eyes that bore into him from all directions, Tynuk fought to keep his focus directed upward toward the figure, as he took each shaking step further into the shadowy unknown depths of the canyon ahead.

8

THE CRACK OF her AR-15 burned in her ears, signaling the final death of everyone she had ever loved. Ari gasped and put her hand to her mouth, choking out a few muffled sobs. Somewhere, a small light of hope deep inside her heart went dark. All the pain, all the loss, all the days before, as they'd struggled to survive, came flooding back. She moaned a sad sound and clutched at her face. She and her brother had always been close, but in the last few years, they'd forged an unbreakable bond of love. They were all each other had left in this dying world. And now it was gone. God had been silent.

Ari could hear the ugly marauders swearing and scrambling up the hillside as they came for her.

Come on, Ariella. They just murdered Aviel. Stand up and fight. Make them remember you.

With renewed purpose, Ari wiped her face, her countenance darkening as she prepared herself for what was to come. Stepping back into the shadow of a nearby tree, the moonless night wrapped her in a murky cloak of disguise. Ari checked the chamber of her AR-15 and the round count in the inserted magazine—two rounds in the magazine, one in the chamber, and no secondary weapon. She waited, poised, every inch of her athletic frame staged for action, as her lips moved, reciting the Hebrew words of an ancient psalm.

"Blessed be the Lord, my rock, who trains my hands for war, and my fingers for battle."

She took a deep breath to steady her heart and hands as the grungy highwaymen approached.

"Hey, there! Don't be afraid. We'll treat you real nice." Two shadows laughed as they came into view. Ari knew without question there would be more. These two would try to draw her out, and the others would make their move. She was trapped, but still had the element of surprise.

"Yeah, just come on out, an' we'll take real good care of you!" one of the bandits crooned.

Stepping from the dark of the shadow, Ari raised her rifle and fired two rounds in quick succession—the muzzle flashes blinding her enemy and illuminating the look of shock and dismay on his dirty face as he crumpled and rolled down the hillside. Not missing a beat, she pivoted and dropped to a knee as the second thug fired over her head. A single round through the teeth froze him in midstep as chunked fragments of his brain littered the hillside behind him.

Screams, like sheer madness, filled the air as the rest of them came for her. The bolt on her rifle was locked to the rear. No more ammo. Groaning and huffing, the first bandit came in and received a savage stroke across his jaw with the butt of her rifle. Ari spun to her left and muzzle punched another in the throat, crushing the wild man's trachea with a gurgled wheeze. Light blazed across her eyes as something hard struck her across the back of the head. She faltered, took one stumbling step, and swung the rifle in an upward arc to the rear, landing a solid strike to the ribs of the man behind her. She spun and brought the rifle across the thug's face, sending him sprawling down the hillside. A handgun was raised in her face as Ari sidestepped and parried the weapon away with the barrel of her rifle and delivered a crushing headbutt to the chin of the gunman. The handgun cracked as it fell, and another bandit behind her went down, grabbing in shock at the open wound in his chest.

Ari growled, ferocious and un-feminine, as the warrior in her came into its full form. Stomping forward she crushed the gunman's tibia at the ankle with a splintering sound as she lunged and delivered a brutal thrust of the weapon's magazine into his face.

But there were far too many. Ari gave a savage groan as the many hands and arms pulled her to the ground. Struggling in vain, she gnashed her teeth, frothing at the mouth like a wild animal.

"Saxon!" one of the bandits called over his shoulder. "Saxon, we got her! We got her alive!"

A well-built man with blue face paint and a braided ponytail approached up the hillside to the edge of the group. "Her?"

"Yeah, it's a woman! Good-looking one too."

The man named Saxon made his way to the center of the small crowd of dirty, jeering thugs.

"What do you think, Saxon? She killed a bunch of our guys. Can we fuck her? Teach her a lesson?"

"Yeah, all of us get to do her," another thug said eagerly as he stooped and groped at her breasts.

Ari's eyes grew wild with fear as she groaned and pulled against the men, shouting in her thick accent. "I'll kill you!"

"Oh yeah, I like 'em with some fight in 'em!" the bandit oozed to the laughs of his fellows.

"Now wait just a second." Saxon turned and spoke to Ari. "First, you tell me who you are."

Ari replied in Hebrew, "Hashem is my stronghold and my deliverer!"

Saxon chuffed. "I'd know that filthy Hebrew speak anywhere. She's Jewish."

Ari pulled hard against her captors again, straining with the effort.

"And by the looks of it, I'd say she's Israeli. Too defiant and well trained to be an American Jew." Saxon knelt close to Ari, his dark ponytail drifting across his shoulder. "I was raised as a Muslim."

Ari curled her lip in anger.

Saxon gestured casually. "The Muslim faith and all that 'Allah is great' stuff didn't really take. But my parents' boundless hatred of the Jews did—to this day I can't stand a fucking Jew."

Ari spat at Saxon. Saxon laughed. "I would expect no different response from a Jew bitch."

Saxon turned to the men. "I agree, gents. We need to break this little vixen. Put her back in her place. Re-establish the natural order of things. And one of the best ways to do that is to give everybody a turn with her and then bleed her dry." The men erupted into slur-filled screams of excitement as they threw their hands in the air.

A pall of despair lay down upon Ari, her fate at the hands of these filthy barbarians now all too clear. The thought of the coming assault soaked into her and made her dead inside. Cold and dead—which was what she'd rather be than have to endure it.

"But first," Saxon continued as he silenced the group. "First, she sees Malak. He won't want to miss this one. And after that, we will do with her as we wish."

More cheers, as they hoisted her up and began to carry her back toward the road, their filthy hands never missing an opportunity to grope and molest her as they went. Ari closed her eyes and tried to hold back the approaching tidal wave of panic. Panic never helped anything. It only served to get you dead faster. She started combat breathing to slow the hammering of her heart, to clear the oppressive distractions swarming through her mind. She had to get free. That was the only acceptable option.

Arriving back at the place where the others had been murdered, Ari was thrown to the ground and cruelly kicked several times before one of the bandits put his foot between her shoulder blades, pressing her flat.

"Don't even think about moving, woman," he said from above her.

Saxon disappeared around the corner for a few moments, and when he returned, a massive muscular, bald man accompanied him. The goons hushed in the presence of this man, who was clearly their leader. He stepped forward and folded his arms across his chest, surveying Ari as she lay prostrate, face down on the ground.

"What do you want?" Ari managed.

"You are a Jew?" Malak growled.

"What of it?"

Malak stepped a few paces away and kicked something toward her. "Do you know this one?"

Ari clenched her teeth at the sight of her brother's severed head as it rolled toward her, his glassy, dead eyes staring up at her, the unmistakable hole from the round she had fired in the center of his forehead. "No," she said and looked away.

"He was a Jew. You're sure you don't know him?"

"I'm sure," Ari mumbled.

"I don't believe you. So you're going to watch what happens next."

Several men dropped down onto her and pulled her hair, forcing her to look forward. Some bandits were bringing out a bunch of wooden planks nailed together in the shape of a star—the Star of David. Ari watched in horror as her brother's body was lashed to the star and then hoisted so that he hung attached to it, upside down, his corpse still draining blood from the neck.

Ari gasped and wrenched her arms against her captors. "You're a monster!"

"Yes, I am." Malak grinned with sinister intent, a darkness festering beneath his skin. "Raise up the others."

Ari watched as several wooden crosses were raised next to her brother; the poor people who hung nailed to them were still alive. The final touch came when Saxon spray-painted a message on the barrier wall below them: "This is what happens to the followers of God."

Some of the bandits around her laughed, others clapped and whistled. Ari thought she might throw up. Malak approached her again.

"Renounce God, and you'll be spared."

The fierce Israeli woman bared her teeth.

"You will be taught a painful lesson for resisting us, for killing my men, and for clinging to your belief in God. Your final moments on this earth will not slip away painlessly. They will drone on and on until the agony is so great that you will beg us for death. This is your last chance. Renounce your God and join me or face the consequences of believing what you believe."

Ari continued to say nothing, her eyes drifting off to land on two small, dust-covered children who seemed so out of place amid the murder and terror. They cried, heads pressed together, as they sat chained to the flatbed of one of the bandits' trucks, eyes cast down like beaten dogs. Ari gnashed her teeth and shook her head.

Malak sighed. "Just as stubborn as those fucking Christians. Have it your way." He turned and looked to one of the drivers. "How far to Arizona?"

"It's still several days' travel, boss, at least."

"It's getting late, and we've wasted enough time on this entertaining but fruitless little exercise. Where's Shank?"

A mush-faced troll of a man shuffled to the front of the crowd. "Yes, my lord?"

"Shank, you have not disappointed me before. Pick four men to help you deal with this woman. Then take a vehicle and catch back up with us on the interstate. We shouldn't be that far ahead of you."

"What do you want done, my lord?" Shank slurred.

"Spare her no pain and humiliation. You're a creative professional. Make good use of her and then hang her next to the other one."

Shank giggled like an adolescent. "Yes, Lord."

Shank called forward the men he wanted to help him, causing the others to grumble at having to miss the festivities.

"Back to the vehicles!" Saxon yelled as the men quickly dispersed behind Malak. Saxon turned and smiled with eyes full of hate. He stooped low and drew close, salivating in her ear. "I'm sorry I'm going to miss out on this one, darling. I'd really love to ruin you personally, but I guess I'll just have to be satisfied with cutting your baby brother's head off."

"You don't know anything—"

"Yeah, I do. I do, actually. He told me everything. Spilled his guts like a fucking Jew coward."

Ari shook her head, her eyes far away, drowning in toxic pain.

"He was sure you'd come for him in the end," Saxon smirked. "He was so sure. The poor bastard screamed your name. He begged for you to save him as I opened the flesh of his neck with my blade—"

Ari erupted, shaking, a storm of fire billowing deep behind her dark eyes as she spat the words: "Understand this, here and now. I'll—"

"You'll what? You're just like all the other followers of God who are too weak to stand against us. What you'll do is hang on your very own star, right next to the others—that is, once the boys here have had their fun with you."

Ari said nothing.

"Cheers, bitch." Saxon laughed as he turned, his ponytail swishing across the hard muscles of his back as he headed for the vehicles along the highway. Engines roared to life, and tires peeled out, the bandit caravan taking off down the deserted highway.

Ari burned with uncompromising fury, her face a mask of hate. The men around her were undressing; the concussive sounds of their belt buckles jingling drowned out all else. It was the sound of her doom. She had one chance to live, and her only plan was something desperate and disgusting.

She waited for the perfect moment; the taillights of the rest of the bandit caravan winked out of sight, signaling that they were at last alone. One of the men, now naked except for his sneakers, stood over her and argued with the others about who got to go first.

It was in this moment that she did it. With one hard push, Ari evacuated her bladder and bowels into her pants, the unmistakable stench of urine and fecal matter filling the air around them.

"What the—" one half-naked bandit yelled.

"You nasty bitch!" cried another.

The two holding her down flinched and loosened their grips—providing Ari with the exact moment she was waiting for. She twisted, rolling hard to break free as she deployed the hidden karambit knife from her waistline and locked it open. Lashing out, she cut the Achilles tendon at the ankle of the closest goon, sending him crying and stumbling to the ground.

Rolling forward and rising fast, she slashed upward with the claw-like knife, opening another man's throat in a spray of gore. The thug gurgled, blood and air mixing in his throat as Ari grabbed him and spun, another goon opening fire on them with a revolver. The thudding concussions of the rounds striking meat in front of her only fueled her fury as she groaned and shoved her human shield toward the shooter. Slamming the bodies together, she saw the revolver knock free and slide across the ground. Wasting no time, Ari dumped the body and lashed out, slicing through the man's femoral artery near the groin and back across his abdomen with the popping sound of his gut bag releasing. She watched as he stumbled away, moaning and clutching his intestines in terror before crashing to the ground. With two steps and a final lunge, she drove her blade through the eye socket of the first man she had wounded, causing immediate brain death. She tossed his lifeless body to the ground and turned.

Shank took a step back and pulled two eight-inch Japanese tanto knives from his belt. "You are adept with the knife. That's good. That's real good. I've been waitin' to test myself against someone like you."

Ari said nothing as she circled him, swinging the karambit to the outside of her hand and back to her palm, regripping the blade.

"That was impressive. An' I gotta say, shitting your pants to get us to back off was pure genius—fuckin' gross, but genius," the man slurred.

"Shut your mouth and make your move, dead man," Ari hissed.

"Heh, you're cute when you're angry." The ugly man spat. "I'm gonna cut your pretty head off just like all the others." He winked at her. "Don't worry, sugarplum. I'll keep it as a souvenir."

With a swift movement that belied his stumpy, troll-like form, the ugly man lunged at her. Only her lightning-fast reflexes spared her a fatal thrust of his tanto to her chest. She felt the blade snag her clothing as she turned and lashed out. But Shank came up quick and met her blade with his, sparks illuminating the darkness. Again and again, they went back and forth, slashing, dodging, and parrying. Ari swiped low, but Shank evaded, landing a solid punch across the jaw, her world spinning with stars and night. He came in fast as Ari deflected the thrust of his blade and hammered him with a powerful A-frame kick to the groin. Shank stumbled back, groaning and clutching his stomach. Ari could tell he was losing steam, the man's labored breathing increasing with each passing moment. With a cry and a lunge, he came for her again in the darkness, and with a brilliantly timed check-parry-pass movement, she ducked beneath his attack and sliced deep into the brachial artery of his arm with her blade. Shank cried out and tried to retreat, but she was too fast, centering behind him with four deep strikes from her karambit to his liver. The bandit groaned, spittle and blood hanging from his swollen lips as his knees buckled. Ari grabbed him under the chin and dropped with him to her knees, pulling his weakened body against her.

"You don't have a clue what you're doin'," Shank wheezed in defiance. "Malak ain't gonna let this slide, you stinking bitch."

"You and Malak, that blue-faced piece of shit, and all the rest of these ignorant pigs have failed to realize something of vital importance here." Ari fumed with menace into the ear of her dying foe, her accented words slicing deeper than the blade she wielded.

"Yeah? And what's that—? Gak!"

Ari silenced the puffy-faced man as she drove her blade deep into the base of his skull and twisted. She took a deep breath and let it out slow. As Shank's hot blood soaked through her clothes, a steely calm settled over her features.

"You picked the wrong girl for this."

9

QUEENASHANO STOOD ON the edge of the Palo Duro Canyon, looking down into the mists below with an obvious expression of interest.

"The boy is dead, then?" A warrior behind the war chief spoke with hesitation.

Queenashano shook his head. "No."

"But it is impossible that he—"

"No," Queenashano interrupted with authority. "No, it is impossible that he was actually trained by the great Nuk'Chala. It is impossible that he possesses such a noble warrior's war belt. It is impossible that a boy traveled alone across bandit and mutant-infested territory to find us here. And it is impossible that such a boy would injure and kill so many of my trained warriors without breaking a sweat. But he has done all of this, and some of it I have seen with my own eyes. So, until I see his body for myself on the floor of that canyon, he is alive."

No one moved, and no one spoke as the group looked incredulously at their leader.

"Mia ranu! We have wasted enough time." Queenashano waved for the group to disperse.

The journey down through the canyon was a solemn one, each step taken in contemplation, every hand placed against the dark canyon walls with an almost painful thoughtfulness. The gray sky loomed overhead and gave the midday light of the canyon a dimness that rivaled dusk.

Queenashano led the group of warriors who had volunteered to participate in the boy's trial, though they would soon find if they were needed at all. Some of the younger warriors, prompted by Neraquassi's snide remarks, laughed in hushed tones about how ridiculous it was that Queenashano had insisted upon finding the body. There was no possible way the boy had survived a fall several hundred feet to the floor of the canyon, all while fighting a lethal dose of poison. The concept was obscene, and they knew that when they found his mutilated body, they could finally conclude this foolish errand.

After a long descent, Queenashano stopped, and the rest of the group came to a halt behind him, watching as he crouched and plucked up a few strands of thick, black animal hair from the sand of the dry canyon floor. He took a moment to roll the strands curiously between his fingers as he analyzed the strange hair.

"Thutseena tsoyaa," Neraquassi said.

"No, my son, it is not wolf hair. We have not seen wolves here in this canyon for many cycles."

"What then? A coyote? Maybe the trickster watches us even now!" Neraquassi laughed.

With animalistic ferocity Queenashano spun and came up hard against Neraquassi, striking him with his palm in the pit of his stomach. Yellow Horse dropped to the ground, gasping for air and digging his fingers into the sand beneath him. Queenashano yanked the young warrior's hair back as the others looked on with mute interest.

"Do you think it's funny to speak of the trickster in such a way? Your foolishness will bring about your doom." He released Neraquassi's hair with a shove as the young warrior knelt before his father, humiliated. "If you weren't my own, I would drain your blood on the floor of this canyon. Don't you ever forget that the role you play in this universe is a *very* small one. There are forces at work here that are far beyond any of us. To mock them is to mock the turning of the ancient wheel of time. There are spirits that have preordained that this must occur. We are already caught up in the winds of fate like the played pawns of some greater game."

Some of the warriors looked on seriously, while others dumbly tried to discern his meaning.

Insulted and embarrassed Neraquassi stood and wiped his raven hair from his face. "What of it then? That doesn't have anything to do with the dead boy you've been so obsessed with since his arrival!"

"No?" Queenashano turned so the rest of the group could see the perfect, shallow imprint of a body in the sand of the canyon floor ahead of them. The indentation was ever so slight, much less than the crater that would have been left by a body falling hundreds of feet. There was no blood or any other sign other than the footsteps that meandered away into the dim, ruddy canyon ahead. Queenashano pointed upward. "Our camp is directly above this place. This is where he fell."

The warriors stood rooted in place, some with their mouths hanging open, their eyes traveling up and down as they tried to make sense of the strange set of events.

"And there, the body of Ito." Queenashano motioned. "It hangs there where the boy tossed him in." He pointed to the mangled, bloody arm that hung exposed from a ledge above them. "This is the place."

"But...there is nothing! Where has he gone?" Neraquassi managed to say.

"This is what I have been speaking of, you fool. There are forces at work here that we cannot explain. But there is one thing I am now sure of: that boy is still alive. And I want to know for sure why the spirits protect him still."

Another warrior spoke up. "What do we do?"

"We are now invested in this. We must see it through," Queenashano said.

"He can't have made it far," one of the more seasoned warriors said.

"Yes, in this you are correct." Queenashano turned to the seasoned warrior. "You will leave now. Follow his trail. Track the boy and kill him before he exits this canyon. We will follow at walking pace, the others releasing after you in timed increments as prescribed by the old ways. They will succeed in the event that you fail."

"I will not fail," the warrior stated.

"That remains to be seen." Queenashano's eyes brightened with a hidden flame. "Either way, the trials of the ancients must continue."

▲ ▲ ▲

The scope of the dream towered over him like an eternal titan, time and the universe washed over him, bathing him in endless secrets unknown, even as he failed to comprehend them. In a strange moment of clarity, Kane knew this was not a normal dream. He felt aware of himself, aware that he was supposed to remember whatever it was that he was about to see.

In his mind's eye, his body elevated, touching both sky and space as the world rushed backward like a bizarre string of reverse time-lapse footage. Back it went, back before a billion risings of the sun, to the beginning. And in this empty void, he saw a splinter of light, single object hanging amid the nothingness. Around the object hung a sprit—no, *the* spirit of God. Formless and yet quite distinct, it spoke to the object in a tongue Kane did not understand. Light bloomed forth in the darkness, and the universe was born.

Kane watched, his mind reeling, paralyzed at the sheer spectacle of creation. And as time flew before his eyes, he saw that it was this device that God used to create the universe and everything in it.

Above, the heavens opened to him, and Kane witnessed a terrible conflict take place, the images filling in the gaps in his mind as he tried to process it all. One army clad in glistening, mirror-like armor and the other black as night as though each twisted creature had been dipped in oil. On and on they fought, never surrendering, never retreating, fighting for the fate of all things—an eternal battle for control of the sacred object. Kane watched as one heavenly warrior broke away and tried to flee with the object. An engine with immense power imbued by its creator—the Machine. A single device with the power to create and, in the wrong hands, destroy and corrupt the universe. Kane watched the angel and demon fight over the Machine as they fell from heaven to earth, streaking across the night sky like burning meteors against the clear, deep black of night.

Then, in a turn that startled him, he too was flying, careening across the atmosphere after them and watching them as they fell. Time sped up and then slowed, revealing the location where the device landed and its recovery thousands of years later by primitive civilizations, after which it was hoarded by kings and pharaohs and buried forever in vast tombs of treasure, only to wait in the silent dark to be discovered again. The celestial warriors that had fallen with it were long gone.

Kane watched the images flash in rapid succession, images of the Machine's recovery by a modern archaeological dig, its seizure by the US government, and subsequent study of it at an underground research facility nestled deep within the bowels of a massive, towering hydroelectric dam.

Kane watched as the End War happened with a stunning quickness, as life as they'd known it ceased to exist, and the pitiful survivors of the world tried to reclaim their lives. Then he saw himself, his Susan, his children, and his friends, as their story was recounted before him in all its desperate hope and savage horror.

And as the vision arrived at the present, Kane watched with grim understanding as Malak and his dark Coyotes marched upon this secret facility, and under a banner of fire and death, claimed the Machine for the powers of darkness. He saw the sky boil with rage, a new evil pouring itself out across the vast expanse of the universe, heralding the coming of the Master. And there he was, alongside his friends, little more than a defiant thread of hope standing between this madness and what was left of their world.

As his mind took it all in, an overwhelming sense of dread overtook Kane. Now, he knew the stakes of this most dangerous game. For the first time, in this moment of clarity, Kane understood the gravity of their calling and the real purpose of his mission. The Machine could not be allowed to fall into the wrong hands—desperately evil hands that had searched for it for so long now. And as he considered this, he realized how all the pain, loss, and misery that had broken him and driven him to this exact place where God would meet him, restore him, and empower him to be the man that heaven needed him to be. This was the moment of truth, and it very well could be his last.

Kane opened his eyes and sat up on his bedroll in the dark of an overcast midnight sky. The camp around him was quiet save for the pop of the fire and the droning of Courtland's titanic snoring. Kane took a moment to compose himself as he brought his hands to his face and raked them through his shaggy, brown hair. The vision still lingered in his mind, the moisture hanging in the air over him like a curtain of silken quiet. And in the humid dark of night, Kane's lips began to move with reverent care.

He pinched his eyes shut and begged his God to spare them from this evil, to bestow upon them all the wisdom and fortitude they would need for this last, unconquerable obstacle. And as he prayed, he felt it descend upon him. Like the soaring answer to his heart's purest hope, he felt it rise inside him: a wellspring of righteous confidence and strength that swelled within his chest and gently drew his wounded heart up and out from the darkest of places.

Somewhere in the dark, an infant was crying. She could hear it's pitiful sobbing, far away from her now. So far away. Jenna awoke with a gasp, her body rigid. She lowered herself back to her elbows, her body relaxing, her nose taking in the heavenly smell of meat sizzling over an open fire. She lay back again for a moment and wiped a tear from her cheek, her fingers touching a child-size silver cross that hung around her neck.

"I love you, sweet girl."

Her life was what it was. No one could change their past no matter how much they all wished they could. Even so, none of it made the nightmares any better. Everyone had lost someone, and some had lost much more than that. It was the cruel nature of this new existence, living after the death of civilized society. They each had to choose to either give up or go on. There was no middle ground.

She rubbed her face and sat up, pulling back her gray wool surplus blanket, revealing several little ones who had snuggled up next to her and each other like a litter of rabbits in the cool of the night. Headed west on I-40, they were now between Memphis and Little Rock. It had been slow going since they had gone well out of their way to avoid the major cities on their journey west. It was for the best. The ruins of civilization were now only burned husks—havens for the depraved and infected.

She tousled the hair of a curly-headed little boy named Curtis as he began to stir. Jenna pulled on her jacket, the cold, damp fabric reminding her of the way her heart felt throughout the night. Her dreams were fantastic and terrible, with angels and demons and a mission from heaven. It was an insurmountable task she could hardly get her head around. How in the world was she ever going to tell Kane and Courtland without them thinking she was off her rocker?

She roused herself and moved across the ashen, gray half-light of the early morning to plop down beside the small fire where Kane sat prodding several sizzling lumps of potted meat.

"Smells amazing." Jenna breathed in through her nose.

"Huh?" Kane mumbled. "Oh yeah, it sure does."

"You doing okay? Couldn't sleep?" Jenna asked.

"Yeah, I'm okay. Sleep isn't so restful for me these days."

"I know the feeling," Jenna said as other members of their group slowly trickled in to sit and stare into the smoking pit of red coals.

"Morning."

"Mornin'."

Kane knifed a chunk and raised it. "Who wants to be the guinea pig and let me know if it's done?"

"I can handle that." Winston smiled and outstretched his hand.

"Alright. It's hot, now."

Winston nodded and played hot potato with the steaming meat as Kane dropped it into his hands. The pudgy man dropped the greasy meat onto his shirt, where he cradled it in the cloth before popping it into his mouth.

"Ish dome," Winston said and smiled, chewing gingerly.

Jenna raised her eyes as a disheveled, groggy Courtland lumbered his way over to the group and sat down with his back to a roadside boulder. His giant bulk dwarfed the sizable stone behind him. He yawned and stroked the gray-white stubble of his beard.

"I think I'd do anything, right about now, for a cup of coffee," the giant grumbled.

Jenna smiled, and Kane raised his knife. "Here, here!"

"But," Courtland continued, "I'll take what I can get. Enjoying a quiet breakfast with my friends, free from fear and oppression—well, that sounds pretty great too."

"I'll drink to that." Dagen shambled up, working his crutches. "Uh, I mean, I would drink to that—if I was still a drinking man."

"Giving it up altogether?" Jenna asked, her eyes checking him.

"Can't find alcohol anywhere anymore. But the stuff's no good for me, anyway," Dagen said. "Never has been."

The group nodded with quiet murmurs as Kane began doling out small chunks of potted meat to the group. A few of the children giggled at a game they were playing. Kane removed the makeshift skillet, a rectangular section of scrap metal, from the fire and began to eat his own meager helping of potted meat. Several plastic water bottles began to circulate. It didn't need to be said that rationing what water they had was of critical importance.

Jenna received a bottle and took two small sips, swished, and swallowed. She took a breath, released it, and passed the bottle. She tried to think through how she'd put it into words.

"I...uh..." She paused and licked her lips as she set her eating implements down. She wiped her hands on her pants. "So, I had a really vivid dream last night."

All motion around the fire slowed to a stop as the eyes of the whole group centered on her. She shrugged off the attention. "It was...um... pretty bizarre. A whole story about—"

"Angels and demons and a battle for the fate of everything— known and unknown," the older gentleman, Sam, said.

Jenna stared at Sam in astonishment.

"I had it too." Sam shrugged his shoulders.

Kane set his plate down, appraising the group. "Who all had this dream?" he asked, looking over the small gathering. "Give me a show of hands." They all watched as every single member of their group, including Dagen and the now-serious-faced children, raised their hands.

"Yeah." Kane wiped his sleeve across his mouth. "Well, it's obviously not a coincidence. We were meant to see it. We were all meant to know the stakes—how important our cause is—how important it's always been."

"The stakes," Dagen repeated with a strange look in his eyes.

"Yes," Courtland replied, "we've become embroiled in something much bigger than us. It's bigger than justice or revenge, even bigger than saving Kane's children." Courtland turned to Kane and pointed, "which is still a priority, my brother."

"Yeah," Kane said, his eyes never leaving the plumes of smoke drifting from the dying fire.

"This is big—like, fate-of-all-creation, scary big, isn't it?" Jenna's voice wavered.

Kane nodded.

"I had the dream too," Winston said. "I saw a hydroelectric dam. It's also a secret government facility. That's where that thing is kept."

"The Machine," Courtland said, "a device with unspeakable power."

"I don't know where that dam was though," Winston started.

"I do," Jenna said. "I've been there. That was the Glen Canyon Dam on the Colorado River in northern Arizona. Charley and I had our honeymoon on Lake Powell."

"Wait. What are we talking about here exactly?" Winston broke in. "What does this mean? That we're supposed to go to war with that psycho and his bandits over this…Machine? What if we fail? I mean, look at us—"

"We won't fail." Courtland smiled, interrupting the pudgy man. "We can't fail. This is just like the greatest stories from the Bible: stories of Moses, Joshua, David, and countless others who all stood where we now stand, terrified and outnumbered by the most horrific enemies they could imagine. Confronted with an evil that threatened to wipe their ways from the face of the earth, they chose to fight. Even amid the darkest of times, these good people clung to their faith in a God who was strong enough to win the day. And win the day he did, again and again, and again."

Everyone sat listening as the giant spoke.

"This is our chance. This is our opportunity in this life to truly do something worth doing. To stand in righteousness when we are commanded by the forces of darkness to kneel."

Jenna placed her hands together against her lips and glanced skyward in a silent prayer. "But are we supposed to be going to war?" Jenna shook her head, a distant tear developing in the corner of her eye. "It's really scary that, after all this, we would deliberately go after Malak with a mission to stop him. I get trying to secretly rescue Kane's kids, but open war? I can't help but think that maybe there's some other way. Is there a way to stop this without going to war with these hateful men? I mean, as Christians, aren't we supposed to be promoting peace?"

Kane remained silent, deep in thought. He took a deep breath and all eyes turned to him, waiting.

"Yes," he said at last, "you're absolutely right, Jenna. We are commanded to establish peace on this earth, but peace has never been the reward for those who sought peace with truly evil men. Evil must be fought. It must be contested. It must be subdued in order for justice to again cover this land. Only when justice is reestablished will we have peace."

Kane considered his next words, rubbing his hands together. "Look, I know the Bible says to turn the other cheek. That's in order to preserve your witness, to be Christ-like. But what of it when turning the other cheek means the annihilation of all the good that is left in this world? What then? Darkness will reign, and the light will be stamped out. Now, I'm not saying God can't prevail without us, but I think he's *choosing* to use us. In his wisdom, he created both the lion and the lamb, and each has its purpose. I think we've come from where we have for a reason. I've known in my heart for a long time now that God had a special purpose for us and that this purpose is to stand against the forces of darkness. It's the only thing left that matters."

"I know. I feel it too." Jenna's gaze questioned his words. "We've all just been through so much…"

Kane looked at Jenna and smiled. "We have, Jenna, and that's all the more reason for it to mean something. If we fight to preserve the way, to rekindle the light, is that not a noble and worthy cause to fight for? If we do it only that the weak and oppressed can live without fear, only to stop the failing of the light across this earth and beyond, is there anything more worthy of our greatest effort?"

Courtland nodded, a faint look of astonishment showing at the wisdom of his friend. "There is no other way. We must find the courage to pursue this darkness and pray that, in being obedient, our God aids us and grants us the power to vanquish it."

"If there's no other way, then I'm with you. You know that." Jenna conceded.

Kane reached over and squeezed her shoulder, and Jenna and Courtland glanced at each other, as a sly look formed across Kane's bearded face. It was a look of sincerity and promise, a hardened look of confidence—a look no one had seen from him in a very long time.

"We're going to do this together. All of us. We can hide and wait for this evil to devour all that is most precious, or we can fight against the fading of the light. We're going be in the history books, one way or another, so I think it's time for us to decide what kind of story we're going to write." He paused, chewing the corner of his lip with a boyish look of daring. "I don't know about you, but I've wallowed in the misery of defeat for far too long already. It's time for a story where the good guys win."

10

*H*E'D WALKED FOR hours, and the sun would be high in the sky by now, if one could see it to measure its progress. With each step Tynuk took, it felt like his foot might step through the floor of the world, and then he would fall and keep falling, forever. The dark sky blurred with the rising wind and twisted together with the walls of the Palo Duro Canyon to create the feeling that he was walking in circles, a rat trapped in a dreamlike maze.

The warrior boy raised his head and squinted, the light breaking into colors that distorted and melted through his ocular nerves and into his brain. He wiped at his dusty, parched lips and outstretched his hand toward the strange figure who continued to lead him forward past the many eyes that watched him from the walls of the canyon as he went.

"Water."

The figure stopped and turned, shaking his noble brow slowly.

"But I don't know that I can continue, without—"

The figure raised a hand as if to silence the boy, the look his face seemed to say, *you must.*

From off to Tynuk's left, a comforting whisper reached out to him, "Come here, boy. I have water for you. Stop and rest a moment."

Tynuk turned his head and regarded the shadows that danced along the canyon walls. He shook his head. "But he said—"

"He is being cruel to make you walk all this way with no rest. Come, have some refreshment with me," the shadow said, eyes laughing in the darkness.

Tynuk turned, delirious, stumbling toward the sound of the voice. "Maybe just a quick drink. I'll just sit for a moment."

"Yes, yes, just for a moment," the voice echoed.

As Tynuk neared the shadowy walls of the canyon, he felt himself start to drift. He was so tired. He would just rest for a moment. Without warning, a vise closed down across his bicep. It was warm and powerful, pulling him hard away from the wall of the canyon. As he turned, he saw the figure staring at him, his displeasure at Tynuk's straying from the path evident in the scowl upon his face.

"But I was just—"

The figure shook his head. He turned with urgency, pointing back up the mouth of the canyon from whence they had come.

Everything moving at half speed, as a demon with eyes full of rage, came howling up the canyon from behind him. With a shriek, the creature leaped at him, but Tynuk was ready, his body moving to a rhythm he'd spent thousands of hours honing. Tynuk spun, and the colors of the world spun with him as he struck the demon and sent it flying back against the nearby wall of the canyon.

He readied himself and half closed his eyes, knowing that in the grip of the poison his senses were of no use to him in this fight. He would have to rely on instinct alone.

As the demon launched it's attack, he ducked a swipe of its weapon and came up inside its guard, slamming into it with a barrage of hand strikes. The creature faltered, stepping back as its chest labored, and it shrieked a terrible sound. Tynuk readied himself as his body continued to operate completely devoid of thought.

The demon came in again slashing and thrusting, attacking him in a fit of rage. Tynuk parried, blocked, and dodged the blows effortlessly as he slipped beneath the demon's arm and rose high in the creature's armpit, wrapping his arms tight around the far side of its neck in a vascular blood choke.

Tynuk now unleashed his fury as he clamped down and bared his teeth, clinging to the monster as it thrashed him about the walls of the dim canyon floor.

With a groan, the demon fell to its knees and then onto its face. Tynuk held secure, giving a few more violent pulls at the demon's neck, to ensure it was indeed finished. The creature shuddered and became still.

Without a word, the dazed warrior boy rose and turned, his chest rising and falling with the effort of battle. The noble figure stood before him, its tattered robe flowing with the canyon breeze. He inclined his head and motioned for the boy to follow him once more.

Tynuk swallowed the dryness in his mouth and followed the figure, running out of the canyon and into the wasteland desert that beckoned them onward.

It wasn't long before the second runner found the body of the first dead Comanche runner, strangled against the red sand of the canyon floor. With an oath of vengeance howled amid heaving breaths, the seasoned warrior exited the canyon, sprinting into the desert evening, furiously driving after the mysterious, unbreakable warrior boy.

▲ ▲ ▲

Kane stepped from the cab of the beaten Chevrolet truck and raised his hand. Behind him, the train of vehicles rolled to a stop. He surveyed the scene of smoke and wreckage with keen eyes, no detail overlooked, no evidence unconsidered.

"What is it?" Jenna called, standing through the top of the Jeep behind him.

"An encampment of some sort. There's not much left to look at, now."

"Is it safe to check for survivors?"

"As safe as it gets out here." Kane motioned for everyone to exit their vehicles and search the camp.

Stepping between the plumes of acrid black smoke, remnants of trash, body, and bone, Kane and Jenna moved together with their weapons at the ready. They stopped, Kane motioning Courtland and Dagen forward across the small camp. There were no signs of life. Nothing.

Lowering his weapon, Kane stepped into the center of the small-ish, ransacked camp and stopped in midstride, the evidence of the crime washing over him in a visual stimulation that he'd never asked for. There was no longer any question if this was the work of Malak and his Coyotes. Jenna gasped and put her hand over her mouth. The lifeless bodies and heads that stood before them, mounted on jagged stakes that protruded from the ground, bore witness to the pain and suffering of so many.

"Lord Jesus, come quickly," Courtland said from across the way.

"Is there anyone left?" Kane managed with his sleeve across his face.

"Those bastards don't leave anything to find but this," Dagen said.

Jenna turned and saw the crude crosses that protruded from the blood-soaked earth, those who hung on them, now long deceased. Beside them, a wooden star sat at a crooked angle on the ground, a loose rope dangling over a headless corpse that was still lashed against the crude wooden implement. It appeared to have been cut down.

"Dear God! I can't look at this anymore. Their suffering must have been...just...just..." Jenna turned, but Kane grabbed her arm. She looked to him, desperate questions lingering in her eyes.

"Jenna, get your first-aid kit."

"Kane, you can't be seeing what I'm seeing. Whom could I possibly treat?"

"Her." Kane pointed, stepping forward toward the base of the star where a woman lay, her chest rising and falling with steady breaths.

Jenna wheeled and ran for the vehicles, throwing the door to the Jeep open and fishing out the black canvas bag with all the medical supplies she had been able to muster. Slamming the door, she ran as fast as her legs would take her back to where Kane stood before the woman.

Jenna stepped forward, but again Kane stopped her with an outstretched arm, motioning to the tightly gripped, curved, blood-covered knife that still rested in the woman's hand.

"Don't startle her. Let's try to give her some room. We don't know what she's been through."

"I think we know," Courtland said under his breath.

Kane knelt down and leaned just a little forward toward the beautiful but beaten, dark-haired woman, as she lay unconscious.

"Miss."

Kane waited as the small group filled in the gaps, watching.

"Miss, please wake up. We're here to help you. Miss?"

No reaction.

"Toss something toward her," Sam said.

"No." Kane glanced over her shoulder. "The last thing I want to do is give her the wrong impression." He took a crouched step forward. "Miss." Then another. "Miss, please wake up. We want to help you."

The movement came so fast that Kane almost didn't have time to flinch back as the furious woman came to life, slashing with the blade where his body had been just moments before.

"Get back!" she snarled.

"Woah, hang on!" Kane shouted as he stumbled and lost his balance, falling backward. Before he could readjust his position, she was upon him, her knife hooked against the side of his neck. He had instinctively grabbed her hand and clenched it tight against his body, leaning his neck as far away as he could from the knife.

"Drop your weapons, or I open him up!" Ari shouted, frantic.

"We don't want to fight you, lady." Courtland held his hands up as Kane gave a suppressive motion with his free hand, and the other members of the group dropped their weapons to the earth.

"Do anything stupid, and I'll do it. You can't stop me!" Ari shouted with a delirium-soaked resolve.

"Look, look at me," Kane said. "I'm going to let go of your wrist, okay? I'm not here to hurt you." Kane released his grip and felt her push the blade flush against his neck. Kane gritted his teeth but said nothing further as he waited, eyes locked with hers.

"Liar! There is no one left to trust in this world. I should kill you now!" Ari cried in her heavy accent, her chest rising and falling with panicked breaths.

"No." Jenna reached out her hand. "No, please, look at my face. Look in my eyes. I promise you that we only want to help you. Please let us do that. Don't hurt our friend."

"Why should I believe you? Why would you help me?"

"Because…" Jenna gave the others a nervous glance, knowing her answer could provoke a terrible response if not well received. "Because our God commands us to. It's what he wants from us now that all else is lost," Jenna said pulling her hands to her chest.

"What God are you talking about?" Ari trembled, her resolve threatening to break.

"The God of the Bible. We are Christians—well, many of us are." Jenna motioned to the group.

Ari looked down at Kane as the blade of the knife trembled and her body began to shudder. "I can't," she cried as she fell back away from Kane and tossed her knife aside. "I couldn't cut Aviel down before I passed out. I can't see him like this anymore!" Ari cried and shielded her eyes.

Kane sat up slowly and touched at a small cut on the side of his neck. Jenna moved forward, her arms open.

"Shh, it's okay. If you let me, I'll help you," she said as she gently placed a hand on Ari's shoulder. "Together we will get him down and find a place for him to rest in peace. You are among friends now."

After a moment, Ari bit her lip and nodded, took a shuddering breath, and wiped the tears from her face. "Hashem. Elohim. My God has spoken and is faithful."

▲ ▲ ▲

Malak stepped out from the passenger side of a rusted junker that had seen better days in some far-removed suburban life filled with groceries and crumb covered car seats. The human skulls that hung as a permanent fixture on the rust-covered steel ram grate on the front remained a warning of the impending doom of all who bore witness to it.

Malak's heavy boot ground the gravel beneath it as he stepped a few steps away from the rusted caravan full of bandits. Psychos and sadists, every last one, they'd submitted themselves to him and had now become a part of something much larger. A dark plan that had been put into motion long before humankind, in all of its arrogance, had even existed. Malak brooded at the thought of the power to come. The sheer lust he felt for it was beyond comprehension. He wanted it all, and there was nothing in this world that could stop him now.

The pain, like a dagger in his brain, caused him to cry out as he stumbled and shook his head. Swarming with unrelenting agony, Malak thought his head might burst from the pressure. When the Voice was ready to emerge again, it would. Until then it would guide him, cloaked in a disguise of flesh and bone. He placed his hands on the side of his head and bared his teeth.

"What do you want?"

For you to remember.

"Remember what? I've done what you wanted."

Remember to whom you belong. Remember this: though you may enjoy the power, it does not, and will never, belong to you.

The entire convoy had now exited and was watching the bizarre exchange along the dusty roadside, as Malak continued to groan and converse with some unseen oppressor. The men didn't understand it, but they also knew not to interfere with it.

"Why do you torment me, Voice? Have I not been faithful?" Malak continued, hissing through clenched teeth.

Oohh, yes, Malak's been sooo faithful. But he never seems to get the job done...

"Do not mock me!" Malak raged.

Touchy, touchy, Lord Malak. Such little faith. You have no idea what is coming. How the Master will cleanse this wretched planet with blood and fire. When he comes, you will be granted all that you desire. You will be a god over these miserable people.

"Yes. I will be a god."

Yes. But you must first complete your task. You must first find the Machine. It is the key to the power you crave.

"And where will I find this Machine?"

It resides where your kind keeps all the things they value—in the secret places of the dark. Keep moving west, and I'll show you...in time.

"I understand."

And, Malak, take care to guard those little ones as though your life depends upon it.

"Oh?"

Malak glanced to see a few bored bandits taunting the two helpless children tied together in the bed of a nearby truck. They sat huddled close, each the other's only and final defense from the evil that surrounded them.

Malak laughed, amused at the irony. "So you would spare them out of love?"

You think me funny? This act is not one of love. Their innocent blood and their pain are necessary for the Master's task. If your dogs corrupt them, it will be on your head—and you, of all people, cannot afford to fail the Master again. Now do as you have been told and be a good, ignorant little host.

As the Voice faded from him and the pain subsided, Malak felt a whole new fury bloom within him. In a fit of rage, he pulled the door off a nearby vehicle and plucked the shrieking driver from behind the wheel, lifting him up for all to see. With one deft movement, Malak crushed the man's head and flung his disfigured corpse down the embankment away from him. The children shrieked in dismay, covering their little faces. Malak watched as the Coyotes dropped to their knees in fear and reverence, chanting for him to spare them, and the fear of all who had seen his power began to calm him. Nothing could stop him. He would be a god. And when that day finally arrived, no one—not even the Voice—would dare to mock him.

11

IT HAD TAKEN hours for Kane and the others to clear the site of all the bodies. That included appropriate burials for those who had been crucified or put on gruesome display, including Ari's brother, Aviel. Ari had cried, trembling and stalling the act of covering him with earth. It was clear that they had been close.

Kane watched the Israeli woman for a moment now, as she sat off to the side, fighting some horrific internal battle alone. She had cleaned up and changed out of her blood and gore-soaked clothes into something cleaner, a rugged button-down shirt and some camouflage BDU pants wrapped at the ankle and tucked into her boots. The change appeared to have helped her regain her composure.

The group had scavenged what food, fuel, and weapons there were to scavenge and prepped the vehicles to roll. He knew there wasn't much time to waste after they spent the entire afternoon here, but he also knew this woman and her brother deserved this attention and care. As much as he disliked the idea of their group traveling at night, it was a foregone conclusion at this point.

Taking a few steps over to the silent female figure now staring off into the distance, Kane tried to rehearse what he should say. He had never been a wizard with words, and most times the filter for his mouth didn't function the way it should. He scratched at the itchy stitches in his abdomen.

"No knives this time, right?" Kane said.

Ari looked up and rubbed her sleeve across the corner of her eyes. She flashed a small but genuine smile. "I've got one. But I think you're safe, for now."

Kane chuckled, touching at the small cut on his neck, and sat next to Ari, with a groan of pain from the healing wound in his side.

"Sorry about all that." She cut her eyes at him, with what looked like a hint of embarrassment.

Kane gave a dismissive wave of his hand. "That's the world we live in."

"You are injured?" She looked him over.

"Huh? Oh yeah, got a few stitches." Kane settled himself next to her and dusted his hands. "I'm healing, but it's slow going."

Ari gazed at him, questions looming.

Kane made a dismissive gesture with his hands. "We've all got scars. None of us would have made it this far if we didn't."

"Your name is Kane, and this is your group?" She said.

Kane gave a nod, stroking his beard.

"Where are you going?"

"West," Kane said.

"What's west?"

Kane grimaced, a look half smile and half pain. He wasn't sure he wanted to tell her the whole bit. "Unfinished business."

Ari regarded him, her thoughts also shrouded in a veil of secrecy. "The man with the crutches—"

"Dagen."

"Yes. I heard him say something about having seen this before." She waved her hand over the shattered camp. "Like he was familiar with the bandits that did this."

Kane didn't respond.

"Do you know who did this, who murdered my brother?"

"Revenge is a difficult thing. It's going to hurt you more than it's worth—trust me."

"You worry about you," Ari cut him short, a coldness returning ever so slightly to her demeanor. "Are you familiar with these bandits, or not?"

Kane took a deep breath and nodded. "Yeah. The Coyotes and their leader, Malak—that's who we're following west."

Ari suddenly came alive. "Why? Why would you court death by trying to stop a group like that?"

Kane took a moment to consider his words. "Ari, I told you: we all have wounds," he said, his face gravely serious. "They have to be stopped. You've seen why."

"But you?" Ari opened her hands to indicate the small group packing up along the road. "You have this, and Malak has an army. How do you expect to take him on with a bunch of untrained civilians?"

"We've been through a lot so far, and it's made us strong. We also have some training. But beyond that, we trust that God is with us. He has brought us this far. He will see us to the end."

Ari's wheels spun, her experience contradicting her faith in a myriad of unanswered questions that all seemed to cross her face at once.

Kane continued. "This is bigger than any of us. It's bigger than revenge or justice or any of the ways we've been personally wronged. Malak has to be stopped. If he isn't checked, he's going to unleash something terrible."

Ari's questioning look deepened.

"Please, don't ask me to explain it further right now. Just trust me. It's worse than you can imagine."

"Take me with you," she said, standing abruptly.

Kane stood to meet her, his mouth half-open. "You just said it yourself—it's a death sentence. Why would you come?"

"You know why. Like you, I have unfinished business. Besides, you may be Christians and I a Jew, but our God is the same God. We all now have a role in this."

Kane regarded the stoic, unflinching nature of the woman before him. She would be an undeniable asset to their cause.

"Yeah, Ari," Kane agreed, "you are more than welcome to join us. We would be honored to have you."

Without warning, Ari stepped forward and wrapped her arms around Kane's neck, clenching him in a hug. He stood with his arms raised, surprised at the gesture.

"The chance to make things right…" Ari fought back the emotion as she squeezed him. "You don't know what this means to me."

"I think I might," Kane reassured her with a small pat on her back, only a little concerned now, that touching this woman would get him cut again.

▲ ▲ ▲

Winston awoke with a start to find a rough hand clamped over his mouth and the point of something sharp pressed into the side of his neck. He moaned, and his eyes flashed wide, the blade threatening to penetrate the stretched skin of his neck if he dared to move.

A female voice slipped into his left ear. "Do what I say, and I won't kill you. Nod if you understand."

Winston nodded, his pudgy body trembling. He tried to clear his mind. He had taken a nap late in the afternoon. He'd pulled his bedroll off to the side to get away from those who were talking or working. Now that it was dark and he had a knife to his throat, he began to deeply regret just how far he had wandered from the safety of the group.

He was jerked to his feet, the knife remaining at this neck as he stumbled and was half dragged farther away from camp. As they rounded the other side of an old convenience store, now deserted and empty, Winston was shoved back against the concrete-block wall.

"Hey, Winston, long time no see," Shana said, sneering.

"Shana? But you were…"

"Captured by the Coyotes, then sent back against them in a rash decision by Kane. Only I wasn't fighting for you people anymore, and Kane got a bunch of his people dead."

"I don't understand."

"Of course not, Winston. That's because you're a sheep. It's remarkable that you've made it this long."

"But—"

"Shh." Shana cut him off and pressed the knife into his neck again. "Look, sweetie, call it Stockholm syndrome if you want, but it goes much deeper than that. Malak took pity on me and opened my eyes to the truth of this world."

"What truth?"

Shana smirked. "Tell him."

"No one stands against the darkness. The world belongs to us now," one of the thugs said.

"That's right, Winston. I chose to be on the winning team, and right now we need you to be a good little squealer and help us out."

"Me? Help…with what?" Winston quivered in terror.

"You're going to hand Kane and the others over to us. We need something to present to Malak, to get back in his good graces. Your information and those people's lives are going be that thing. You understand?"

"I can't do that!" Winston stammered.

"You can't, or you won't?" Shana snapped. "You know Kane and those people aren't going to make it anyway. You know they have no chance out here, how stupid it is to go against us. Now, there are only two ways this is going to go. One, you tell us everything, and I mean *everything*, and we not only spare you now but also when we return to destroy these people. Or you give us *nothing*, in which case we're going to cut your throat and leave you in this ditch."

The fat man shook with fear and indecision.

"You want to die for nothing? Is that what you want?" Shana snarled in his face. She paused and gave a flick of her head. "Fine. Bleed him."

The rough men pulled him from the wall and dragged him to a nearby ditch where they grabbed a fistful of his hair and yanked his head back. The fat man cried out as they put the blade to his neck and began to pull.

"No!" Winston shrieked. "I'm not ready to die," he sobbed.

With a flick of Shana's head, Winston was snatched up and forced back against the wall again.

"Okay, fat boy, ready to play ball or what? Don't waste my time," Shana said, taunting him.

"Wait. Just listen to me."

"What?" Shana said.

"Spare Jenna and the children too. If you do that..." Winston could barely get the words out.

"Not going to happen! The deal is for your life—or nothing!"

"But the children..." Winston stammered.

"They're going to die anyway, and there's nothing you or anyone else can do about it," Shana hissed. "Now deal or die, fat boy—*those* are your choices."

"I...I can't."

"Hold him down." Shana said.

Winston moaned as the men pulled him to the ground and pinned his arms and legs. Shana slid on top of him and pinned his shoulders to the ground with her knees.

"OK, fat boy, you're going to work for us whether you like it or not. Open your mouth."

Winston quivered in terror, refusing to cooperate.

"Do it!" Shana siad as one of the thugs grabbed either side of his jaw, forcing it open. Winston moaned in desperation as Shana cut her own hand, dripping her tainted blood across Winston's face and into his open mouth. The pudgy man thrashed his head and tried to spit it out, but he was choked and forced to swallow it. As he did, he felt it affect him. Deep inside, he felt his heart grow cold, a creeping sickness overtaking him one inch at a time, until there was nothing left but sorrow, shame, and defeat. His thrashing slowed and grew still.

Shana looked into the now-darkened eyes of the fat man before her and smiled. "I'll be damned. Let him up."

The thugs backed away as Winston stood, wiping his face.

"It worked just the way it does for Malak. You can feel the darkness inside you now, can't you? You can feel it like a cancer, growing with every hopeless thought. You belong to us now. You understand that?"

Winston nodded his head reluctantly.

"Now listen up. Doing anything other than what I tell you to do will result in a slow and painful death for you, Jenna, those kids, and everybody else. But if you do exactly what I say and you keep your fat mouth shut about it until we return, we'll let *you* live. You got that? Not a word to Kane or anyone else."

Winston nodded, and Shana continued as she explained the plan and what was in store for the people who had become like family to him. But Winston was only half listening now, his mind descending into a mire of despair, knowing full well that there was no cure for the disease of fear that was now swelling inside him.

They'd forced him to make a deal with the devil, and the devil always collected his due.

▲ ▲ ▲

The reality of the situation, the dire hopelessness of it all, still failed to take root in the depths of his mind. Tynuk stumbled over a low scrub brush and fell to all fours as vomit, thick and milky white like old pancake batter, poured from his throat. He wretched, his insides cramping in pain and exhaustion as they worked to expel the toxin that still plagued him.

The warrior boy sat back on his haunches and wiped the spittle from his face, his head lolling in dizzy circles. The dark of night surrounded him as he searched the desert horizon for any signs of movement. His strange companion had left him hours ago, motioning for him only to continue west. His focus drifted in and out as the shadows laughed at him from the darkness beyond. Placing his hands on his face like some old drunk trying to find his way home, he rubbed it to try to clear his mind.

This pestilence, the devil's snare, as Queenashano had called it, would neither finish him, as it should have long ago, nor release him from its grasp. He was a prisoner in the clutches of the poison, a bystander witnessing the events of his life as they played in front of him on a great cinema screen.

Tynuk vomited again, his body quaking and groaning with the effort. There was no question that he would not make it much farther without water.

Suddenly, before him stood Grandfather Nuk'Chala, his figure, though aged, still regal and full of power.

"Grandfather, help me," Tynuk begged. "I came all this way. I did what you said."

"You failed the trials, boy. Die and release yourself from this purgatory."

"Why would you say that? After all the training, after you told me my destiny was to lead our people?"

"That has passed. You are a failure—a waste of my time and effort."

Tynuk tried to stand before the old man. "No. Grandfather Nuk'Chala would never say such a thing! Away from me, foul spirit!" Tynuk lashed out, swinging his fist in an arc that passed through the hallucination, causing it to evaporate like a specter in the still of thecnight.

"What then of your mother?" Grandfather's voice spoke to him from the darkness all around him. "The woman who bore you, the mother you left to die."

"Stop it! Leave me, demon!"

Now the voice of the boy's mother spoke to him from the depths of the night, her cries echoing against the barren hills of the surrounding landscape. "Reno? Reno, are you there? I'm so scared, Reno."

"Stop!" Tynuk stood, stumbling forward as he cupped his hands over his ears, groaning. "I don't want to hear this!"

"Why did you abandon me, Son? Was I so evil that you would leave me to die?"

"Mama!" Tynuk shrieked as tears ran down his face. "I didn't mean it. I never wanted you to get hurt!"

"You could have taken me with you. But instead, you left me to burn in the fire!"

"No, I wanted to take you with me, but I couldn't!"

"Face it, boy!" Grandfather's words cut like a knife. "You're a failure! You don't have the strength to fulfill your destiny!"

"Please!" Tynuk gasped, as he stumbled blindly across the desert, desperate to escape from this hell.

"You've failed already! Give up and let the desert take you!" Grandfather's voice yelled after him.

"You left me to die!" his mother's voice screamed.

"You failed us!" Grandfather howled.

"You left me!"

"You failed!"

"Leave me, demons! In the name of the Great Spirit, I command you!" Tynuk's feet left contact with the earth as he ran, tumbling headlong into an ancient crevice carved by centuries of flooding watershed.

"Spirit, protect me!" The boy's cries disappeared into the depths of the trench and the failure of his own heart—a darkness that no longer allowed him to see any hope for the future.

12

THE GROUP ACCEPTED Ari into their midst without so much as a vote. It was as though they all sensed that she had as much a right to be a part of what they were doing as those among them who had been embroiled in this mess from the beginning.

Courtland stood, watching, his passive demeanor in stark contrast to his gigantic, almost-mythic size. He eyed the new dark-haired woman as Kane helped to find her a vehicle to ride in. As a result of her coming on, they had had to do some chinese-fire-drill-style seat shuffling.

The giant watched as Winston wandered out, disheveled and shuffling toward the vehicles. He looked terrible, absorbed in his own thoughts as he made his way to the caravan. Courtland felt a twinge of sympathy for this man, who looked as though he carried the weight of the world on his shoulders.

"Hey, Winston, get some good rest?" Courtland said with a good natured smile.

The man continued to shuffle, entranced.

"Winston? You okay, big guy?" Courtland tried again.

"Muh? Wha—?" Winston turned and blushed, embarrassed he'd been caught off guard.

"Are you alright?" Courtland emphasized.

"Oh yeah, yeah, I'm fine, thanks." He turned away and entered a tarnished sedan of unrecognizable make.

Strange.

Courtland landed a huge booted foot into the cab of the old diesel Ford F-350 and craned his neck to look at the sky. The ribbons of smoke and cloud cover left ragged holes in the ceiling of the world just big enough to see a few stars now as the sun dropped out of sight, melting beneath the black horizon. Above, the small, uneven pockets remained remarkably clear against the darkening sky. A host of stars glittered like tiny diamonds flung against the dark unknown reaches of space. They stood in stark contrast, single points of illumination, lighting an otherwise dark and uninhabitable landscape.

It had been so long since he had stopped to gaze at the stars. It made him think of his daughter, Marissa, years ago when she was just a girl, giggling and lying against his massive chest as she pointed up and asked him about the constellations. They lay on the front lawn for what seemed like hours, snuggling, tickling, and enjoying each other's company. Each was all the other had after Marissa's mother passed— a loss Courtland thought he might never recover from. But the difficulties and loneliness of single parenthood were nothing compared with the beautiful, all-consuming joy of being a father. Courtland cherished it, knowing that like all things on this earth, one day, this phase of his life too had to end.

Sadly, it ended much sooner for him than he would have liked—his daughter killed in a terrible car crash that he'd miraculously survived, only to face the End War and the death of modern civilization that followed. Through it all Courtland never lost his faith, never stopped believing in a God who acted with purpose and love. He always reminded himself that he deserved nothing and that his sin was enough to condemn him for eternity were it not for the redeeming blood of his savior, Jesus. He knew that he existed on this earth to further the kingdom of God, and if that was in the Crushball arena, the church pulpit, or a wasteland nightmare fighting the deranged forces of evil, it was where he knew he was supposed to be. It was what he was born for. It was why God had chosen him and imbued him with uncanny superhuman strength. Just like Samson. And Courtland knew that, just like the long-locked hero of old, should he lose his way or his faith in God, so would he his strength.

"Hey." Jenna's voice broke his concentration and snapped him back to the present. "Dagen is going to ride with you, since Ari and Kane are now in the Jeep with me. We've had to shuffle a few folks around since we're taking on Ari and the few others we found. I figured Kane and this one probably shouldn't ride together." She gave a half smile as she patted Dagen's shoulder.

"Yes, probably a wise move," Courtland responded. Dagen slipped his crutches into the vehicle and took his seat. He appeared to be miffed at the change. Jenna winked at Courtland from across the cab and made her way back to her vehicle.

Well, this is going to be interesting.

Courtland heaved his massive bulk into the truck that rocked hard to one side with the addition of five hundred human pounds and pulled the door shut with a clink as the diesel rumbled to life and began to roll west down Interstate 40.

⋏ ⋏ ⋏

Hours of silent, ruined highway had passed beneath the tires of the caravan that had passed into New Mexico a while back. Courtland and Dagen led the way, cutting the night with the bulk of the heavy F-350, the skipping yellow line disappearing from their headlights into the the desert void ahead.

They had gone out of their way to avoid Oklahoma City, Amarillo, and a few other cities. It hadn't even been a discussion since by now they all knew the drill. Large cities or significantly populated areas were to be avoided at all costs. They were the areas that had been hardest hit with plague, famine, riot, and death. They would also have the highest concentration of highwaymen and mutant Sicks. It was never worth the risk.

It had taken an extra hour or two, but Courtland had safely led the group around the southern perimeter of the two cities through the broken, smoldering suburbs, a chilling reminder of how many people, how many unprepared and unsuspecting families, had perished in the days since the end began. The simple, now-ransacked neighborhood subdivisions passed without further thought, ghosts of a previous era, remnants of a better time.

Dagen sighed and rubbed his eyes. What was he doing? After all that had happened in his life, how had he come to this place? How had he become a part of this group? No longer just tagging along, he was now a member of these people, these Christian survivors. It was, of course, Jenna's influence that had spared his life on more than one occasion. He owed her too much. They were debts that would never be paid, no matter what choices he made in this life. She was a saint, his angel. He had tried to tell her, but the words never seemed to come out right without being creepy. He knew he wouldn't ever be able to voice what it was that he felt inside.

But as much as he knew that it all began with Jenna and that she was the catalyst of everything that he felt inside, he also knew now that there was something else at play here. It was a presence that he couldn't quite put his finger on. They all called it "God," and Jenna had told him that it was Jesus that he saw in her. Dagen wasn't sure yet, but he couldn't deny that there was a greater power at work around them. What they had all done and overcome—it was beyond reason that any of them were still alive. Not to mention the strange visions and dreams they all had received. It was like some greater being had designed it that way like they were all meant to see it. He just couldn't make any sense of it, and the more he did, the less he felt he understood it.

"You know," Courtland said, interrupting Dagen's pondering the mysteries of life, "I don't think I ever said anything to you, but I was impressed at how you stepped up to defend our people during all that mess with the mutants and Jenna being kidnapped and all that."

Dagen said nothing, unsure how to respond. He hated awkward conversations, but the giant didn't seem to have a problem expressing himself.

Courtland cleared his throat. "I just wanted you to know that it was my honor to stand with you through that."

"Yeah, well, don't get too excited," Dagen said, blowing him off. "I'm not the guy to make the sacrifice play. It's not me."

"Well, whatever it was, I was grateful to have your help. God called us to be there in that moment, to stand together."

"Sure thing."

"You don't think so?"

"I don't know what I think, Courtland. Forget about it."

"Then what is it?" Courtland looked over at him, his massive frame comically wedged into the cab of the truck. He couldn't be comfortable.

Dagen turned to look back out the window, the dark landscape outside passing without a sound.

Courtland glanced at Dagen again. "Come on, friend. I can see your wheels turning from here."

Dagen turned to look at the giant. Something about the demeanor of the man called to him, urged him to trust the gentle giant in confidence. "Okay, if you're not going to let this go, can I ask you a question then?"

"Shoot," Courtland said, looking back forward as he veered left to avoid some wreckage in the road.

"When you believe in God, how do you know your belief isn't misplaced? How do you know that it's real?"

Courtland considered this for a moment. "I think you already know the answer to that," the giant said. "You ever had someone love you? Not in a way that was artificial or selfish or purely sexual. I mean really love you, even though there was nothing you had done to deserve that love?"

Dagen immediately thought of Jenna. "Let's say I have. What of it?"

"Well, knowing that we deserve to spend eternity in hell for our sin, and knowing that the God of the universe paid that price for us so that we could be saved from that fate, it feels the same way. You trust in it because you feel it in your heart. You know that God loves you even though there's nothing good in you apart from him."

"But what if it's not that simple? What if a person has never been to church or been baptized or any of that other holy roller stuff?"

"Don't worry about that, Dagen. The condition of your heart is what is most important. If you are sorry for your sin and you truly desire forgiveness, then all you have to do is ask for it."

"That's stupid. There has to be more to it."

"Not really. That's the most important part."

Dagen seemed exasperated as held his palms up. "Okay, just for the sake of argument, wouldn't you feel cheated if you had been a good person your whole life, but you just didn't believe in God, so you couldn't go to heaven? Or what about if you were a devout believer your whole life, and then some loser who had lived a rotten life believes at the last moment—you think that it's fair that they both get to heaven just the same as the other?"

Courtland smiled, patiently considering Dagen's earnest questions and obvious irritation. "It's not about fairness, my friend, and it's not a race or a contest. Everyone, regardless of how good they think they are, is in need of the saving blood of Jesus. He is the only way. There is no other. And if you come to him as a child or on your deathbed, in the end, you have still come, and that's what matters."

"That's ridiculous," Dagen said, turning back to the window.

"Yes, sir," Courtland said, chuckling, "it truly is."

Courtland's radio crackled to life as Kane's voice washed through the static. "*Hold up right here, Court.*"

He slowed the truck as they came to an exit ramp off the interstate with a dust-coated sign that read, *Hwy 14, Cedar Crest, next right.*

After a long pause, Kane's voice came through the radio once more. "*Albuquerque is not far ahead. We are going to need to detour north around the city and head toward Farmingdale. According to my ancient, half-mutilated road atlas, Highway 14 north to 536 to 550 should work, as long as they all are passable.*"

"So we're taking the next exit, right?"

"*Correct.*"

"Copy. We're going to need to scavenge for gas soon too, we're running low."

"*Okay.*" There was a pause before Courtland's radio crackled again. "*It's been a long haul, and we've made it relatively unmolested. It's probably time to make camp and get some rest for now. Let's exit here and see what's what.*"

"Copy that."

Courtland set the radio down and steered the heavy truck toward the ramp and down to the dark wreckage of post-civilization below.

The inhuman shriek echoed across the dark of the landscape and froze every member of the group where he or she stood scavenging. Whether it was PTSD or just the sheer terror they all associated with that sound was irrelevant; the reaction was the same. The children burst into tears, Kane and Courtland exchanged worried glances, and several people swore under their breath as they picked up their weapons and waited.

"Infected?" Ari asked.

Kane nodded. "Yeah, we call them Sicks. We had a bad experience with them."

"That's putting it mildly." Jenna huffed.

One scream was followed by another—its long, low warbling ending in a painful, animalistic groan.

"Everyone, rally up on me," Kane said in a forced whisper. "Get close enough to hear me."

Everyone shuffled close, careful not to make too much noise as they listened for what Kane had to say.

"Listen, don't wig out. This is not going to be a repeat of what happened at the station; that group was organized by the Father. Without him and his control over them, they're just hungry freaks. If we stay calm and stay quiet, we will get out of this."

"Let's just get in the trucks and go!" Sam urged, a little too loud, as the others motioned for him to shut up.

"Courtland is almost out of fuel, and we haven't found any diesel yet. Several other vehicles are about dry as well. We won't make it much farther if we don't siphon some."

"So what do we do then?" Sam asked.

"We take up positions here, 360-degree coverage, and we wait. Put your firearms down but keep them close. Firing them will bring any others within earshot." Kane said.

Moving quick while maintaining their sound discipline, the group circled the wagons with the children in the center. Staying low and quiet, they watched and waited in the thick, silent dark.

It felt like they waited hours, each contemplating the unknown outcome that lay before them. Then they heard it. The shuffling, scampering, and snuffing of what sounded like a pack of wild animals. They could just make out their haggard silhouettes, as a moderate-size group of Sicks crossed the road in front of them, some walking upright like the humans they had once been and others scrambling about on all fours like hybrids of human and beast.

Kane swallowed away the old feelings of terror that threatened to steal his resolve as Courtland leaned in and whispered in his ear.

"I forgot just how much I hate those things."

Kane said nothing, waiting for the monsters to see them. One by one they crossed the road, meandering into the dark hills before them. After a few tense moments, they were gone, not a single one alerted to the humans in their midst.

"Are they gone?" someone asked.

"I think so," Kane glanced around and pointed to a nearby convenience store, an A+ Mart. "There. Take what you need and as fast and quiet as you can, move to that store. We will clear it first and make sure it's safe, then we'll fortify it for the night. Rummaging around in the dark for supplies is a sure fire way to draw more unwanted attention. When we get some light, we will find some fuel and be on our way. Now, everybody, go and be over at the store in no more than five minutes. Stay quiet."

There it was again, that repetitive grinding sound that seemed to scratch it's way into his troubled dreams. Kane shifted his position, leaning his back against an interior wall of the dirty, trash-filled store. He hadn't thought he'd sleep, and yet sleep came for him before he'd known it. Sam was on watch, he'd let them know if there was danger.

The sound continued grating, pulling on the unraveling seam of his unconsciousness as it grew distant.

What is that?

Kane flicked his heavy eyes open, at first seeing nothing but dark.

"What is that damn noise?" he said with a groan, looking toward the rear door of the shop, which was now being pushed open. He could just make it out: feet sliding across the floor, the door edging wider, eyes like flickering flames.

Kane flew to his feet, crossing the lobby of the store in a dead run. Slamming into the closing door, he collided at full speed with the slick, leathery flesh of a mutant Sick, as it dragged Dagen from the store, its clawed hand clamped over the crippled man's mouth as he moaned and squirmed.

Scrambling on top of the thrashing creature, Kane drove his knife between its ribs, twisting the blade to the chorus of cracking bones. The monster howled just before Kane silenced it with a stab of his knife through its temple.

Dagen rolled to his belly on the ground. "Motherfucker tried to abduct me!"

Kane, head still swimming with disorientation, shouted, "Courtland, check our people! See who's missing. They're trying to take us!"

The inside of the store came to life as people scrambled for their weapons, shouting.

"Who's coming?"

"Where's Sam?"

"Somebody get a head count!"

Something inhuman shrieked in the darkness beyond. Kane scanned the horizon and dropped his gaze to Dagen.

"Are you injured?"

"I...don't think so."

"I'm going to drag you back inside."

"Fine."

Moving as fast as he could, Kane dragged Dagen back into the store and bolted the door behind them.

"Jenna?" Dagen called out.

"I'm okay," she replied.

"Keep ready, there may be more out there," Kane said to no one in particular.

"Sicks?" Courtland looked at Kane.

"Yeah, I've never seen them do this before. That one, just now, was dragging Dagen right out from under our noses. Had a hand over his mouth and everything." Kane was still out of breath.

"Sam's gone too," someone said.

"And Brian. I can't find Brian," cried another.

"Alright, everybody stay calm." Kane swallowed, wiped his mouth, and tried to forget that his side was aching like he'd been kicked by a mule. He checked his stitches and tried to get his breathing under control. "Sam was on watch, Brian was sleeping under the open window, and Dagen was closest to that rear door. They went for the easiest prey first."

The Sick howled as it came running out of the dark towards the front windows, frothing and foaming, its ugly gray lips peeled back over sharpened teeth.

"Behind you!" Ari called, acquiring the amber dot of her AR-15 optic and firing a round through the monster's head. The freak took another clumsy step and fell, sliding across the ground to the front of the store.

"I'm going after them." Kane did a round check of his Glock and looked up.

"Me too," Ari said.

"I'll go," Courtland said, nodding.

"No, you stay here, big man. Protect everyone else. Ari and I will handle it."

"Godspeed, brother," Courtland said.

Without wasting another moment, Kane and Ari climbed through the broken window and set out to find their people. Tracking the distant cries for help, it didn't take long. With a muffled groan here, a cry for help there, they tracked their quarry. They just reached the top of a nearby rise when they saw it, a group of about fifteen of the creatures gathered together in a huddled mass. Kane could just make out Sam's haggard voice naming the saints near the center of the swaying group.

"We don't have much time," Kane started.

"You have enough ammo?" Ari interrupted him.

"No. Two topped-out mags. That's it."

"I have about the same. It's enough. We'll flank them. Interlocking sectors of fire. Head shots only. Get ready to move."

"Yeah," Kane said. There was no question—the woman knew how to take charge. "Let's do it."

Moving down the short slope at speed, but not so fast that they lost their point of aim, Kane and Ari descended upon the fragmented swath of savage mutants. Each moving to the outside, Ari fired first, and Kane opened up from the other side. With both of them striking good head shots, the plan was working, the freaks fleeing in all directions. In moments, each and every Sick had cleared out.

Kane and Ari moved to the downed men, stepping and jumping over the massacred Sicks that lay all around. At their feet, Brian lay in a pool of blood, his pearly white intestines strewn about in the dirt.

Ari swore as Kane checked Sam.

"Sweet Moses! Are you guys a sight for sore eyes," Sam stammered.

"We've got to get you out of here." Kane stooped and started to help Sam to his feet when Ari stopped him.

"Kane."

"What?"

"Look."

Standing, Kane noticed the eyes before he saw the shadows. Soulless, fiery embers staring back at him from the dark. He raised his weapon but didn't fire. All around them, the eyes of forty or more of the mutants looked on. Likely come to investigate the noise, hoping for an easy meal.

"We're screwed," Sam moaned.

"Hang on. Let me think." Kane glanced at Ari and checked his round count. "Seven."

"Four," Ari said.

"Alright. Before you tell me I'm crazy, just hear me out. These things are more animal than man. I think we should posture."

"What?"

"Posturing. Like you would if you ran into a grizzly while hiking. We scream, wave our arms, and fire our weapons in the air."

"You *are* crazy! Shoot all our ammo?"

"They don't *know* how much ammo we have."

"What if they come anyway?"

"Then we didn't have enough to fight them, and we'd never make it back to the others anyway."

"Just give me a logical reason why we should do this."

"They're not organized—not like before. They're just hungry freaks. I think we can scare them off."

"Organized like before?"

"Look, it's way too long a story. Just trust me."

Ari bit her lip. "I'm going to be pissed at you if you get me killed."

Kane forced a laugh. "Yeah, I figured. Sam, you get in on this too. Stand with us."

Sam stood with them, and Kane counted down from three. In unison, Kane, Ari, and old Sam raised their arms in the air, screaming mightily. Even cloaked in shadow, the Sicks flinched, some shuffling away from the outpouring of noise. A few bolder creatures nudged forward baring their teeth.

"Louder!" Kane shouted, firing his handgun into the air. Ari followed suit, firing her rifle. The many flickering eyes shifted, departing, and after a long, tense moment of collective shouting, the last pair turned and disappeared into the dark.

Silence held.

"You lucky idiot," Ari said, huffing. "I can't believe that worked."

Kane was already pulling her and Sam in the direction of their people. "Let's not stick around to find out if they change their minds."

Beyond them, daybreak was but minutes away, the darkened landscape stark against the thin line of growing light along the horizon. They would get their people together, find more fuel, and keep moving. Anything was safer than staying here.

13

TYNUK GASPED AND waking in panic in the darkness of the rough sandstone crevice. He was still alive, somehow, and for the first time, he felt as though his head was starting to clear. It would appear that the poison had run its course, and he was beginning to regain control of himself. He raised his head from the soft sand of the crevice floor and felt a wet suction pull against his cheek. Wet. He turned his face and smelled the liquid that trickled with a gentle flow around him. Pushing his swollen tongue from his mouth, he tasted the coolest, cleanest water that had ever made its way to the desert that was his throat.

Gasping with a moan, Tynuk buried his face in the crystal-clear spring. He gasped a breath, bubbles forming on the surface of the small pool. Smothering himself in the intoxicating pleasure of the moment, he bathed his face again in the shallow spring as it continued to flow its way through the wash.

His eyes caught the tiniest flicker of movement along the water's edge above his face. Tynuk focused his eyes and watched the tiny shadow skitter this way and that, it's pink tongue flicking into the water as it moved. A lizard. Tynuk remained still as a statue, waiting. He shot out his arm and snared the creature in his hand, shoving it in its entirety into his open mouth. He chewed vigorously, the tiny bones snapping as the thing wriggled in his mouth. He shook his head with a grimace, swallowed, and drank again from the stream. The nourishment would do him well.

A shuffling movement above him along the edge of the crevice brought back the reality of his perilous situation. He rolled his body, twisting his head so he could see above him. Faint at first and then more pronounced, a shadow moved along the rim, only twenty feet above. The figure moved with practiced care, analyzing every aspect of the terrain as it tried to determine the fate of the maker of the tracks it followed. Tynuk knew without question that he was the quarry and that his pursuer intended to kill him. It was the ancient way.

It was possible that the shadow would believe that he had leaped over the crevice and continued west, but should it choose to investigate further, he would be trapped in the narrow cut with scarcely enough room to turn or maneuver. The warrior boy rolled back to his belly and lay still, the cool water flowing with a healing power against his skin. He took another quiet drink and waited.

After a long moment, a thud against the wet sand of the crevice floor confirmed his fear. He had been discovered. With any luck, his pursuer would believe that he had finally expired, falling into the unmarked grave that was this ditch.

He listened as the figure stooped upstream, scooping water into his hands that he first smelled and then tasted, before gulping several handfuls. The figure wiped his face with his arm and looked at the shadowed form of the dead warrior boy lying in a crumpled heap just a little farther down the cut.

Tynuk remained still as the shadow approached. He knew that, in his current, weakened state, he would be unable to put up enough of a fight to defeat this shadow in a stand-up fight. He had to end it as soon as possible or things would get ugly for him. Such was the nature of extreme survival.

The figure was close now, standing just outside the boy's reach. Raising a short spear, the warrior jammed it down with lightning-fast precision through Tynuk's hand—a test to see if he yet lived. A blast of searing pain roared up Tynuk's arm, setting his body ablaze. It took every ounce of self-control for him to remain unflinchingly still, a dead boy against the floor of the wash.

The spear was jerked free, causing another shock wave of pain. Tynuk shook inside, his mind wild with the overwhelming sense of injury. The shadow gave a grunt and raised his spear again. Tynuk knew he might not survive another thrust of the weapon. He also knew without question that he would scream if he were hit a second time—a move that would surely prompt his aggressor to strike again before he had a chance to react.

Tynuk knew his one option lay in the advantage of surprise, an advantage he still possessed but was losing with every passing moment. In a moment born of sheer will, Tynuk rolled and deflected the short spear as it stabbed down at his back with surprising speed. As he rolled he flung a handful of mud upward that landed with an audible smack in the center of the shadow's face.

His pursuer stumbled back, cursing him in their native tongue and clawing at the mass that was now adhered to his painted face. Tynuk was up and moving, but his body ached, and too late he realized the poison wasn't quite done with him, a wash of dizziness and nausea covering him as he shot forward.

Slamming against the howling Comanche warrior, Tynuk latched onto the spear. His body crashing backward into the wall of the ditch. The shaft of the spear snapped against the rock like a dry twig. He had sorely underestimated this warrior's size and power. Gasping, flailing against this larger, superior warrior, Tynuk knew he was doomed if this fight wasn't over quick.

Squaring his shoulders, the warrior pinned him against the wall with the weight of his forearm against Tynuk's neck, the pressure causing Tynuk to gag and froth at the mouth.

"This is where your journey ends, child!" the warrior snarled in his native tongue as he pulled a knife from his belt and stabbed in toward the boy's chest. It was in that moment that Tynuk realized he was still holding the point of the broken spear in his other hand. He dropped his arm and knocked the stab of the knife away, sinking it into the dirt next to his torso. Torquing his body, he swung his opposite arm in an arc and jammed the spear point into the large warrior's neck. The man released him immediately, pulling the bloodied spearpoint from the side of his neck. Blood sprayed from the wound in pressurized spurts, and the warrior feebly tried to cover it in his final moments. He did not attempt to conceal his shock that he had somehow lost this contest to a boy half his size.

Tynuk, still dizzy, vomited watery bits of lizard and wiped his face.

The warrior stumbled to his knees. "Ketokwe hina haniitu."

Tynuk took a step forward, a twinge of sympathy in his heart over killing another one of his own. "I am not a devil. I'm sorry for this, brother, but I cannot fail. I must go on."

Tynuk took a deep breath and tried to steady the hammering of his heart as the warrior dropped before him and flopped to his belly, bleeding the last arterial pumps of his life against the sand. Tynuk composed himself, rinsed and wrapped his injured hand, and began to search the dead man for food, useful items, tools, clothing, and gear. When he had gathered what he could carry and refilled the warrior's empty waterskin from the creek, he looked on the dark form of the warrior one last time and felt compelled to lay his hand on the man out of respect.

"You fought bravely and with great power, my brother. But in the end, you could not stop me." The boy gathered his gear and began walking down the trench away from the brightening of the horizon.

"None of you can."

▲ ▲ ▲

The walls were thick. Thirty feet, he had been told. Concrete so thick you couldn't hear the outside world even if you wanted to—not that there was anything to hear out there anymore. At this point, he'd sacrifice a body part to hear another human voice, a car in motion or a jet passing overhead. He looked at the expired calendar on the cluttered desk in front of him. He made a quick estimate of the time he'd been here, marooned on his own desert island. About a year.

Son of a bitch. Has it been that long?

Nick Corvaleski leaned back in the springy metal-framed desk chair and tented his fingers against the tip of his nose. It was a position he had taken to years and years ago as a kid when he needed to think. All the school, the training, the PhD in electrical engineering, it had done nothing for him when the world ended. Now he was just a warm body without a function apart from eating, defecating, and using up oxygen.

He glanced around the stark, gray interior of the lab. The cold, gray concrete had a way of stealing away any sense of warmth or joy. He wasn't sure why he stayed. Except, that wasn't true. He knew. Divorced, no kids, no real friends outside of work, and no living family to speak of, he didn't have any reason to go rushing off to save people who couldn't be saved when the attacks came. Many of his coworkers did, and they'd never come back, just as he'd expected. A few had stayed: Joseph in hydro; Nikki, one of the nuclear physicists;

and several of the military personnel, air force, he thought but had never been bold enough to probe.

All of them were now dead or gone. After a few months, Nikki and the remaining soldiers left. Said they were going to Washington, DC, to do something about this mess. Joe had stayed the longest but had a heart attack of all things and died on the floor in the bunk room. Nick thought it was funny. He and Joe weren't really friends, and he found it ironic that the man survived the death of civilization only to die of a stupid heart attack. It was like he always said—life sucks, and then you die.

Everyone being gone didn't bother him much. He was a pretty serious introvert, so it was just a matter of time before he ran off the people who surrounded him anyway. Most folks only dealt with him in a professional capacity because it was a requirement of the job.

The job. It had seemed real important at the time. He'd been hired to be one of the project leads at a "secret facility" in Arizona. At first, he thought it was a joke when the nameless voice on the telephone offered him a job with "top-secret" clearance at an undisclosed facility but refused to answer any questions or discuss it further over the phone.

Because he'd hated his job at the time, he accepted the offer without much thought, knowing full well that he was going to work for the government on a project that involved weapons of mass destruction or something. Little had he known that this secret facility was hidden deep beneath the walls of the Glen Canyon Dam on the Colorado River in northern Arizona. Or that the project he was hired for was just one of many that were being worked on there. He'd even heard rumors that it wasn't just *a* secret facility but *the* secret facility—that there were crazy things housed here in the bowels of the dam, things that weren't supposed to exist, like the Ark of the Covenant and alien artifacts from Area 51. But that was all probably just the blind super-stition that surrounded this place.

Nick stood from the chair and plucked up an MRE from the table, pulling the tab and examining the nitrogen-packed contents. "Beef stroganoff. Meh."

He crunched the dry MRE crackers, spilling crumbs down his shirt. With power generated by the hydroelectric systems of the dam, which he'd been smart enough to get running again, clean moun-tain-cleansed water running beneath him, and a stockpile of food, he could live here like a king for quite a long while.

He gave a guffaw, spitting dry cracker bits across the room and pushing his glasses further up his nose. Unless someone decided to come and kick him out, he could stay here, problem-free, maybe forever.

Everyone else out there could deal with the horrors of the outside world. That was for them. Life sucks, and then you die.

▲ ▲ ▲

After the close call with the Sicks, the group decided to pack up and move on as soon as possible. Partially refueled and with some extra supplies and even a small quantity of scavenged water, they were ready to roll once more. Rest could wait, especially since Kane had the sneaking suspicion that no one would get any real rest with those things lurking about.

The dark mesas loomed in the distance against the brightening skyline as the caravan of vehicles wound their way north on the lonely, debris-filled state highway.

Kane shifted his position and pawed again at the wound in his abdomen. The struggle with the Sicks had aggravated the pain, and even though it was pretty much healed, it still maintained a considerable ache the radiated outward.

Ari looked at Kane, her eyes casting over him from the passenger seat of the Jeep. Jenna had ridden with Courtland and Dagen to see how they were faring, which left Kane and Ari of them alone for the time being.

"What?" Kane glanced at Ari.

She ducked her eyes, a little embarrassed that she had been staring so long. "You keep touching your side. I know the running and shooting back there probably didn't feel very good."

"Not so much."

"For what it's worth, you shoot pretty well, for a man."

Kane smirked. "It's a good thing I had such a strong and confident woman with me to call the play."

"True." Ari bobbed her head. "If you hadn't, you'd likely be mutant food right now."

Kane shook his head, still smiling good-naturedly.

Ari motioned to his side, her face a bit more serious. "Your wound—it still aches?"

"A little sensitive still, I guess."

"What was it from?"

"A bullet," Kane shrugged. "I had soft armor on, but it still penetrated at close range."

Ari nodded, her wheels turning. "It seems like you guys really had a hard time of it before."

"Understatement of the year."

They rode on in silence for a few minutes, both at war with their own thoughts. Along the horizon, the faint swell of the sun was just visible through the hazy cloud cover as it began its ascent into the darkened sky.

Ari screwed up her face and shook off her morbid thoughts. Kane took notice. It was his turn to ask.

"You had a bad go of it yourself the other day."

"I'm alright. I just…I, um…" Ari couldn't decide if she even wanted to say anything.

Kane waited, staring straight ahead as he drove.

"Tohar ha'neshek."

"What was that?" Kane glanced over as Ari shifted position.

"Tohar ha'neshek. In Hebrew, it means 'the purity of the weapon.' This is the concept that an Israeli soldier is not permitted to use his or her weapon in a way that desecrates the name of God. Technically that means we are prohibited from intentionally killing noncombatants."

"Okay," Kane waited.

Ari wasn't sure why, but she had to get it off her chest. "So, this principle is ingrained into the IDF soldier. Forget what the news used to say or what our enemies would have you believe; Israelis are trained to show unbelievable restraint in battle because of this. Tohar ha'neshek is of vital importance to every IDF soldier." She paused, considering her words. "A few days ago, I killed my baby brother. I shot him in the head before they could torture him." Ari swallowed a lump in her throat and turned so Kane wouldn't see the tear that she quickly wiped away.

"But I thought your brother was murdered."

"It was a mercy killing. He was having his throat cut, but he wasn't dead yet. I couldn't let him go through that anymore…"

"Oh."

"By military standards, a mercy killing doesn't violate this code, but I did choose to kill my baby brother, and I can't see the difference right now. There's a storm inside me."

Kane let a long moment of silence pass before he spoke. "You had a tough choice to make."

"That doesn't excuse it."

"I know it doesn't, but you're human. Just like the rest of us. We've all had to make hard decisions. For what it's worth, I understand where you're coming from." Kane looked deep into her troubled eyes. "Trust me on that."

Ari averted her eyes, changing the subject. "So what is your story here, Kane? Why are you so motivated to catch up with this Malak character?"

She immediately regretted asking when she saw his face.

Don't let her in. Don't let anyone in.

Kane glanced at Ari, whose rugged militaristic appearance failed to conceal the exotic beauty beneath. Her long, dark hair pulled back in a loose ponytail flopped over her shoulder and caused his eyes to wander toward her breasts.

"Look," Kane said, pulling on his neck and sighing, "Malak murdered my wife and my friends and kidnapped my children right in front of me. Then he tried to off me too. That part didn't take." He stoically delivered the horrific news like he had just ordered a burger with fries and a cola.

Ari didn't try to conceal her pity. She shook her head, "I had no idea. I'm very sorry, Kane."

"You asked, I answered. They're gone. There's nothing I can do now but hope that my kids—"

Ari interrupted him, an instant revelation spreading across her face. "Your children! How old are they?"

"What? Why?"

"Are they young? Four or five? A boy and a girl—twins maybe?"

Kane looked at Ari with nothing short of desperation.

"I saw them," she said with surety. "I saw them tied to one of Malak's trucks."

Kane pulled the wheel hard and locked the brakes up. The Jeep slid to a stop on the dark stretch of road. The rest of the caravan came to a stop as Courtland's voice crackled over the radio.

"Kane, is everything okay?"

Ignoring his friend, Kane searched Ari's eyes, scouring the woman's words for truth. "Don't lie to me," he said, his words carrying a lethal edge. "Don't you lie about *this*."

"I would never—"

"How did they look? Were they...Did they..." Kane's face was drawn, his eyes filling with tears.

Ari placed a hand gently on his arm. "They looked really scared but otherwise alright. I don't think they had been badly harmed. It's like he was saving them...for something."

Kane wept with relief at the news. He knew they were far from safe, but they were very recently alive, and for now, that was enough. The radio crackled again.

"Kane, I need to know you guys are alright," came Courtland's voice. "I'm walking back to you now."

The giant reached the Jeep and opened Kane's door. His surprise at Kane's tearful face, which was now morphing into joyous laughter, caused Courtland to look to Ari in confusion.

"They're alive! My kids are *alive*, man!" Kane blurted out.

"What?"

"Ari saw them. She saw them," he mumbled through the tears.

Courtland immediately responded by pulling Kane from his seat and shaking his friend in a great big hug. The infectiousness of the giant's booming laughter drew the rest of their group out of their vehicles and into the street.

Winston swung his legs out of the car and watched the group cheering and hugging in the middle of the road. Time was growing short. The Coyotes would soon return and butcher these good people. He bit at this fingernails, cracked his knuckles, and tried with feeble determination not to throw up. Swallowing hard, Winston produced a fake smile and walked slowly toward what would now be an unavoidable but cherished moment of celebration—for everyone who didn't know what lay ahead.

14

UEENASHANO DISMOUNTED HIS unshod and unremarkable dapple gray mustang. By all considerations, it was one of the most nondescript horses he had ever laid eyes on. But he was old enough to know that, in the ways of life, looks can many times be deceiving. Just as this ugly horse was also one of the fastest he had encountered, a young boy, an outsider, who'd claimed to be half Comanche had proven himself to be a remarkably skilled warrior, tactician, and survivor.

The war chief stepped to the edge of the crevice, rubbed his hairless chin, and twisted his face into an expression that melded astonishment with confusion. It was as though fate needed him to learn a lesson from this. Nodding his head, the war chief took a moment to recount the facts.

This boy who called himself Tynuk had arrived one morning at his encampment indicating he was one of them. He had claimed to be the half-breed son of Nachona Yakeschi, Queenashano's own brother and the immediate student of the great Nuk'Chala. Queenashano turned and reached into a bag that was tied to his bedroll. He removed the dusty war belt that the boy had produced, claiming it had belonged to the old man. Working the leather, beads, and thread beneath his callused fingers, he looked the belt over for any tell. There was no doubt in his mind. He had even had another elder verify his thoughts. The belt was legitimate. But the question remained—how had this boy come to be in possession of it?

Queenashano peered into the crevice to where the body of yet another warrior lay against the blood-soaked sand of the ditch. The child was special. There was no other way to consider it. As bizarre as it all seemed, he could not help but believe that this boy had some-how actually been the protégé of Nuk'Chala, one of the great sages of his people, a relic of their oldest ways and deepest secrets. A man unsurpassed in skill and wisdom—a man who just happened to be Queenashano's uncle.

The war-party leader cursed under his breath and allowed him-self to think of his uncle for the first time in a long while. Their final words to each other had not been ones of love. Nuk'Chala had become infatuated with the idea that the Great Spirit lived inside him. That it was somehow invested in him. And though the other mem-bers of the tribe believed that the old man was losing his mind, there was no question that a strength of belief empowered him. He had been the very best of them, until he had strayed from the direction Queenashano felt they should go. In a moment of fury between uncle and nephew, Queenashano, with the support of the tribe, demanded the old man renounce his love for the Great Spirit. When the old man refused, he was cast out and threatened with death if he ever returned.

Queenashano took a moment and observed the awe on the faces of his warriors and the uncontrolled fury on the face of his own son, Neraquassi, upon seeing another body of their own and knowing that this outsider had prevailed, yet again.

No, Nuk'Chala may not have returned in the flesh, but some-thing of him had. The boy was a reminder of the past, of their peo-ple's waywardness. They had strayed from the oldest ways, and this was their punishment. And if Queenashano was correct, this boy, his own nephew, would survive the trials of the ancients and supersede Neraquassi to become…

"Father, what are we waiting for?" Neraquassi fumed. "By standing around, we are losing ground to this child!"

Queenashano acknowledged the impatience of his son with a staying motion of his hand. The boy had not survived the trials yet. There were two tests left, the final obstacles that the boy must overcome in order to complete the trials. A few days ago Queenashano would have thought this feat impossible, but now the war chief was not so sure.

"Bring up the wolves." Queenashano motioned as several men pulled a wooden cage forward. Inside it, three large, but skinny, gray wolves shuffled back and forth, snarling and biting at the wooden bars. "Everyone, behind the cage," Queenashano called out. The cage was pushed forward, its mouth facing the direction the boy had fled. One of the men pulling the cage extended his hand to Queenashano. The war chief reached into this satchel and produced a piece of clothing he had taken off of the boy when they had stripped him. After he handed it over, the silent man tossed it through the bars, where the wolves snarled and foamed, tearing the cloth to shreds.

"They will stay the course?" Queenashano asked.

"They are hungry for his blood, war chief." The silent man spoke at last. "They will not stop until they have tasted it."

Queenashano didn't choose to question the trainer further. "Good. We will see if this 'Wolf Born' can survive his namesake."

With a nod, the man yanked the strap that held the door closed. In a bawling, whirling maw of fur and teeth, the imprisoned, starving creatures burst forth from the cage. Without a rearward glance, they fled at full speed down the path the boy had traveled, away from their captors.

"The wolves will finish him, Neraquassi, but in the event that they do not, he will at least be weakened from fighting them. I want you to be the final solution. Take three of your best and double up on horseback, but when you are close, separate. Two will go on foot, and two will remain mounted. Use your bows and short spears and overwhelm your prey in the event that the wolves do not succeed."

Neraquassi gave a sharp nod; the acknowledgment that this was his opportunity to finally prove himself glowed in his features.

"Go. We will give you a head start and follow on horseback. Ensure that he is dead by the time I arrive."

Neraquassi nodded again and mounted his horse. He jabbed his finger at three separate warriors: one took his weapons in hand and mounted Neraquassi's steed, and the other two mounted another. With a cry from their riders, the horses were off with uncanny swiftness, delivering their human burdens across the barren dessert.

Queenashano waited until the men were out of sight and the dust began to clear before he called over his fastest rider. Placing a hand on the man's opposite shoulder, in a method indicating that important information was about to be delivered, he spoke just low enough that no one else would hear the message conveyed.

"Take your best horse and ride to meet Penateka and the rest of our people who have made camp in the north. Tell them to break camp and meet us where the sun kisses the horizon in the place of our ancestors. He will understand my meaning."

The young rider, understanding the implication of rallying the whole tribe, began to stammer, "But that means you expect this boy to..."

Queenashano nodded and made a sharp motion for the young rider to be silent. The rider mounted and was gone in a matter of seconds.

Queenashano was beginning to understand that there might be far more to this boy than the eye could behold. For if he was correct, this Tynuk possessed something great, something that had been foreseen and predicted many years ago by the wisest of the ancient priests: a power of belief so strong that it would take their people back to the glory days of old, back to the oldest ways, to times they had all long since forgotten.

▲ ▲ ▲

His father was a fool, an old man who had forgotten the way of things. His unrelenting belief in that stupid prophecy was what blinded him. Neraquassi saw this Tynuk for what he was: a lucky child. Alone and afraid, the boy now fought only for survival, as any hunted animal in his position would.

Neraquassi spurred his mustang onward, his companion hanging on to him, silent and strong as they rode west, following the boy's trail. Whether the wolves finished him or not, it wouldn't take long for them to find him.

There was nothing special about this child who had tried to lay claim to their proud heritage, not a single bone or breath. He was not on a special mission or empowered by anything beyond his own will. He was not of the same bloodline as Neraquassi and his father, and he certainly was not *the one* the prophecy spoke of. It was beyond absurd that a simple half-breed boy could be the one.

Neraquassi shook the tasteless thought from his head. The fact that the boy had survived what should have been a fatal dose of poison meant nothing. He would be hunted down like a dog and surrendered back unto the earth. Big Father was not interested in the games of men. Neraquassi spat and glanced at the brightened patch of thick, dark cloud cover where the sun lay cloaked in the midmorning sky. Big Father had but created them and then set them about their ways, caring no further about their deeds or misdeeds. Neraquassi's destiny was his own, and he would not be controlled by the will of some disinterested God.

Soon, Queenashano would see the truth. He would be blind not to recognize Neraquassi's skill, ambition, and ruthlessness. Neraquassi would be the next war chief of the last survivors of their great people. It was his birthright and his claim. He would, without incident, take the life of this child, setting in motion the events that he knew would follow. There was nothing now that could keep him from claiming his rightful place among their people. Only a boy, tired, scared, and alone, now remained between him and his destiny.

The thunderous boom from above him caused Nick Corvaleski to drop his canteen. The container struck the ground and bounced, splashing water across the floor. He stood, fear filling his limbs like poured concrete, his body rooted in place. Another boom echoed inside the walls of the massive dam, the sound of someone breaching the concrete barriers at the main gate. The terror of what he had worked so hard to avoid, was overwhelming—imminent contact with the outside world. And it sounded to him like the outside world had not come in a display of peace.

"Hit it again," Malak growled, dropping a heavy, muscular arm to his side. The bandit with dreadlocks and a bandanna over his face reloaded the Russian-made rocket-propelled grenade into the launcher and shouldered it. With a whoosh and another deafening concussion, the final concrete barrier blew into a hundred scattered chunks that haphazardly fell as they littered the entrance to the Glen Canyon hydroelectric dam.

"Saxon," Malak motioned for his second in command. "Take thirty men and secure the arch bridge that the highway travels, parallel to the dam. Its position will give us a second angle of fire on both entrances, as well as give us control of the highway and anyone traveling it.

"Yes, my lord."

Malak swung his arm in an arc over his small army of over three hundred. "Take the dam. Subdue any personnel here who may be of value and execute any who try to resist you. This facility now belongs to me." He turned his attention toward the dam, grinning with malevolence. "Do not hide your secrets from me, my dear."

Malak's lustful thoughts of limitless power were interrupted as a beaten Datsun pickup truck screeched to a stop behind them. The smoking engine sputtered and died with a cough, and the occupants exited with their hands in the air.

Malak's Coyotes rushed the vehicle, the occupants yanked from it and pressed to the ground. One of the occupants screamed as his throat was cut in a spray of blood, the thugs laughing over him.

"Do another!" a bandit screamed, mad with lust for blood.

"Lord Malak!" a voice screamed amid the shouts for death.

Malak turned his attention to the boil of madness around the truck.

"Kill that bitch!"

"Lord Malak, I have information!"

"Stop!" Malak commanded, and the furious mass of squirming bodies ceased immediately. "Let her up."

The men pulled Shana to her feet, and a broad smile spread across Malak's face.

"Well, well, look who decided to show back up. Did you forget where we said to meet, my dear Shana?"

Shana bowed her head before the imposing tattooed warlord. "No, my lord. I was wounded carrying out your orders. I couldn't make the rally point before you had gone."

Malak nodded, "And of what use are you to me now?"

"I faithfully carried out your orders, my lord. I returned to Kane's group and assisted in their division, a move that helped to separate Kane from the others. It was all done for you, Lord."

Malak brooded. "What a loyal soldier. But why should you still be valuable to me?"

"I have information you will want to hear."

The bandits around her snickered, all knowing that she would be dead if this information wasn't valuable.

"Out with it," Malak said, crossing his massive arms over the tattoo of a large, coiled viper in the center of his chest.

Shana swallowed. "Kane is alive. His group pursues you as we speak."

A strange hush fell over the group.

"Liar," Malak said, the rage building inside him.

"No, Lord!" Shana fell to her knees. "I saw him with my own eyes."

Malak's eyes flared as he remembered what the Voice had said to him: *Malak'sssss been sooooooo faithful. But he never seems to get the job done...*

Balling his fists, it took every ounce of control he had to keep from lashing out and destroying the lot of scum that stood before him. The massive warlord took a deep breath and then another as he regained control of his emotions. His normally fearless Coyotes cowered before him, anticipating the outpouring of his volcanic temper. He mastered himself and lowered his head in meditation.

Kane was alive. It couldn't be possible, and yet, why would the woman make up such a foolish, audacious lie? If Kane was alive, then he would be coming for his children.

Malak looked at Shana, the weight of his words palpable. "Tell me everything you know. Leave nothing out. Your pitiful life hangs on this moment."

Shana bowed in submission and recounted her story, moment by moment, up to where she now stood. Malak listened, and when she'd finished, he waited for a reflective moment before speaking.

"Is that all?"

Shana bowed low. "Yes, Lord. Kane and about thirty survivors from his group are traveling west on I-40. They are coming here. It's how we found you."

"Which of them survived?" Malak intoned.

"Kane, Courtland, Jenna, Dagen—"

"Stop—what did you just say?" Malak stood stunned at the realization.

"Kane, Court—"

"The last name you said."

Shana swallowed. "A man named Dagen. He's been with them since I first arrived—sort of a loner. His legs are jacked up, so he uses crutches to get around. He's Jenna's pet project for some—"

"Silence." Malak groaned, his face the visage of pure hate. So, Dagen, his own lieutenant, was now a traitorous member of this group that opposed him. The Christian woman had succeeded in wearing him down at last with all her talk of grace and salvation for all. Malak boiled with dark power, millions of years of hate flowing within his veins. He ground his teeth and longed to pull the traitor's heart from his breast. Yes, soon enough.

"What about the Indian boy and his beast?"

"They've been nowhere to be found since before the mutant siege, my lord. They are not with the group now, and there is no one else of interest."

Malak raised himself, brimming with terrible power over the woman. "So this is what you bring to me—news of these insufferable Christians? How they keep on and on, like a fucking disease."

"There is something else, Lord, something that will please you."

Malak's eyebrows rose. "Oh, do tell," he mocked.

"I have a man inside now. He is working with us and has given me detailed information about Kane's group—where they're traveling and what they're planning. If you give me some men, I will slaughter them before they ever make it to this place. You will never even have to lay eyes upon them again. It will be as though we never had this conversation."

Malak considered it long, before answering with a nod. "Do it. Take the men you need and end this blight upon my kingdom. Do not fail me again, woman."

"I won't, my lord!" Shana turned gratefully and quickly began to gather men, arms, and vehicles for her assault.

With long strides, Malak walked toward the dam, his thoughts centering on what rested deep inside; the cosmic device the Voice had spoken about. The timetable had changed. He would have to move now to activate the Machine and put the Master's plan into motion.

There was no doubt in his mind that though Shana's move would slow and maybe even cripple Kane's group, her efforts would ultimately fail, and Malak would be forced to confront Kane and Courtland once again in a fight to the death. And though he had superior men, technology, and a fearsome dark power flowing within him, he also now had just the smallest twinge of doubt that the champions of God could be destroyed at all. And this, more than anything, stirred a restless fear deep inside his heart of darkness.

Part 2

A Time for War

But if thou do that which is evil, be afraid; for he
beareth not the sword in vain: for he is the minister
of God, a revenger to execute wrath upon him that
doeth evil.

—Romans 13:4

And the battle is my way,
I will go this path alone.
I will take unto my prey,
This I know—
All my life will sing the pain,
My suffering will show.
In the fight I find my name,
This I know—
The weight of my call.
One name above all.
All others will fall.

Excerpts from "This I Know" by Demon Hunter

5

STEPPING BACK FROM the mirror pool, the towering figure of stacked muscle and glistening armor turned and leaned against a stone rail, looking out upon the high realm, a place of heavenly lights and untold magic. It had remained unmolested for eons, so why was the Dragon moving now? The earth had been destroyed numerous times over in its brief history. The ravaging of the human race was at times necessary in order to support its continued existence. It was a cycle that went on and on, which was why this event was not the true end of days, at least not in the ways it was portrayed in the holy tomes. That would come later.

"Commander," a voice said, strong and confident as it echoed across the stone corridor.

Michael the archangel, high commander of the forces of heaven, raised himself from the rail and addressed the messenger as he approached. It was Jophiel, one of his personal guard.

"Commander," the angel continued, bowing, "we picked up a trace signal but immediately lost it. It could have been angelic."

"What do you mean *could have been*?"

"As you well know, the signatures of the fallen appear as a variation of ours, similar but different." Jophiel continued, "This was something else. We just registered it for a moment, but it wasn't human, and it wasn't a part of scheduled patrols."

"Speak freely, Jophiel. We've known each other far too long." Michael softened his gaze.

"Yes, Commander," Jophiel said. "I believe we might have found Raziel. I can't prove it, so, call it a hunch."

Michael took in the words, his thoughts far away. "He never returned from his mission those many ages ago. But his spirit never left him either since his name has never been recorded in the pages of the Lekshueh."

"The record of our lost brothers." Jophiel raised his eyebrows.

"Yes. Though this would seem to go against reason since Raziel never tried to contact us or return with news of the Machine's safety. Raziel may yet be alive, but to what end? If he has not perished, then what has he been up to all these years?"

"Maybe something happened," Jophiel said. "Maybe he hasn't been able to contact us for a reason. Our last reports of him indicate he fled with the Machine and fought with Abaddon while trying to protect it. Then they were gone and neither has been heard from since."

"So?" Michael crossed his muscular arms.

"Well, Commander, that was their final order—one was charged to protect it and the other to seize it. Could it be possible they've been at it all this time? Trapped in the earthly realm, searching for the Machine across that entire plane of existence?"

"It is possible. Raziel knows it is a violation of his code to reveal his true form to any human without the express permission of the high king, maybe he is hiding in plain sight, fighting the powers of darkness from the shadows. He could be the signature you picked up."

Jophiel nodded in agreement, his regal, mirrorlike armor glinting in the glow of a nearby white-fire sconce that hung against the ornate stone of the celestial fortress.

"But Abaddon…" Michael turned and motioned to the mirror pool. "Abaddon no longer follows such a code, which brings us to this."

Jophiel turned his attention to the giant stone bowl filled with shimmering liquid. As he watched the images spread across the surface of the water, he saw the death and destruction of humanity the world over, as it struggled to survive in the aftermath of such catastrophic societal collapse, disease, and war.

"The humans appear to be purging themselves again. What of it, Commander?"

"Here." Michael waved his hand over the pool, and Malak and his forces came into view, ransacking and pillaging the Glen Canyon Dam. "I've been watching this one," Michael said, pointing to Malak. "He is a warlord and a criminal by human standards, but there's something else. He is possessed by one of the fallen."

"Many humans are possessed by evil."

"This one is different. This creature is very powerful, so powerful in fact that my sources indicate that it may be connected to Lucifer himself. It makes open displays of its power before the humans who worship it."

Jophiel looked up. "You're saying that could be Abaddon?"

"I'm saying that we need to keep an open mind. The Machine that was lost before our great war was designed so that it could be located by neither angel nor demon using the powers of the spiritual realm. It must be seen or touched for us to find it. Which is why it has remained hidden for so long. Now, this demon appears to be trying to find it, which of course we can't allow. Which brings us to the other side of the coin."

On the other side of the pool, Kane, Courtland, and the others appeared as they moved through New Mexico, toward the dam.

"What do you make of this, Jophiel?"

Jophiel shrugged. "I don't know. How is this group different from all the others struggling to survive in this world?"

"I'll tell you," Michael answered. "This group is made up of believers, keepers of the way. They are on a mission to confront this demon and his brood."

"But why?"

"They have been personally wronged by this warlord, but there is something else at play here as well. The high king has seen fit to reveal to them the magnitude of their true purpose."

"Truly?" Jophiel said.

"Yes, and would you believe me if I said I have already received orders direct from the king that this group must be under the strict supervision of our very best?"

"But why this sad lot? These people look terrible, wholly incapable of facing a demonic tyrant such as this."

"I know." Michael waited.

"Are you saying we should help them?" Jophiel replied in astonishment.

"Not directly, no—at least not yet. But if the creature that resides in this warlord has already shown its true self, if it was the first to interfere in the humans' struggle, we may have recourse to act in the believers' defense."

"Commander," Jophiel said and indicated the pool, "do you think that we should be involved in the petty conflicts of the humans? If Raziel is down there, do you believe that he's mixed up in this?"

"My brother, this fight no longer belongs only to the humans. If the Machine *is* there, and it *is* activated by the Dragon's forces, well…" Michael smiled, placing a powerful hand on the armored shoulder of his standard-bearer. "We cannot allow that to threaten everything that our high king has done."

Jophiel gave a quick nod. "Shall I prepare a legion of our finest and have them on standby, Commander?"

"Make it two, and see to it that a request for elite support is processed as well. I want you and Zadkiel on the ground leading our warriors if things go bad."

"Understood, Commander," Jophiel responded, waiting.

Michael paused long before raising his intense gaze. "I cannot say if Raziel is down there or not, but if he is, and he needs us, then we will stand with him, wherever."

"Without question, Commander," Jophiel said, then spun, marching with purpose to his task, when the voice of his commander summoned him again.

"And Jophiel?"

"Yes, Commander." Jophiel stopped and turned.

"Should the need arise, I expect to see these human believers with more power at their backs than they can possibly imagine."

"I will see it done, commander." Jophiel smiled, with a gleam in his eye, as he turned and pushed through a heavy crimson curtain and disappeared like a phantom in the night.

16

IT WAS WELL into the day when Tynuk stopped for the first time to rest and drink from his appropriated waterskin. He slurped at the nozzle like a baby calf suckling at a swollen teat, dangerously close to becoming intoxicated with the cool, clean taste of the water as it trickled down his throat. Coughing, he sputtered and forced himself to stop, wiping his face.

The warrior boy gave a quick 360-degree survey of his surroundings. By his estimation, he had traveled close to sixty miles due west of Palo Duro and was somewhere in far northwest Texas close to the New Mexican border. The desert wind whipped up, tossing debris into the air in a quantity that was just enough to be annoying. Tynuk squinted and looked to the sky. He judged that it had been about seven hours since he had killed his last pursuer at the bottom of that drainage ditch. It wouldn't be long before the others came to fill his body with spears and arrows.

Now, for the first time since this ordeal had begun, he could actually think with clarity. His thoughts, no longer clouded by the fog of battle or the pain of the datura poison, now began to convey to him the grave urgency of his situation. He'd known that he had to survive through this, that no matter the cost it had to be him. What eluded him, even now, was the why. What was the endgame with his people, and why had he been having visions of a place, a giant concrete hydro-electric dam? Sooner or later, it all had to—

Tynuk instinctively froze. Something was off. There was a scent on the wind, a hint of danger. He was being hunted. He had been hunted by Queenashano's men for days, but this feeling was different. The feeling was similar to when he and Az had toyed with each other, training each other's senses in a not-quite-lethal game of cat and mouse. Az always got the jump on him, but that was because stealth and patience came more natural to the beast than to him.

Tynuk turned, scanning every rock and bush that surrounded him. Again he smelled it, the faintest aroma of musk riding on the wind. He saw nothing.

The attack seemed to come from directly beneath him, as the hungry gray wolf launched itself at his throat from under a nearby bush.

Twisting his body hard to the inside, the knife at Tynuk's waist flew from its sheath with blinding precision just as the wolf's jaws snapped shut where the boy's throat had been only moments before. The wolf cried out, the cold steel of the blade piercing through the soft underside of its neck. Tynuk landed to face the vicious beast, the end of his blade dripping liquid crimson. The wolf landed on all fours and faltered, its muscles quivering. It blinked hard and, with overwhelming exhaustion, lowered itself to the ground. It licked its lips, breathing deep, heavy breaths as thick clumps of blood poured from the small but deep wound in its neck onto the ground around its feet. He had struck a fatal blow.

Tynuk cautiously regarded the creature that had just tried to kill him. It looked back at him, its gaze unwavering, as blood continued to flow in globs from the wound. The wolf rolled with a lazy motion onto its side, now completely resigned to its death. Strange, Tynuk thought, how animals knew how to die with such grace, unlike the begging, pleading squalor that preceded the death of men. The wolf's eyes were heavy now, blinking slow, when Tynuk heard the movement behind him.

This time Tynuk didn't have time to turn as the wild creature slammed into him from behind, its foaming jaws savaging the flesh of his back below the shoulder blade. As he was knocked forward, the knife flipped from his hand into the dense Texas scrub that surrounded him. He landed hard, face down, crying out in pain as the wolf dipped its teeth again and again into the meat of his back. He became light-headed, his mind swimming with pain and the overwhelming, starved savagery of the thing upon him.

Unarmed, wild with the fury of battle, Tynuk rolled to his back and grabbed the jaws of the wolf, which was foaming a mixture of saliva and blood. Tynuk did the only thing he could think of: he drove his hand deep into the throat of the beast, sinking it in all the way to his shoulder. Wide-eyed, the wolf spasmed, thrashing its head as the boy clamped down, the two nearly equals in size and weight. He grabbed everything he could inside the belly of the wolf, as tissue tore and the wolf groaned in agony. Yanking his arm free, his hand full of the creature's guts, the third wolf slammed into him at full speed, sinking its teeth into the flesh of his ribs on the opposite side.

Shrieking with rage and pain, Tynuk rolled with the beast, snagging a rock the size of a softball from the dusty ground. Righting himself, he slammed it down into the hungry beast's skull. The wolf cried out in pain and tried to flee, but Tynuk knew he was too weak to chance another attack. Again and again, the feral boy slammed the rock down against the broken skull of the dead wolf until he dripped with the creature's blood and brain. The boy shuddered, his own wounds still streaming blood. He tried to stand but dropped back to the ground, where he placed his head against the warm body of the brother he had just been forced to kill. His body gave him no choice; he would have to rest for a spell.

Tynuk's eyes fluttered open in the thick warmth of the oppressive, overcast afternoon. Thunder rolled across the sky and spoke to him of the storm that was moving in. The body of the wolf below his head had long gone cold. He had to get up. The wolves, though starved and locked on his scent, were not random scavengers; they had been sent to kill him by Queenashano. He wasn't sure how, but he knew it to be true. This was all part of the trials.

He struggled to his feet and felt the freshly clotted scabs of his wounds pull. Taking the remaining water in his skin, Tynuk swallowed a gulp and used most of the rest to rinse clean his wounds, starting the bleeding anew. Though the pain of his injuries burned through him, he could do nothing further for them now. He had to continue on.

He had to think ahead for once. His pursuers would come again, and he would need to be ready this time. Sheer luck, good fortune, or even force of will alone wouldn't be sufficient any longer. If he were to survive this ordeal, he would have to reach deeper within himself, to the spiritual, the eternal. It was time to dig in and make a final stand. These trials couldn't go on forever.

It only took a moment for Tynuk to locate a nearby rise, steep and alien in its jaggedness; it would make difficult terrain for horses. Slinging his nearly empty waterskin across his body, he jogged, wincing with the pain, to the place and quickly climbed to the top of the plateau. There were only two true ways to ascend: a thin game trail he initially missed for its obscurity and the short, near vertical face he had climbed to get to the top. All in all, the plateau wasn't more than a hundred feet up from the valley, but with a flat summit, only two approaches to it for him to defend, and a small animal cave below at the base of the trail, perfect for staging a trap, Tynuk knew this would be as good as it got. He found himself wishing he had his fearsome companion Azolja to face the coming battle with him.

The odds might then not seem so daunting. However, the boy took comfort in the knowledge that his friend was close, always watching, forever vigilant.

Tynuk turned his mind to focus on the task at hand. It would take a few hours of hard work, which by his estimation should be plenty of time to prepare, before the rest of Queenashano's warriors arrived to put an end to him. And then the true test, for all of them, would begin. Who would be the last man standing? The warrior boy swallowed the dryness from his throat and gave the few remaining ounces of water in his skin a shake.

"Spirit, sustain me," Tynuk sighed through the dust that blanketed his round face. He crouched, his worn hands scooping a handful of ruddy earth that trickled through his boyish fingers. Only the Great Spirit knew how this would all end, and only time would tell.

▲ ▲ ▲

Neraquassi stopped his mustang short of the plateau before him. A moment later, the second horse bearing its riders strode alongside him. None of them said anything as they stared at the three dead wolves lying in pools of blood among the scrub brush. Neraquassi followed the defined tracks against the sand as they meandered from the killing ground and noted how they abruptly ended before reaching the hill. He dismounted, stepped over the wolf carcasses, and knelt, examining the tracks in the desert sand with his fingertips. Another warrior dismounted and took up his short spear.

"He has gone to the hill," the warrior grunted.

"Are you so sure?" Neraquassi countered.

"Of course. He killed these three and swept his tracks before taking refuge in that cave." The warrior pointed at the dark hole at the base of the plateau.

"Give me a moment," Neraquassi muttered with exasperation, as he turned back to the tracks. The other warrior gave a huff of impatience. Neraquassi ignored it.

While only a boy, this Tynuk was not to be misjudged. Too many powerful warriors had gone after this child planning to kill "just a boy," and look where it had gotten them. No, Neraquassi would handle this the right way. Today would be the day he would prove himself to his father and to the rest of the tribe. After this grand victory, there would be no further question as to who was most worthy to be the next leader of the New Comanche Nation.

A sharp scream jolted him from his thoughts and brought Neraquassi whirling to a defensive position, his lance pressed in front of him. Another groan brought his eyes upon the warrior he had just spoken to as the man exited the mouth of the small cave, clutching his chest.

"Fool!" Neraquassi spat.

"What happened?" one of the mounted warriors called out, dismounting.

"Stay on your horse!" Neraquassi stopped him with a sharp thrust of his palm. "And be on your guard."

A long moment passed as the three Comanche warriors held their positions. Aside Neraquassi, the two mounted warriors, with their short bows, arrows notched and half-drawn, stood ready to strike. The wounded warrior groaned something unintelligible and continued to stumble toward them. They could just see the broken, jagged edges of three wooden stakes jutting from his impaled chest.

"A trap..." the warrior managed as he flopped against the dusty turf and became still. The others refused to move, expecting an ambush at any moment. But nothing came, the wind twisting miniature cyclones in the dust at their feet.

"He's—"

"Dead," Neraquassi confirmed. "This Tynuk must have used a bush or root with a trip wire to deliver the stakes."

The two mounted warriors glanced warily at each other.

"Don't lose your nerve. The child is on foot and still outnumbered. You two," Neraquassi said, pointing at the two mounted warriors, "flank the base of the hill, and be prepared to engage the boy from horseback with your bows. I will go on foot toward the summit. Remember, though he is a boy, he has been lucky enough to kill many of our warriors. Do not underestimate him, and do not hesitate if you have a chance to kill him."

The mounted warriors grunted an acknowledgment as they spurred their horses onward toward the base of the slope. Neraquassi took up his spear and made for the faint game trail that wound its way up the side of the dusty rise. He moved with slow precision, his eyes scanning the plateau above for any signs of the dangerous warrior boy.

▲ ▲ ▲

As their convoy of battered vehicles made its way up the lonely dust and debris swept New Mexico State Highway 550, Kane brought the vehicle to a sudden stop. Behind him, the others' vehicles veered left and right to avoid collision.

"Whoa." Ari placed her hands on the dash.

"*What is it?*" Dagen's voice crackled over the radio.

"Stand by," Kane replied as he continued to stare straight forward, watching the hazy formation of dust rising from the highway along the horizon before them. Something large was moving, and it was moving in their direction.

"Somebody's coming," Kane said into the radio. He scanned the roadway and the mountains beyond the highway, looming like ancient titans in the distance. There was nowhere for them to divert, flee, or hide. They would have to confront whomever or whatever was coming toward them.

"*Call it, Kane.*" Courtland's voice popped over the radio.

Kane glanced at Ari sitting next to him as she did a quick function check of her rifle and stuffed an extra magazine in her left cargo pocket. She did not return his glance or say a word.

"Okay, here's how we're going to play this. We don't want to provoke a confrontation with whoever this happens to be—friend or foe. If we stay here blocking the road, then that's what's going to happen. We'll pull our vehicles down to the left and as far from the road as we can. Keep them in formation. When you exit, arm yourself and take cover behind your vehicle, facing the road. We will give whomever this is as wide a berth as possible and we will let them pass, if they so choose. If they stop to offer anything but peace or engage us, we must be prepared to fight to the death."

Kane paused and could sense Ari nodding in his periphery. He keyed the radio again. "Look, we don't want this fight, but we will fight it if we have to. Minus the kids, we have almost thirty shooters, which isn't anything to scoff at. Let's hope these folks don't want a fight today, and hopefully, we'll be on our way soon. If there are no objections, everyone acknowledge."

The voices came in quick succession.

"*Got it.*"

"*Sounds good.*"

"*Dagen and Courtland—copy.*"

Kane listened as someone from each vehicle acknowledged the plan. "Alright, everybody on me." He set the radio down and pulled his vehicle as far as he could off the road—approximately fifty feet. The others behind him followed suit and set their vehicles and themselves according to plan.

Then, crouching behind their vehicles, with the children hiding between them and behind the engine blocks of the vehicles, they waited.

As the dust rising from the road drew closer, Courtland turned toward Kane. "What if they think we're lying in ambush?"

"Everybody," he called out, "lower your weapons and keep your heads low. We want to appear as non-threatening as possible."

Everyone murmured their consent. All eyes watched the slow-moving convoy of large vehicles as it drew closer.

A few people shuffled, their nerves getting the better of them, the children huddling in groups like squirming piles of kittens.

"Those vehicles are huge, whatever they are," Kane whispered.

Ari spoke up. "Looks like military."

"Or militia," Dagen added. "Whoever they are, they're serious, rolling in MRAPs and Humvees like this."

A hundred yards back from their vehicles, the convoy stopped. A moment passed, then another, as the convoy seemed to assess the threat Kane's group posed. Kane watched as manned turrets, one at the top of each vehicle, swiveled toward them. The barrels of the mounted M2A1 .50-caliber heavy machine guns looked like stove pipes as they pivoted in their direction.

Kane felt a cold chill descend upon him. If these weren't friendlies, this wouldn't be a fight. It would be a massacre.

"Set your weapons down. We couldn't fight this if we wanted to." Kane laid his pistol down on the ground. The others followed his lead.

"Stand and raise your hands—kids too," Kane said.

Again his group followed suit, standing with their hands in the air, some of the children's hands rising alone above the hoods of the vehicles.

After a bloated pause, the convoy rumbled with a groan and closed the gap between the two groups, all the while training their overwhelming firepower on the small group of survivors. Pulling parallel, the convoy stopped once again, the sounds of the huge, rumbling engines striking an uneven cadence. To Kane and the others, the wait felt like an eternity.

"This is the United States Army National Guard!" a voice rang out. "Do as you are told, and you will not be shot!"

Kane couldn't contain his relief as he smiled and pushed his hands high in the air. "Guys, I think we just found a unicorn."

17

IN THE DARKNESS of the closet, Nick Corvaleski sat hunched, waiting. Beyond the dark safety of the closet, beyond the dark office of some long-dead administrator in which the closet resided, people were running everywhere, searching for something, maybe him. He pinched his eyes against the thought and found the inky black no different from that of his surroundings.

What had these people come for? To the outside world, the Glen Canyon Dam was just that. Nobody without top-secret military-level clearance knew that this place was used for anything other than the standard processes of a hydroelectric dam.

The psychotic whoops and screams echoed distant and forlorn within the concrete bowels of the dam. These people had used massive amounts of force to gain entry into a facility that Nick previously thought impenetrable. They weren't here to make friends.

Suddenly, he wanted to be anywhere but here. He was trapped like a hunted animal. There was no longer any escape for him. They would find him sooner or later, and then, he would be at their mercy. All he could do now was sit and wait.

The men could feel it. With every passing hour, Malak was losing a little more of himself to whatever it was that gave him his monstrous power. The Coyotes avoided him, fearing their own death and dismemberment as the focus of his unbridled rage. He'd spent the last half day huffing his way through each room on each floor of the dam facility, tearing doors from their hinges and destroying anything that got in his way as he searched for the device he claimed was hidden here, somewhere.

"I know it's here. Where is it? Why would they keep it here? There is nowhere here to store something so ancient."

Saxon stood back with his arms crossed as he watched the massive warlord pacing and speaking to himself. He knew better than to interrupt.

"It won't show itself to me now, but it will. It will when it is ready." He laughed, giddy like a deranged man.

There was a shuffling of feet at the door behind him as a thug dragged up little Michael and Rachael Lorusso. With eyes cast down, their filthy, torn clothes and dirty faces masked the innocence of their youth. Together, in unison, they whispered the Lord's Prayer.

"What do you want?" Saxon looked to the thug pulling them along.

"Lord Malak said to secure them."

"Then what the hell are you doing here? Go secure them."

"Yeah," the thug mumbled.

"Stop," Malak said from behind them.

The men turned. The children continued to pray.

"Stop!" Malak clenched his teeth.

"What?" Saxon said, bewildered.

"Stop saying that!" Malak put his hands over his ears.

Saxon looked at the children, pinching their little eyes shut as they continued to pray. The thug covered their mouths, but the muffled words were still audible.

Without warning, Malak flung himself toward them. Saxon fell away in fear, the thug still trying to muffle the children's prayers.

"Stop it!" Malak shrieked, the darkness drifting from his lifeless black eyes. He stopped short, seeming to swell in size before the children. Overcome with fear, the thug now shrank back, but the children continued their cadence.

"Look at me, children," Malak snarled. "Look at me. Look at me!"

The children stopped, their eyes opening to take in the massive, demonic man, his appearance far more like the boogeyman's than any child's mind could ever attempt to conjure.

"Do I frighten you?" the warlord whispered in a voice that was not wholly his own. "Do you fear the darkness that you behold? Will you look on in terror and agony when I bathe in your little souls?"

Unflinching, Michael began to sing, "Our God is greater. Our God is stronger. God, you are higher than any other…"

Malak gasped and shook his head back and forth as though he'd just stuck it inside a hornet's nest.

"God won't save you now! Jesus is dead! Your mommy and daddy are dead! You belong to me! You are mine now!"

Michael pinched his eyes and continued to sing, with Rachael joining in. Malak huffed and grabbed his head as the children's words slipped into his ears like the blade of a knife, cutting, cutting…

With a roar, Malak lunged forward as the terrifying demonic presence poured from his features. He raised his fist to obliterate the tiny voices. To make the singing stop—

Destroy them, and the plan is ruined. Get them away from us.

"Make them stop!" Malak screamed.

"We can't, Lord. That's the problem." The thug whimpered.

"Get them away from me, and make them stop, now! Beat it out of them!"

"Yes, Lord."

As the singing continued, Malak whirled in a frenzied panic and grabbed the closest thug, squeezing him by the neck and shoving him back. "Stop fucking around, and get them away from me!"

Shuffling in the chaos, the thug grabbed the children and fled, pulling them down the hallway as they sang, louder and louder. Saxon looked on in absolute bewilderment.

"I will drink of them soon enough. Yes, soon enough," Malak chanted. After a time, Malak seemed to shrink, his demeanor calming. Saxon slipped away from the mad titan and left him to his mutterings and ramblings.

"Childish songs cannot stop me." He clenched his fists. "I will find the Machine. I will find it. It's here. I can feel it. Nothing will keep it from me."

▲ ▲ ▲

Kane sat on the ground next to Jenna and Courtland, their hands behind their backs in flex-cuffs. Around them, Army National Guard soldiers in ACU digital BDUs stood guard, watching them with their weapons at the ready.

"What is so funny?" Jenna whispered to Kane, who had a wry smile plastered across his face.

"I can't believe our luck," Kane said from the corner of his mouth. "Well, that...that and the fact that they tried to put Courtland in flex-cuffs."

Courtland turned his head and smiled.

They had tried but had not been successful in finding restraints that fit the giant. The giant now sat peacefully with his hands in his lap and with four soldiers and their issued M16 rifles trained on him.

"Stop talking," one of the soldiers said.

Kane bobbed his head, and they all sat as several men who looked to be in charge talked about what to do with them.

After a moment, one soldier with a lean, muscled appearance and an angular jaw approached. The sharp-featured man was flanked by two solidly built men who were unquestionably part of the operational leadership of this outfit. The man eyed Kane's group for what felt like an eternity before he spoke.

"I am Second Lieutenant Ryback with the United States Army National Guard, Eight Hundred Fifty-Sixth Military Police Company. I need to speak with whoever is in charge." He looked the group over.

There was some shuffling, and all eyes shifted toward Kane.

"I'll speak for the group," Kane said.

The lieutenant turned his attention to Kane and paused. "Very well. Stand him up," Ryback said to his men, who stood Kane up and walked him away from the group. Upon stepping away from the others, the lieutenant stopped and turned toward Kane. "What's your name?"

"Kane Lorusso."

"Are you bandits? Was this an ambush you set up here?"

"No, sir."

"Then what is it?"

"We saw your vehicles coming. Call me gun-shy, sir, but we've been through the ringer. We were on the road and had nowhere to hide, so we took up defensive positions instead. Just being prepared for the worst."

The lieutenant considered this for a moment. "Are you active or a vet?" Ryback's said.

Kane shook his head. "Neither, sir. Law Enforcement."

Ryback nodded, seeming to have arrived at some sort of a decision. "We've taken up all your weapons. When I remove your restraints, you'll remain calm, or you'll be shot—your people too. Is that understood?"

Kane nodded. Ryback's men clipped his flex-cuffs away.

"We may be on home soil, but we don't take any chances these days."

"I understand," Kane said, rubbing his wrists.

Ryback turned to another man, heavily built with a commanding presence. "Take care of the men, Sergeant. I'll handle Mr. Lorusso."

"Yes, sir." The platoon sergeant turned and immediately began belting commands to the men. "Alright, people, I want a close perimeter up with loose inner security for our guests. Check your weapons and ammo and drink water. We won't be staying long."

As the platoon sergeant stepped away, Lieutenant Ryback turned his attention back to Kane. "In a moment, we will be on our way, and we'll leave you and your people to whatever it was you were doing."

"Lieutenant," Kane replied, "I have a lot of questions."

The second lieutenant gave Kane a stern look. "Go ahead."

"In over a year, I haven't seen anything like this—nothing to indicate that anything resembling formal government or military entities still existed. I was just resigned to the fact that they didn't anymore, which is why a military convoy was the last thing I expected to see."

The lieutenant continued to gaze coolly.

"Is there anything you can tell me?"

After a long pause, Ryback gave a small inclination of his head. "Since you don't have a need to know, I'll have to keep things general.

After all this country's been through, I think folks have a right to know something."

Kane nodded.

"I'm sure there are other military enclaves still out there, but we haven't had any contact with anyone since this mess began. Second Platoon is all that's left of the Eight Hundred Fifty-Sixth. We've waited here long enough. We're headed to Washington, DC, to see what we can do."

Kane shook his head. "DC is a glass crater. It took a direct hit."

"I heard, but we still have to go. There's nothing left for us here." Ryback said.

"We sure could use your help."

"I wish we could, Mr. Lorusso, but I don't have the resources or people to spare to protect you. Unfortunately, for now, you'll just have to do like everyone else out there and find a good defensible location you can hole up in till this all blows over and the United States reestablishes itself."

Kane hung his head. "I wish it were that easy. How much have you seen?"

"What do you mean?"

"How much out there have you seen? We just traveled from the East Coast, and it's a wasteland—from Miami to New York. The cities we've circumnavigated on our way west haven't fared much better. How much have you seen of it?"

The look on the lieutenant's face was his answer.

"This is the first time you've left your base, isn't it?" Kane sighed.

"Our last orders were to hold our position. The base was strategic. But yes, you are correct. We've regularly sent scouting parties out in the area, but this is the first time we've actually left to go somewhere else."

"You're in for a rude awakening, sir. This isn't something that's going to blow over," Kane shook his head.

Ryback glanced over his men, his wheels turning. A lot appeared to be riding on the man. "You said you wished it was *that easy* to hunker down. What do you mean by that?"

"I mean we hunkered down once. We did okay for a while, but they came and tore us apart anyway."

"They?"

"Savage feral mutants, wasteland bandits—take your pick," Kane said.

"You mean the Night Walkers?"

"Yeah, sure. We call them Sicks. They're mutated people, gone mad."

"We've just run into a few of them up here."

"Well, you're in for a treat when you hit one of the large metro areas. They're overrun with the things."

The lieutenant made a disgusted snarl. "That's why you said your party circumnavigated major cities?"

"That's right."

"Why are you headed west?"

"It's a long, sad story. Suffice it to say, we got caught up in an ugly conflict with some nasty bandits, and we can't let it go."

Ryback replied with detached confidence. "Letting it go is as easy as letting it go, Mr. Lorusso. There's no room for egos out here. It's much safer to just mind your own business."

Kane's face was pained, drawn, as the days, weeks, and months of agony he'd already endured came pouring through his exhausted features. "I can't let it go, sir," Kane said, his voice frail. "These bastards took my kids."

Had Kane hauled off and punched Lieutenant Ryback in the stomach, he would have likely gotten the same response. The lieutenant, who only seconds earlier had been far too cool and distant, suddenly deflated, his posture sagging with the weight of the revelation.

"Shit," Ryback muttered to himself. "They were kidnapped?"

Kane nodded, the knot in his gut tightening.

"Shit." Ryback looked at his men and rubbed his chin. He turned, scanning a quick 360, and clenched his jaw.

Ryback turned back to Kane and lowered his voice. "Look, I can't help you, but say you were to find this lying on the ground somewhere..." He produced a chipped ID card and discreetly dropped it at Kane's feet. "You could probably use it to access the secure facilities at Camp Navajo, about ten miles that way." He motioned with his head in the direction that he and his men had come.

Kane, stunned, placed his foot over the ID card and pulled it with his boot under his foot.

"If someone were to find that place and have the ability to gain entry, they could gain access to all kinds of resources—food, water, vehicles, and arms and ammo," Ryback continued. "Of course, *if* this ship that we call the United States of America ever rights itself, I would have to officially condemn such actions. Additionally, any unauthorized use of my *stolen* ID to gain access to such a facility or utilize anything found within would be swiftly and severely punished." Ryback paused, staring intensely at Kane.

"I can see how that would be necessary, sir," Kane replied.

"Good. Well, my men and I have to be going now. Good luck, Officer Lorusso."

The second lieutenant turned to leave when Kane spoke again. "Lieutenant Ryback..." Kane paused as the lieutenant met his gaze. "Why?"

Ryback paused, his thoughts far away, lost in a better life—a life now long gone. "Because you seem like a good man," he cleared his throat, "and because I never had the chance to save my kids."

The lieutenant turned and rallied his men as Kane's group was cut loose. The soldiers moved to and fro and back to their vehicles, where they loaded up and brought the convoy rumbling back to life.

As he watched them pull away, Kane swallowed the lump from his throat and waited till they were nearly out of sight before he reached for the ID card under his boot. Second Lieutenant Ryback of the US Army National Guard might not ever truly know the magnitude of the gift he had just given.

18

*A*THUNDERCLAP SPLIT THE air above their heads, tearing the heavens asunder and rolling into the distance like battle drums. Fat raindrops fell against the thirsty earth in sheets, culminating in a soaking downpour. A heavy, cloud-covered sky reached out against the horizon, black fingers scratching the distant mountaintops. Below it, three men and a boy moved, silent cogs in a machine that could not be stopped, not even if any of them were to desire it.

Neraquassi's two warriors circled the base of the hill, drawing farther apart and losing sight of each other, the only sound the clip-clopping of the mustangs' hooves against the hard earth.

Tynuk watched from his place of concealment as one of the riders approached, howling into the air like a wolf. After a moment, the other warrior on horseback gave a distant howl in response. They were communicating.

As the warrior passed beneath him, eyes scanning warily, Tynuk launched himself from the embankment. Dropping like a mountain lion with claws extended, Tynuk snarled as he flew through the air. The Comanche warrior pivoted in the saddle, quick firing an arrow that pierced Tynuk's side just below his floating ribs. He screamed and collided with the rider as they both fell from the horse to the ground. The horse, now thoroughly spooked, began to run.

Groaning, struggling amid the dust and scrub, Tynuk wrestled with the warrior across the ground, gyrating and fighting for a better position. In a flash, the warrior grabbed the arrow protruding from Tynuk's side and pulled. Tynuk shrieked in pain and brought his hardened fist across the jaw of the fighter, dropping it with a bladed hand to shear the shaft of the arrow from where it protruded from his own body. The warrior fell back howling, still clutching the broken arrow shaft as Tynuk flung himself forward and drew his knife, slashing like a frenzied beast. The warrior screamed as Tynuk blocked a strike, drove the knife into the warrior's side, and then drove it again into his skull below the ear. Silence.

Tynuk scrambled from the dead warrior and grabbed the man's bow and quiver. It was rudimentary, like all Comanche bows, but still highly effective at close to medium range. Tynuk scrambled up the hillside back to the summit as the hoofbeats of the second warrior galloped closer. Tynuk readied himself and notched an arrow. He pushed his mind away from the flaring pain in his side, a wound that streamed blood and still harbored a spearhead inside it. His wounded hand ached with the pull of the bow, pulsing to the rhythm of his pounding heart. He calmed his mind and steadied his nerves.

As the second rider approached, Tynuk loosed his arrow, a perfect shot that lanced through the rider's neck as the rider fired back. Tynuk lunged to the right, snatching his enemy's arrow from the air and notching it in his own bow. He fired three more arrows in rapid succession, all landing with the thud of pierced flesh and broken bone. The warrior appeared dazed, detached, as he dropped his bow and murmured something indiscernible. A thin string of blood streamed from his lips as his hand moved to one of the arrows but stopped when he slumped forward in the saddle, dead.

Tynuk lowered the bow and took a breath. Neither of these fighters had been Neraquassi, which meant—

Tynuk spun at the last moment, deflecting the knife that Neraquassi intended to bury into his spine. He cried out as the blade slashed back again across his face, and he felt the blood begin to spread down his chin. How could he have been so stupid?

No time to consider his failings now. Tynuk lunged forward, stomped into Neraquassi's pelvic bowl, and then kicked him hard to the inside of the thigh, the femoral nerve motor point. He side-stepped, his eyes taking in the shattered bow on the ground next to him, now made useless. This would be a close-quarters fight to the death.

Tynuk wiped the blood, and it smeared like savage, hot war paint across his round face. He watched Neraquassi try to put weight on the leg that had just been kicked and saw him falter. Good. Motor dysfunction had been his goal, and it would aid him well in the next few moments.

"The wolves wounded you dearly, boy. Your strength fails you as we speak. Surrender your life to me!"

"You would not recognize true strength even if it should suddenly flow within your own body, Yellow Horse."

"You are a dog!" Neraquassi spat. "I will mix your blood with this sand!"

"Here I am! Come and finish it!" Tynuk snarled.

As they lunged toward each other, the rain streaked down, covering them in a wet sheen as bodies collided against each other yet again. Like wolves fighting over the last scrap of meat, this contest would only be settled with death.

Tynuk rolled, grabbed Neraquassi's short lance, and turned. Neraquassi came for him, knife drawn as the warrior boy thrust with the lance, just missing flesh when Neraquassi spun and lashed out with the knife. Ducking the swipe, Tynuk swung the shaft of the

11

spear back across Neraquassi's face, knocking him to the ground. Seizing the opportunity, Tynuk threw himself on the warrior and bore down with the point of the spear. With a shout, Neraquassi stabbed up with his knife, and Tynuk deflected it back down with the spear. In a silent, locked struggle, they wavered, pushing, pulling, neither giving an inch of ground.

"You don't deserve to live! You aren't true blood!"

Something snapped inside Tynuk. With a savage blow, he struck Neraquassi across the face and then again at the neck; he knocked the knife from his hands and seized the warrior by his hair. The point of the spear was not far behind as he pushed it flush under Neraquassi's chin.

"My heart is true! Have I not proven myself? How many of my own people do I have to kill? How many?" Tynuk screamed, tears, rain, and blood flowing down his face. Neraquassi could do nothing but close his eyes and wait for death.

"You have killed enough, my nephew." The voice came from behind him.

Tynuk, stunned at receiving an answer, stayed his hand. He turned to see the noble Queenashano standing behind him, flanked by many warriors.

"Nephew?" Tynuk stood, releasing Neraquassi, who groaned in shame.

"Yes," Queenashano said and smiled, "I am your father's brother, and I myself am a nephew of the great Nuk'Chala—like your father."

"My father...Then that would make..." Tynuk looked down at Neraquassi, who was now sitting up.

"Your cousin." Queenashano nodded.

"No, this isn't right." Neraquassi stood, wiping his face.

"Silence, boy," Queenashano barked.

"No!" Neraquassi snapped back. "I will not acknowledge this dog as my blood!" He moved and picked up the spear.

"Neraquassi, your heart has become poisoned against the truth. This boy is the one! Set the spear down," Queenashano said.

Neraquassi was breathing hard now, a furious rage billowing inside him. He pointed the spear at Queenashano. "You couldn't even let me die! Couldn't even let me have an honorable death on the battlefield. You *stole* that from me!"

"You forget your place! Lay down your weapon!" Queenashano yelled.

"I will not! You are an old man and a fool! This child deserves to die! He is not and will *never* be one of us!" Neraquassi turned and raised his lance, aiming it at Tynuk.

Tynuk raised his hands in submission. "I will fight you no longer, Cousin."

"You are not my blood!" Neraquassi shrieked as he prepared to spear Tynuk through the heart.

A rushing sound filled the air. Tynuk closed his eyes and waited for the pain. Slowly he opened his eyes to see Neraquassi standing before him, a shocked look on his face. More than seventeen arrows protruded from his chest—fired by Queenashano's own warriors, at his command.

"Father…" Neraquassi wheezed and fell to the ground, a crimson fan spreading out beneath him.

Queenashano lowered his head. "I release you, my son. Your heart is filled with too much hate. Maybe you will find peace in the next life."

Neraquassi rolled to his side, gasped his last, and became still.

Tynuk was still trying to overcome his own shock and physical pain when Queenashano spoke again, raising his eyes to the boy. "My own son was not worthy, but you are, Tynuk. You have passed the trials of the ancients. You have survived these trials because you are special. I think it's time you found out why."

Tynuk tried to speak, his mouth forming soundless words. His body sagged with the pain of his many wounds, slumping to the ground in exhaustion. Mercifully, the trials of the ancients had come to an end.

▲ ▲ ▲

Kane slowed his vehicle to a stop in front of the barricaded steel gate with a sign on it that read "US Army Restricted Area. Deadly Force Authorized beyond This Point." Behind him, his small caravan of beat-up, dust-covered vehicles rolled to a stop. Kane sat for a moment and looked at the massive automated gate and down the fence line rimmed in concertina wire; then he looked down at the chipped ID card in his hand that bore the picture of Lieutenant Ryback.

"This has to be it," Kane muttered to himself. He still couldn't believe the events that had transpired to bring them to this place, but he wasn't about to argue with it either.

"Has to be," Ari said and tossed her head as if to say, "Let's do this already."

"Yeah," Kane said as he got out of the truck and looked around. It only took him a moment to locate the nondescript gray panel set against a nearby wall. "Here goes nothing," Kane said and waved the card over the reader. Kane realized he was holding his breath. Behind him Ari and the others had opened their doors and were watching with eager looks on their faces. None of them wanted to believe it was real, that they could have found somewhere safe again.

Kane sighed, the frustration at another dead end was overwhelming. He waved the card once more and perked up at the sound of a chime and the sight of a small green light on the edge of the panel.

With a clunk and the sound of gears grinding and wheels pushing, the gate clinked open, revealing a quiet, secure facility.

Kane threw his arms in the air. Everyone cheered, laughing and whooping, as they hurried back to their vehicles, all eager to see what unknown treasures waited inside those gates.

▲ ▲ ▲

The bulk of the low, gray concrete buildings at Camp Navajo were just inside the main gate down a short road. Beyond the buildings, a dead forest stretched on into the distance opening into a vast amount of acreage on base. Kane and the other new residents of this hidden gem busied themselves exploring every inch of the recently abandoned military facility.

It hadn't taken them too long to get a feel for the place. With banks of solar panels covering every roof of every visible building, there was abundant power. Kane discovered that there were high-tech, motion-activated, turret-mounted M240 machine guns along the walls. Powered by the camp, these weapons systems could be activated or deactivated, functioned day and night, and could be programmed to recognize RFID-chipped friendlies.

Courtland found the kitchen and the stores of canned, dry, and frozen foodstuffs. He was so overcome with joy he began singing in his marvelous baritone as he brewed a large pot of coffee and started a huge cauldron of his mama's world-famous vegetable stew.

Dagen and Ari found their way to the armory and the stockpile of military small arms, mortars, C-4 explosives, armored vehicles, and anything else one could imagine. Waiting on the rails behind the main complex, they also located an antique steam-engine locomotive with a series of attached cars that felt alien and out of place in the surrounding modernized military complex.

The children were laughing and running, playing in the court-yard with a found ball, while Winston, Sam, and the other survivors rested on actual beds, talked together, or cried tears they tried to hide, thankful for a single moment in time free from fear, uncertainty, and desperation.

Jenna knew her moment alone wouldn't last long. She would be needed to help with the children, assist Courtland, or do some other important task. But for now, she just wanted to be alone. She wanted to be unneeded by anyone, just for a few moments. She slipped into the barracks where they determined the women and children would stay. It was empty, silent, and wonderful. She moved to the back and found her way into the large block shower. She stood for an eternity, staring into the open space lined with multiple showerheads. Without a sound, she shed her clothes in a pile at her feet and stepped onto the cold tile of the large shower. Eagerly, Jenna reached for one of the knobs, unsure whether she should get her hopes up. Life had been quite cruel to her. There was no reason for it to improve now. With a twist, the faucet head sputtered to life. Jenna gasped as the cold water hit her skin, stinging with frigid life. But then, the temperature began to rise.

"Oh, you've got to be kidding me!" Jenna called out with a squeal as the water went from warm to gloriously hot. She shuddered, gasping at the euphoric sensation that flooded over her as she pushed her face beneath the beautiful downpour. Laughing, Jenna let the wonderful hot water cascade over her skinny frame, a body that felt like a half-starved shadow of what it had once been.

Amid the beautiful, hot cascade, drowning in the glory of it, she began to remember all the other wonderful things that she could no longer enjoy. She had once been a wife. She missed her dear husband, Charlie. The way he was so gentle with her, how he always listened when she has something to say, and the way he would pull her close against him in the dark of the night. She had also been a mother. She missed the sweet, soft breaths of her innocent baby girl, Lynn. The way she seemed so content, so safe in the arms of her mother. Jenna gasped a painful sound. No, it was too much to remember, and she couldn't ruin this moment now. Not now.

It had been over a year since she had enjoyed a long, hot shower. She'd really believed that she would never have another, and yet here she was, moaning and swishing her hips like a girl in the embrace of this perfect respite. She wouldn't waste a single drop.

19

WINSTON SLIPPED AROUND the farthest building and into the edge of the woods as the evening grew long and the dimness of the day began to fade. He produced the two-way radio the woman, Shana, had given him and turned it on. It gave a loud bleep, and the chubby man jumped, jerking his head about hoping no one heard it.

What he was doing was treason. He was going to sacrifice these good people, his family, so he could live—so the darkness could destroy them. Why was he doing this? He didn't want to do it. These were people he had lived with, fought with, and survived with, and here he was ready to offer them all up as a sacrifice on the altar of his own selfishness. The thought made him sick to his stomach. Why hadn't he just let the woman and her thugs kill him? He could be lying facedown in a ditch right now, and his pain would be over, and these people could live. They didn't deserve what the Coyotes were going to do to them. No one would be spared—not those who surrendered, not the women, not the children. It was going to be a massacre, and their blood would be on his hands.

Winston felt his stomach roll with the thought of it. He wished he was dead. There was no hope for him. He dialed the channel to six and waited, listening to the static. With a trembling hand, he keyed the radio.

"Winston to Shana, do you copy?"

The radio was supposed to have a ten-mile range under good conditions. Winston waited. The radio crackled.

Shana's voice slid over the radio. *"Well, well, if it isn't my best buddy, Winston."*

"Uh, yeah. Look—"

"What's taking so long, Winston? Where are you?" Shana snapped.

"It's complicated."

"What the hell do you mean it's complicated? Where are you?"

Winston swallowed. "On an army base called Camp Navajo in Farmington."

"What the fuck are you doing on an army base, Winston?" Shana shouted. *"This isn't looking good for you!"*

"I know. I know. Look, it's just temporary. It was a fluke thing. I had no control over it!"

"Winston, I swear to God, if you don't produce those people, I'm going to have these savages turn you inside out and hang you by your guts. Do you hear me!"

"Okay, alright." Winston motioned for her to calm down as though she could see him. "Are you close?"

"I'm talking to you on this radio, so what do you think, fatso? We looked for you up and down the highway and wasted our fucking time. Now my boys are getting restless, so you'd better speed things along, dipshit."

"I will. Look, just wait close by. We can't be staying long. Kane wants to get his kids something fierce."

"You let me know, fat boy. I don't want any more surprises."

"Okay," Winston managed and then snapped the radio off, coughed once then vomited the contents of his stomach onto the ground.

As the light faded, the last rays stretching across a rolling black sky, the bonfire in the courtyard began to grow, its flames licking into the air. They had decided to rest and recover for twenty-four hours before resuming their journey toward the dam. Kane had initially been resistant, restless to secure his dear children, but ultimately consented, giving in to his own exhaustion. They were on the final leg of this crazy journey, and they would need their rest for what was sure to come next.

Full on Courtland's stew, the bulk of the group was now sat around the fire, drinking hot coffee, telling stories, and laughing like a bunch of old, carefree friends on a retreat.

Kane sat, staring into the fire, his body the most relaxed it had been in months. Amazing what a shower, a belly full of food, and a cup of steaming, fresh coffee could do for a person's spirits.

The others were enjoying themselves. The older gentleman, Sam, was telling some funny prewar story about a dog he'd once taught to sit at the table and eat like a person.

Kane smiled faintly, the others laughing around the fire. His fingers thumbed the pages of Courtland's old Bible, his mind entangled in thoughts of his beautiful children—not the terror they must now be enduring but the memories he had of better times. All together with him and their mother, Susan.

Susan.

Kane furrowed his brow.

Save them, Kane. Everything I've done has been to save our children, to spare them. Don't let it be for nothing.

He looked down at his hands and touched the rope-scarred flesh of his palms, the skin still tender to the touch. It was a wound that was as much in his heart as it was deep in his flesh. He didn't know what the next few days had in store for all of them; he didn't know how the will of God would align with the course of his life. What he did know was he had a promise to keep.

"I'll save them, baby," Kane said only to himself. "I won't stop until they're safe and this evil has witnessed the glory of our Lord." He nodded to himself and wiped the moisture from the corner of his eyes. "I'll be the man you believed I could be. I'll be the man God needs me to be to finish this. That's a promise. "

▲ ▲ ▲

Jenna watched everyone around the fire from the window next to her cot. She wiped the tears from her face and placed the small silver cross and chain back around her neck. The shower had been a wonderful detour from her pain, but now it was pursuing her heart again with a fearful hunger.

Though she had been able to go on after her loss, the pain never seemed to get easier for her to carry. The loss of her family had left her broken. But she hadn't *lost* them. They had both been murdered by Dagen—the same Dagen who tortured her, looking on as she was beaten and raped. She remembered some of the very first words he had ever said to her.

Maybe it's fate or karma, or maybe God just hates you. Maybe that's it...Making sense of it doesn't change a thing.

Jenna stifled a sob and begged God to take her sorrow from her, to carry her burden and stifle the resentment that swelled inside her. There was nothing that could change any of that now. She would have to make the best of it, however difficult that might be.

Dagen had caused her so much pain, yet she had devoted herself to helping him, to showing him how he could be restored. But she hadn't considered the personal cost to herself. Even after he had made so much progress, even after he had risked his own life to save her from the Coyotes, she still struggled with hating him—even as she hoped for his redemption. Her heart felt so clouded, twisting with pain, grief, and hope.

As if in answer to her inner torment, a knock came at the door. She turned to see the very object of her thoughts, crutches under his arms as he leaned against the doorframe.

"You going to come join everybody out here?"

Jenna wiped her face and stood, busying herself about her cot. "Uh, sure, maybe in a minute." She turned away from him.

Dagen furrowed his brow. "Okay, well, we're actually having a good old time out here. You should come."

Jenna said nothing but continued working on some imaginary task.

Dagen smiled again, a strange, almost foreign, expression on his worn face. "You're not going to believe this, but Courtland and I have kind of hit it off. I never in a million years would have thought I'd like hanging out with a Baptist preacher, but the guy is something else. And after all that mess with the Sicks and fighting to save the station and you, we've kind of bonded. Weird, huh?" Dagen rubbed his head.

Jenna said nothing and wiped her face again.

"Are you alright?" Dagen paused. "Is there something I can do?"

"Dagen, leave me alone. You've done enough," Jenna said.

Dagen's face went slack.

"I don't even know what I've been doing." She shook her head.

"I'm sorry. Did I miss something?" Dagen said, confusion spreading across his face.

"No, Dagen, you didn't miss it. You were there for all of it. I can't fill the black hole inside me—that empty space in my life where my husband and daughter used to live. *You* took them from me!"

"I thought we...You said you forgave me." Dagen lowered his head, his eyes half-closed.

"I know I did. But I don't think I can survive this. My heart is broken. Why, Dagen? Why did you have to murder my Charlie and my baby?"

Dagen had no words. He simply stood and took it.

"You've got nothing to say—after all this? After I break my own heart every day just being around you?"

"I don't think there's anything I can say," Dagen whispered.

"You said you loved me. In so many words, you said it. But I have to tell you something. I hope the best for you, but I can't love you, not like you want me to. I can't. It's too much."

Dagen swallowed. "I didn't expect—"

"But you did. You thought there was some version of this where we could live happily ever after, and I'm telling you that we can't. Not us. Not after what you've done."

Dagen nodded, his face cast down.

"I'm not sure I can even be around you anymore. I don't know how to continue dealing with this, over and over again, every time I see you," Jenna mumbled through the tears.

Dagen was speechless.

"I think I need some time alone now," Jenna said with a huff, keeping her composure as best she could.

"I'll go," Dagen said weakly as he turned and hobbled from the room, his new grip on life and all the hope in his world slipping from him in a single instant.

And in the lonely silence of the barracks, Jenna wept.

20

"OPEN IT." MALAK smiled as his goons brought forth a huge duffel bag and unzipped it. Large, silver aluminum-foil-wrapped bricks slid from the unzipped opening.

"Oh yeah, that's the stuff!" one of the thugs called out, crooning with pleasure.

"What are your orders, Lord Malak?" Saxon added.

"Take ten bricks. Keep one for yourself. Begin distributing the twenty for the men to share. Tell them they've done well and that my orders are for them to enjoy themselves for a while." Malak smiled greedily. "The rest is for me." He motioned to a nearby goon. "Prepare me a dose."

He looked over the last remaining stash of Z, a lethal and hyper-addictive narcotic developed at the beginning of the twenty-first century: a potent and destructive blend of PCP, methamphetamine, ecstasy, steroids, and several other choice drugs. It became a valuable resource for criminals who relied on its beneficial properties, such as numbness to pain, prolonged adrenaline surges, and heightened awareness. But if a user were also mentally unbalanced or unstable to begin with, the effects could be catastrophic. It was well-known for either killing a person outright or enslaving them to it forevermore. There was no middle ground.

Malak liked to use it as a proving ground for his men. Some would inevitably die upon their first use, and the rest would become unstoppable. It was a purging of weakness for his Coyotes. Malak had saved this final duffel for the right moment. This was the last of the mother lode he had stumbled across months ago in the basement of the DEA headquarters on his way to the East Coast. He himself had forced his men to wean off of the drug in order to conserve it. This had only made them crazier and more desperate. He had, for a time, felt that the darkness was enough, that he didn't need the drug anymore. Now he wasn't so sure, and he was going to exploit every possible advantage at his disposal.

Recently the darkness had been uneasy, volatile, almost as if it wanted complete control of him. He needed to take the edge off.

"Here, boss." The thug handed him the loaded syringe, and Malak without hesitation gave himself the direct injection.

Grunting, Malak gasped and opened his eyes wide. In moments, the tremors started to cascade through him, rippling through his body and setting his nerves on fire. His Coyotes watched on with anticipation as their leader shook and frothed at the mouth, growling like an animal.

You're weak.

"No, Voice. I am in control. You may live here, but I will control my destiny!"

You just keep thinking that.

"I am in control!" Malak raged.

The Coyotes tossed glances at each other as Malak screamed at himself. The Voice was not for them to hear. They loaded their own syringes and began to get high.

Malak took a deep breath, and as the thickness of the smothering yellow fog began to clear from his mind, his desperation began to calm. He was all-powerful. He was in control. He looked around the interior station room, and everything sparkled and shone with a golden hue. The glow had returned to him once again, and with the strength of the drug and the fearsome dark power he now possessed, he would rule the remains of this feeble world, unchallenged.

After a few moments, most of his men had recovered. The ones who didn't make it were carried out and unceremoniously thrown over the wall of the dam.

"What is the status of the search?" Malak growled to Saxon, who still appeared dizzy after the initial trip.

"We...uh..." Saxon steadied himself. "Boss, we have searched everywhere that I know to search."

"And you haven't found anything yet?"

"We will search again, Lord Malak."

Before Malak could answer, a bandit interrupted from the far side of the room as he entered, dragging a skinny man who appeared to be reasonably terrified at what was about to happen to him.

"Lord Malak, I found this scared little shit hiding in one of the conference rooms. Said he works here."

"Doing what?"

Nick Corvaleski licked his lips. "Electrical engineer."

"Yeah," the thug continued, "says he can run this place."

Malak grinned with malevolence. "Of course he can." The war-lord pointed at the cowering engineer. "And for his next trick, he's going to find what I'm looking for, or he's going to experience pain and fear like he's never imagined."

Nick could do little more than swallow and nod his head. "I'll do anything."

"Yes," Malak intoned, "I know you will."

She remembered it like it was yesterday. The dream, now more like reality than anything else she knew. She turned on her shallow cot, her mind recounting every moment in excruciating detail.

Groaning, Ari hung from the pull-up bar, her hands aching with fresh blisters. It was the first day of boot camp, and she couldn't do a pull-up. So she hung there, embarrassed, as the instructor screamed at her and someone in her squad snickered—a poor soul who was immediately snatched from formation and made to run.

Ari swallowed and tried again, her arms screaming, her will forcing her onward. She raised a few inches, and then a few more, till her arms bent past forty-five degrees.

You can do this.

"Get up! Get your chin over that bar! We will stay here until you do!" the instructor screamed at her.

Her momentum stalled, progress thwarted. Ari groaned, kicking her legs.

"What is that? That's not a pull-up!" the instructor screamed.

She dropped from the bar and fell to the ground, exhausted.

"Get up! Why are you so weak? You will never make it here! Get up and run until I'm tired! Get up, Princess! Go, go, go!"

Princess. The nickname had stuck. For two weeks she was berated, challenged, and forced to spend mealtimes at the pull-up rack.

"Let's go, Princess!"

"Any day now, Princess!"

"Get your chin over that bar, Princess!"

The taunts were incessant, the drills punishing, and the nickname infuriating. But Ari was not one to be beaten. She never had been. For as long as she could remember, she had wanted to be a soldier. This pull-up rack was not going to stop her.

Twelve weeks later, she could do twenty without stopping. The proud, strong Israeli woman graduated from IDF boot camp as a squad leader and went on to be an exemplary soldier in the famed Caracal Battalion—though, much to her chagrin, the nickname Princess would stick with her throughout her military career.

After three years and many engagements with terrorist cells along the Egyptian border, she finally received the coveted letter from Mossad, one of the most elite intelligence agencies in the world. She knew they recruited straight out of the military and that they targeted females; she just never thought it would be her. The choice had been easy.

It had been the most intense journey of her life. All the training in hand-to-hand combat, special weapons, survival, surveillance and countersurveillance, counterterrorism operations, and espionage—it now seemed like a distant trial by fire, one that culminated in her being black bagged, transported in restraints, and illegally inserted into a hostile Arab nation with only the clothes on her back.

She had run, hidden, fought, been captured and tortured by the corrupt national police, subdued the guards, broken out, and disappeared into thin air. They never determined her identity. While a manhunt raged for *the foreign spy who was still in the country*, she slipped across the border back into Israel and was immediately picked back up, black bagged again, and taken back to Mossad. She had passed her training.

The next few years had been filled with mission after mission of cloak-and-dagger tactics, espionage, high-profile assassinations, and all sorts of other things she could never speak to any other living soul about. She was a warrior, a tactician, and a survivor. She was indomitable.

But Ari was not superhuman, and as she lay there tossing and turning on her military cot, her mind turned back to her baby brother. She had murdered him—at least that was how she felt. She tried to tell herself it was a mercy killing, that she had not violated the purity of her weapon, that she had done what was necessary, but she wasn't sure she believed that anymore.

She shuddered in the grip of the dream, her body quaking as she saw the blue-faced bandit sawing at Aviel's neck, and she listened in horror as her brother gurgled her name for the last time.

Ari sat bolt upright in her bed, her chest heaving with exertion. She put her hands to her face and exhaled, saying, "I'll kill him. I swear I will, Aviel. I swear it." She swung her legs over the edge of the bed and steadied her breathing. "I will avenge you, my brother."

There was no more sleep to be had this night. Ari stood from her bed, slipped into her clothes and shoes, and made her way outside. It was early, just before sunrise, when she exited the women's barracks and moved to slip into the men's housing.

It only took a moment for her to find Kane, his still form twitching under the thin, military-green wool blanket. She stood for just a moment, watching the pained expression on his face, noting each twitch and muscle spasm, knowing full well what it meant. She had just endured the same.

She reached out and nudged him. In a movement so fast she didn't have a chance to react, Kane snagged her wrist and produced a Glock from beneath the blanket, which was pushed flush against her face beside her nose.

"Excellent," Ari whispered.

"Good grief, Ari. I could've killed you."

"You wouldn't have had a chance to pull the trigger," she said and smiled.

"At least you're not cocky," Kane said with a huff, setting the weapon down.

"Come on, let's go," she said and motioned.

"Go where?" Kane sat up.

"Anywhere. How about for a run? If your dreams are anything like mine, then you're ready to get up."

"Yeah," Kane sighed, "you got me there. A morning run it is then."

"First things first," Ari said, pulling her knife and lifting Kane's shirt in the front.

"Whoa, hold on there," Kane quipped.

"Relax, cowboy. It's time for these to come out," she said, swiping the top stitch with her knife and pulling the thread from his skin. She repeated the process until she had removed all of them.

The scar would be ugly, but Jenna had done a solid job. Kane arched his back, testing the new scar with a wince. It held.

"Better?" Ari smiled.

"Oh yeah, much better." Kane smiled back. He shrugged into the rest of his clothes, threw on his boots, and together they headed out into the dawn of a new day.

▲ ▲ ▲

The early morning light stretched across the sky casting small rays of sunlight, like spiritual pillars of hope, through the dark cloud cover and across the central buildings of Camp Navajo.

Courtland had long since been the first to rise and was now hard at work on a large batch of biscuits and gravy for everyone. He paused, pulling a worn photograph of a teenage girl from his pocket. He gazed at the picture with nothing short of sheer admiration. It was a photo of his Marissa, the teenage daughter he had lost just before the world died.

"One day soon, sweetheart," Courtland whispered, a lump of emotion lodged in his throat. "When this is all done, I'll see you again." He smiled and lovingly touched the photograph, its worn and ragged edges speaking volumes about how often this ritual was performed. "I'll fight the good fight, and I won't ever give up. I know I'm here for a reason, but that doesn't make it hurt any less. I love you, baby girl. I'll see you and your mother soon." Courtland kissed the photograph and placed it with great care in the pocket of his flannel shirt, patting it.

He paused and glanced up to see Ari and Kane running back up from the woods. They were both covered in sweat and looked worn out from their morning jog. Ari was giving Kane a good-natured ribbing for being "too slow."

"What's going on there?" Jenna asked as she entered the kitchen and glanced at Kane and Ari.

Courtland smiled. "I don't know."

"Do you think they're ah…"

Courtland ducked his head to level his eyes with Jenna. "I don't know, Jenna. Kane just lost his wife. I don't think it's like that."

"So what then?"

"I think they get each other. They understand each other's loss. They've bonded over it."

Jenna shrugged.

"I'm happy they get along. Kane needs more than an old man to take care of him anyway," the giant said, smiling a toothy grin.

"I guess so. Hey, have you seen Dagen? I can't find him."

Courtland pursed his lips.

"What?" Jenna questioned.

"I saw him leave in a Hummer early this morning."

"What!" Jenna gasped. "He left the base?"

Courtland nodded.

"You didn't try to stop him?" Jenna said, her words desperate.

Courtland shook his head. "He was at the gate and then gone before I had the chance to say anything. I'm sure he's coming back," Courtland said.

Jenna bit her lip. "Oh no, this is my fault."

"What's your fault?"

Jenna couldn't suppress the tears as they welled in her eyes and splashed down her cheeks. "I had a bad moment. I said some stuff…"

"Jenna, what did you say to him?" The giant became stern.

Jenna wiped her face. "Courtland, I'm so mixed-up. He murdered my family, watched as I was…as they…"

"Shh…" Courtland grabbed Jenna in a viselike hug, and she erupted into a geyser of tears. "It's alright, dear. Hey, I know you've got a lot on you."

"Okay, yeah, I do, but I also said some hurtful things to him before I thought them through. If he's gone, if everything we've done to show him God's love has been ruined by me being stupid and selfish—I'll…I don't know if I could forgive myself."

"Hey, look, let's not go there yet," Courtland said.

Jenna nodded and wiped her face.

Courtland let her go and caught her eye. "We'll just hope he's blowing off some steam and that he's coming back—that's all we can do. Alright?"

"Alright," Jenna sobbed.

"We need to pray for him though, Jenna. Right now we need to pray for his heart."

Jenna wasted no time, bowing her head and begging for forgiveness for her own weakness and anger. Courtland placed his arms around her, and they joined in petition on behalf of a man broken by life and lost to the pages of time. Dagen now had an opportunity to choose his own fate, for better or worse, for good or for evil. And somehow they knew, this choice would affect them all in the end.

21

THEY RODE AT a trot through the night and into the next day. The morning gave way to midday and stirred a restless wind as Queenashano's war party continued to ride northward, further into the snowcapped mountains.

Upon waking, Tynuk had found himself lying in Queenashano's personal shelter and tended to by his wives and his people's healer. Initially confused and frantic, the boy calmed when he remembered the events of the day and how he had finally prevailed. He graciously accepted water from the women and salve from the healer. The latter was pressed into his wounds, after which they were wrapped with clean dressings. Queenashano let him rest but woke him later in the day and told him that it was imperative that they continue on if the boy was to finally understand his purpose. They traveled through the night and into the present day. The healer's attention had done him good. Even now, traveling with these people to an unknown location, he felt rejuvenated, renewed, and relieved to know that he was moving on from the trials.

Tynuk looked down at the clip-clopping dappled mustang between his legs. He was amazed at the resilience of the ugly unshod beasts. He had never seen horses so fast and maneuverable and yet so robust in constitution. They were and had been, the Comanche's choice of steed for hundreds of years—capable of handling long hauls over difficult terrain while also remaining quick and agile in battle. Now he could understand the Comanche's affinity for them. They had covered a remarkable distance on horseback, and though they were all exhausted, he had the feeling they were finally drawing near to their final destination.

Tynuk was still having trouble wrapping his head around all of it. He had gone from fleeing and fighting for his life to, in an instant, being accepted. No, it went beyond being accepted; it was more like being honored. This stood in stark contrast to the fact that Queenashano had just left Neraquassi's body where it lay. There was no burial, no last rites, nothing but a buffalo robe laid over Neraquassi's ruined body. Queenashano left the body of his own son to rot upon the desert sand. That's how important their current mission was to him, whatever it was. Queenashano had said it was time for him to learn what his destiny was. Maybe that meant someone finally had some answers to his many questions.

Breaking the silence Tynuk looked to Queenashano. "Where are we?"

"Nearing the home of the ancients."

Tynuk's confusion held.

Queenashano smiled. "Northern New Mexico, approaching the Carson National Forest."

"But how is this the home of the ancients? Wasn't this Pueblo territory?"

"Yes, most recently, but long ago, before white men roamed this continent, it first belonged to our ancestors."

"Our ancestors?" Tynuk raised an inquisitive eyebrow.

"Yes, our ancestors, all of us. Is it such a hard concept to grasp that many Native American people originally came from the same place?"

"Central and South America?"

"There were several influxes of indigenous people into this land, but one of the largest came from the south. We are the descendants of the Aztecs and Mayans and other South American cultures, and while the Comanche are the strongest and most pure, the other tribes, factions, and peoples we have allied with and fought against for hundreds of years are, in truth, not so different from us in ancestry."

"So this 'home of the ancients' was where the original native settlers from South and Central America stopped in their push north, then," Tynuk said.

"Yes, and then over time, rifts and divisions occurred, and the larger group separated and became many."

"Sounds so simple."

"That part is. What comes next is a little more...supernatural. Much like your Great Spirit." Queenashano smiled. "Tell me more about this."

"It is difficult to put into words." Tynuk shrugged.

"Try. My uncle, your mentor, Nuk'Chala, taught you of it?"

The boy bobbed his head. "He did."

"And this Great Spirit is the same as our Big Father?" Queenashano gestured at the sun hidden in the cloud covered sky.

"Yes and no. The spirit is abundant, the bringer of all life and the author of our purpose."

Queenashano looked on in thoughtful silence.

"The Great Spirit created everything. It breathed life into all of creation, but unlike Big Father, it is deeply interested in each one of us. It knows that we have the capacity for great evil, but it still loves us enough to live withing us—if we so allow it."

Queenashano made a face and touched his chest. "It lives inside you?"

"In a manner of speaking, yes. It is a guide and a teacher. It is a nudge that pushes you in the right direction when you falter."

"How do we bring this Great Spirit into our chests?"

Tynuk smiled. "You must only accept the spirit and it's ways."

They rode on in silence for a spell, the flat red-rock valley ending before them in magnificent, towering mountains that pushed straight up from the earth thousands of feet into the sky. The dingy, snowcapped mountain peaks towered high above them, the low-lying clouds swirling like dark halos about their summits. Though the weather was mild, grayish pockets of snow still hugged together in nooks and crannies, nestled in the shade of the great mountains.

"Queenashano," Tynuk said and turned to the war chief, "I must ask you...about..."

Queenashano finished the boy's sentence. "Your father, one of my lost brothers."

Tynuk nodded and did not raise his eyes, afraid the war chief would see his shame.

"Your father was not a bad man, but he was a full-blood Comanche and prone to the excesses of our people. During the days before the End War, Nachona grew weary of our people and our ways. He felt that he had to leave us to join the civilized world—just as he would later feel that he had to leave you and your mother. He was always this way. His name among our people had even been Restless One."

"So, after he left my mother and me..."

"He did not return to us. That is all I know. He may still wander, out there, somewhere."

Tynuk screwed up his face and pushed his mind from the subject. There was nothing further to say about the honorless man who was his father. The boy looked down; the wound in his side had been superficial. And now, though well tended to by Queenashano's healer, it had begun to ache during the long ride. He tested it, wincing with fresh pain.

Hours passed as they ascended farther into the perilous, craggy mountains on horseback. Above them, lone boulders stood, jutting from the rock-covered hillsides that towered high above the ravine. With an ancient omnipotence, they seemed to watch the meandering train of men and horses, threatening to topple in a massive landslide at even the slightest disturbance.

"We'll dismount here," Queenashano said, breaking the silence and pointing, "we'll go the rest of the way on foot."

Tynuk nodded and dismounted with the others. Before them, a large group of mustangs already stood, rooting and foraging in the short scrub, an indication that a sizable force was already here, awaiting their arrival.

The climb up the mountain was strenuous and, several times, nearly perilous. Tynuk hiked, the strong, lean muscles of his legs pushing and pulling as he followed his uncle, and the rest of the war party followed him. It was the work of several hours to climb hand over foot, well up into the crevice of the mountain to the base of a large bald face that extended upward to the snowy peak above.

The path below their feet was worn into the rock from years of use by pilgrims, priests, and wanderers seeking answers. As Tynuk looked ahead, he saw where the path disappeared, twisting into the rock itself. He couldn't imagine, for the life of him, what secrets this place held or, what discovering them might mean for him.

Slipping into the rock passage, they then began a short ascent into a hollow chamber lined with torches. The ceiling of the cavern rose above them, towering in the flickering light.

Arriving on the floor of the cavernous sanctuary, Tynuk saw a large group of warriors waiting for them. Queenashano raised his arms as he approached the squat but heavily muscled man that led them. "Penateka! How are you, my brother?"

"Far better than I deserve, War Eagle," Penateka responded, clasping Queenashano's arm and slapping his shoulder. "Where is he?"

Queenashano turned and gestured to Tynuk. "I present to you, Wolf Born. Tynuk, this is my brother, Rolling Thunder."

Penateka marveled for a moment. "He is just a child! Are you sure this is him?"

"He is the son of Nachona, and he has been extensively trained by Nuk'Chala. I will recount the story to you in its entirety, but yes, there is no doubt in my mind," Queenashano replied. "You have seen his likeness in this very place—have you not? You tell me."

Realizing that all eyes were now upon him, Tynuk looked around in anticipation as the numerous warriors stood in silence.

"Are you ready, Tynuk? Are you ready to see what you were brought here for?"

"Yes," Tynuk said, hardly able to contain himself.

"Then look at your feet," Queenashano replied.

In all the strange newness of this place, Tynuk had never noticed the floor. The many warriors stepped back to reveal an elaborate mural painted on it. Tynuk stepped back, his mouth dropping open, his tongue sticking in his throat. Below him, just beyond his toes, a part of this massive floor painting, was the image of a wild-looking, breechclout-clad warrior boy, who unmistakably bore the image of his own face.

⋀ ⋀ ⋀

There was no question that the base had been a beautiful reprieve from the unknowns and the fear of the outside world. Rested, clean, and with full stomachs, everyone in Kane's group was in better spirits than they had been in months. They'd been able to replenish their arms and had the ammunition to actually train with their weapons for the first

time since the mutant siege. Under Kane and Ari's direction, they had
fired over five hundred rounds each that morning, working accuracy,
speed, malfunction, and magazine change drills for rifles and handguns. He now had all the confidence in the world in his people.

It would be all too easy for them to stay here in this place, but
Kane's dear children were still out there somewhere, held in the
clutches of a demonic despot. They could wait no longer.

Kane looked down the line and did a final head count. He
counted twenty-eight adults—everyone but Dagen. He looked at
Jenna but said nothing.

She caught his gaze. "I know. It's time to go," she said. "I just keep
thinking he'll come back."

"Maybe he will, but we can't wait for him any longer," Kane said.

Jenna acknowledged, touching her fingertips to her lips.

Kane turned to survey the old train, which included seven boxcars
and five flatbeds, plus the engine. While the fancy, modern, comput-
erized trains were all dead, this old World War II–era, steam-pow-
ered, 5011-class locomotive wasn't. Somehow it still functioned. They
had found it, unloaded, on the rails inside the base. The idea of trying
to use it had been a moot point until Sam spoke up. It turned out the
old guy had been a caretaker at one of the largest railroad museums in
the nation—the National Railroad Museum in Wisconsin. Sam was
familiar with steam engines, after a thirty-year career working on and
helping to restore locomotives of all kinds. But now standing before
the great steel beast, Kane began to have questions.

"Why is it here?" Kane asked.

Sam scratched his head. "It's on the rails and in working condition. The best I can figure is maybe a bunch of people came up here
on it from the railroad museum in Albuquerque. I would guess after
all this mess started. They were probably looking for refuge here at
the military base."

"Then where are those people now?"

"Your guess is as good as mine," Sam shrugged.

"And you can drive this thing?"

Sam chuckled. "I haven't driven one before if that's what you're asking, but I think I can figure it out. I'll just need some help with keeping the furnace hot."

Kane nodded. "You have what you need?" He noted a few people carrying wood logs up to the storage hold in the engine compartment. They had been hard at work cutting down trees and loading the logs onto the train for the past few hours.

"Yep. Marcus and Carl are loading up the last of the wood for the furnace, and I just topped off the water tank with the base's well water."

"I know I asked before, but you're sure the railway goes to the dam?"

"No doubt," Sam replied. "I verified it on the map. Besides, I remember hearing that they used trains back in the day for hauling all the raw materials necessary for pouring the concrete and building the dam itself."

"Good deal, Sam. You're a lifesaver."

Sam bobbed his head. "I'll go get the furnace started." He said moving up the ramp onto the engine.

Kane looked to Courtland. "Alright, big man, everything loaded up?"

"Ari is loading the last of the Humvees now."

"Weapons and ammunition?"

"More than we could use in three lifetimes," Courtland said.

"Food, water, fuel, and other supplies?"

"We're good to go. It's all on board."

"Security in place for our journey?" Kane asked.

"We've got it all buttoned up, my friend." Courtland smiled.

"I knew you would." Kane smiled back. "Let's get everyone loaded up."

"You got it," Courtland said and then turned, bellowing, "Everyone who is going to the dam, load up on the train! We're heading out!"

Courtland reached over to pick up two enormous, black, scimitar-shaped blades and hefted them over his shoulder. Each was five feet long and looked to weigh a hundred pounds, easy.

Kane grinned. "You're still hanging on to those things?"

Courtland leveled his eyes at his friend. "Do you remember how I got them?"

Kane stifled a laugh. "As bizarre as all that was—yes, I remember."

"Then you've seen what I can do with them?"

"Oh yeah, I've seen it. You don't forget stuff like that, my man."

"Then you know why I'm bringing them." The gentle giant smiled with a spark in his deep brown eyes that wasn't so gentle.

"Absolutely." Kane saluted good-naturedly. "Very good, sir."

Courtland lumbered up and onto the train as the others followed suit. Kane watched as all the familiar faces, some of whom had been with them from the very first days at the radio control station, moved toward the train. These people's loyalty was remarkable. Even now, they volunteered to fight, and maybe even die, for the cause of heaven and the safety of another man's children. The support overwhelmed him and he took a moment to thank God for it.

Turning, Kane noticed Jenna boarding the train.

"What are you doing?" He gazed at her with concern.

"I'm going with you guys," Jenna said.

"I thought you'd stay here with James and Marilyn to look after the children. Maybe see if Dagen showed back up."

Jenna shouldered a military M16 rifle. "I'm probably better suited for those things, and I do hope Dagen shows back up, but I'm not going to stay here while you guys confront Malak."

"Are you sure about that?" Kane asked, placing his hand on her shoulder.

"No," Jenna swallowed, "but I trust that our God will win us the day. Besides, there's no way I'm going to miss the moment when my king shows these monsters who's boss."

Kane smiled. "Welcome aboard, Jenna."

Jenna walked up the steps and onto the train. Kane took a last look about. Sam gave him the thumbs-up as the engine chuffed to life, black smoke billowing into the air. Swiveling the other direction, Kane watched as Ari repeated the gesture from the rear of the train. Kane reciprocated and moved to the base's main gate to open it.

On one of the flatbeds next to a secured Hummer, Winston looked around anxiously before snapping on his radio with a bleep and a wash of static.

"Winston to Shana. We're leaving the base by train. I repeat we are on a train. We're headed west toward the dam. That's all." The chubby man didn't wait for a response before snapping the radio back off and swearing under his breath. He hated himself for what he was doing, but like this train, it couldn't be stopped now.

With a squeal, the ancient, tar-black steam train lurched forward, the cars clanking and grinding as they began to move. Kane was ready, scanning Ryback's ID and opening the gate for it as the train huffed past. Kane snagged a rail, pulled himself up into the train, and turned to see James and Marilyn with the children, waving good-bye from the center of the base's courtyard. Above them, fluttering at full mast, a tattered American flag rippled, its faded colors still striking as they flapped in the wind. Kane waved back, and the gate shut behind them with a clunk of finality. It was time to finish this fight.

22

NICK CORVALESKI POINTED to the vault. "The…uh…Okay, so…" He licked his lips.

"Spit it out, queer." The bandit behind him jerked his collar, jostling his frail body.

"Yeah, man, look, you need to get to the lowest level of the facility."

"And how do we do that?" Malak brooded.

"You're not going to get there without a security access key for the elevator."

"Do I have to pry everything out of you? Where is the key." Malak snarled.

Nick shrank back, his fear bringing on a whole new wave of stuttering. "In…In…In the vault." He pointed a shaking finger at the thick plate-steel vault at the far end of the room.

"In the vault, you say," Malak cooed, turning his greedy black eyes to the door.

"Want us to blast it, boss?" a thug nearby said, shouldering an RPG.

With a wave of his hand, Malak dismissed him, lumbering forward and gazing at the steel door that had to weigh thousands of pounds.

"Nothing can keep me out!" he growled, grabbing the upper corners of the door and bending them downward as though they were made of flexible plastic. With each pull, the door bent farther, the metal screeching as it distorted. With a shout of fury, Malak jerked the door open, the bolts popping in unison and revealing an empty vault. All the valuables had been removed long ago, everything but two identical red key cards hanging on opposite ends of the vault.

Malak glanced at Nick, and the thin man nodded his confirmation. The keys were retrieved, and they made their way to the service elevator, where Malak and Nick swiped their cards against the internal card readers of the elevator. The elevator lurched to life as it began its descent into the bowels of the dam. There was no floor button for where they were going.

The descent took longer than expected. Malak and his small crew of thugs, along with the electrical engineer, waited in anticipation as the elevator began to slow. It came to a stop with a ding, the doors sliding open to reveal the open corridors of an underground lab.

Malak took in a sharp breath, his eyes widening. He could feel it, calling to him, begging him to find it. He stormed from the elevator, overcome with the desire to have it. Passing isolated labs, one after another, he entered the last room off the hall, a prison gray room with a magnetically sealed storage vault. A note on the outside of the door read, *Do not touch the device without protective equipment. No one has done so and survived the interaction. In the event of an emergency in which the device must be moved, wear gloves, use tongs, and transport it in a level-four, secure-locking, hazardous-material case.*

It was stronger now. He could feel the Machine reaching out for him, longing to be found after all this time. After waving his red card over the lock, the bolts released with a clunk, and the door parted with a sigh. Malak reached forward and eased the door open. Everyone else looked on in awe.

There before him, nestled in a custom-made depression, was the Machine. Malak spoke but did not take his eyes off the Machine. "What else is down here?"

"Other high-priority projects," Nick said, his voice wavering.

"Like what?"

"Well, I had a friend who told me—I mean, he wasn't supposed to, but he told me—that they were working on an active HPM project down here."

"High-powered-microwave technology doesn't work," Malak mumbled, still gazing at the device.

"My friend said it did—that they were weaponizing it." Nick gulped.

"Can you make it work?"

"If it runs on electricity, yeah, I think so. But I don't think it's stable—or safe."

"I'm not worried about all that. Find it and have it taken topside. Anything else that may be of value to us, as well." He stared at the Machine and marveled that it was actually here within his reach.

"Finally," the possessed warlord intoned with malevolent intent, "the time has come."

▲ ▲ ▲

"Is it not your life?"

Tynuk took another step back, the surreal nature of the moment overcoming his resistance to it. He couldn't find the words to answer. He looked over the elaborate floor painting again. It was incredible, an elaborate work of art, far removed from what one would expect to be painted on the floor of a cave in the middle of nowhere.

"Everyone against the walls, so he can see all of it." Queenashano motioned out with his arms.

As the warriors shuffled back, the whole scene came together. Tynuk scanned his eyes back to the first image—a Native American man and woman in modern civilian clothes, holding a newborn child. They were both smiling. The next image was of the man leaving as a young child reached for him, the mother crying behind him. Then followed images of the bullies, his mother's drunken fury, and his harsh training at the hands of Grandfather Nuk'Chala.

Tynuk scanned the images from left to right, recounting every major event from the moment of his birth to the present. He saw it all: Azolja and then Kane and Courtland, the initial fight for the station, his fight with the mutants in the woods, his trials at the hands of these very people—all of it was there, painted into the stone *hundreds of years ago.*

He marveled over the accuracy of it all, surreal in its complexity and entirety. He peered at a depiction of this very moment, an image of a warrior boy peering at the floor of this place while many eager faces looked on.

He shook his head and stepped back. "This...This is too much."

Queenashano smiled. "But is it not correct?"

The boy was quiet. "It is, but—"

"Do not ask how," Queenashano replied with a smile. "That is for the ancients alone to know. What matters is that it is true."

Tynuk remained silent.

"Allow me to dispel any remaining doubt, Tynuk," Queenashano said. "You are the one. It is you who will unite and lead our people to greatness." He stepped forward and presented Nuk'Chala's war belt to the boy. "I believe now that this was given to you by the great Nuk'Chala when you earned its trust. I am sorry for having taken it from you and for any mistreatment you received at our hands. It was necessary for all of us to understand what you really were."

Tynuk took the belt in his hands, his heart swelling at its return.

"Will you lead us, young Tynuk?" Queenashano bowed his head and took a knee. The entire cavern of warriors followed suit.

"But you are their leader." Tynuk looked around in astonishment.

"I was. But I am growing old. It is time for new blood to direct us. It is time for the prophecy to be realized."

After a reluctant moment of deliberation, Tynuk placed his hand on Queenashano's shoulder and nodded. "I will lead my people."

Smiling, Queenashano stood and embraced Tynuk as his own blood. Then, grasping his shoulders, he asked, "What would you have us do, Wolf Born?"

Tynuk scanned the myriad of images depicting his future and saw several that appeared quite terrifying. He looked to the final image, a depiction of a massive battle. In it, Tynuk was depicted riding fearlessly atop Azolja toward a towering dam, his Comanche brothers charging on horseback behind him.

"Where is this?" He pointed to the image.

"Our elders believe it is the Glen Canyon Dam, about three hundred fifty miles due west of here in northern Arizona. The battle, I cannot say."

"I think I know. I have felt pulled to reunite with my friends, our allies, who may have now journeyed west to this place. They will need our help in this conflict. They are involved in something very big, something that concerns us all."

Many faces looked on, puzzled.

"May I ask how this conflict concerns the New Comanche Nation, war chief?"

"It affects us because they fight the forces of darkness. We could allow them to be consumed, saying it is not our fight, only to have to face this same evil ourselves in the future. But instead, we will join them in this fight and see this blight vanquished."

"Very well," Queenashano said, ducking his head. "This battle was predicted long ago by men much wiser than I. Who am I to question it?" He motioned toward the images on the floor of the cavern. "We are with you and at your command, young Tynuk. The battle does not frighten us. We were born of war."

Tynuk nodded and surveyed the large group of warriors, one hundred fifty in number. "Then this dam is our destination, and we will leave for it at once."

"Very well, war chief, but before we do there's just one other thing I must ask," Queenashano said, "There is one part of this great image that none of us, not even our elders, have been able to explain."

Tynuk raised his eyebrows.

"What is *this*?"

Tynuk followed the steady hand of the former war chief to where it stopped, his finger pointing to a black presence in the mural. Like a large, shaggy coal smudge, it appeared with the boy more often than not in the images, a white morning star emblazoned in the dark fur of its chest, a mark that was set below silvery eyes and huge dagger-like fangs.

Tynuk broke into a genuine smile. "You don't know what this is because you have yet to truly experience the supernatural, dear uncle." He pushed his fingers into his mouth and whistled.

From somewhere above them, a shadow leaped from a ledge, unseen until this moment. With catlike grace, Azolja landed in the center of the floor with a thud that shook the room. The Comanche warriors gasped, squeezing themselves against the walls of the cavern as they backed away, raising their weapons. The great beast swung its massive head, taking in the smallish brown men around it, looking

far more like some ancient shape-shifter than anything that belonged
in the natural world. Tynuk placed his hand upon the massive beast's
dark flank of solid muscle.

"This is Azolja. He is with me," Tynuk stated with utter confidence, "and though he is quite fearsome, he is not to be feared—by
you. The Great Spirit, in all its wisdom, knew we would need his
help."

"You could have called on this great beast for aid throughout the
entirety of the trials?" Queenashano was breathless.

"I could have, but I did not."

Not a breath was taken in the cavernous space for what seemed
like an eternity, and for just a moment, Tynuk secretly reveled in the
unconcealed looks of shock and terror on everyone's faces, including
that of the great Queenashano.

▲ ▲ ▲

In the deserted ruins of what had once been Farmington, New
Mexico, Shana waited. She pulled at her short, unkempt hair, her
tongue stroking across blistered lips. Behind her were no less than
fifty dirty, rabid wasteland bandits—some of the Coyotes' finest.

She'd received Winston's last transmission. Kane and his group
would be leaving the army base aboard a train. She couldn't believe
her shitty luck. *A train.* She had sworn on her life that she would
produce Kane's head on a stick and that not a single member of his
group would survive.

She was beginning to regret those promises. And now she also had
to figure out how to assault a moving train. Not an easy feat. Shana
had to assume they were already beaten down from their journey,
that they wouldn't have much fight left in them. Once she coupled
that with the sheer surprise of an ambush, this little group wouldn't

be able to resist the Coyotes for long. Her men would board the train and slaughter everyone on board.

She looked over her group again—disgusting, ugly highwaymen, each and every one. They were a violent bunch, but success was not guaranteed, and there were no other options. Her skin tingled at the thought of how pleased Lord Malak would be when she arrived with news of Kane's death while also producing a loaded train as a bonus.

As if on cue, the piercing whistle of the steam train cut through the air, the chugging of the engine loud and powerful, the sound so strange in the silence of the new world. Kane was headed toward the dam. She had to stop him, and suddenly, she knew just how to do it.

23

"HOLD UP, SAM," Kane said, leaning his head out of the window to get a better look at the debris that was blocking the track. It was a foregone conclusion that sections of the track would be blocked along their route. Kane had just hoped that they could make it out of town first.

Kane scanned the horizon as Sam began to gradually apply the brake lever, the train squealing and slowing to a stop. Farmington, New Mexico, hadn't been much to look at when it was alive: a small mountain town with squat, square one-story buildings and little definition in the way of architectural diversity. Now the abandoned adobe structures appeared like the stone dwellings of some long-forgotten indigenous people who'd left long ago in search of greener pastures.

"We're going to have to remove it from the tracks." Sam looked toward the broken-down, rusted sedan that straddled the tracks before them.

"Yeah," Kane muttered. His portable radio crackled; it was Ari.

"What's going on?"

"There's a vehicle blocking the tracks; it's going to have to be moved. I don't like it. It looks placed to make us stop. Keep security tight." Kane said catching a flash of movement from behind the vehicle. Someone was crouched down, waiting.

Ambush.

"Ram it!" Kane bared his teeth and grabbed the throttle, forcing it open.

"What?" Sam cried out, grabbing Kane's arm. "It could derail us!"

"Do it! It's a trap!" Kane yelled as the train screamed a trail of steam, picking up speed. "Everyone brace for impact," Kane called into his radio. "We've been set up. Get ready to fight."

Two bandits popped up, firing from behind the abandoned vehicle, the bullets striking the front of the train and bouncing off the interior walls around Kane and Sam.

"Get down, Sam. Keep us going."

Sam ducked his head, and Kane rose, shouldering his M16 rifle. The first shot was dead on, a fine pink mist spraying from the first bandit's skull as the other broke from the cover of the vehicle and began to run. Kane tracked him, firing single rounds to conserve ammo. With a jarring concussion, the train slammed into the sedan, shoving it down the tracks in a squalling grind of steel against steel. The vehicle was stuck sliding down the track as they went.

"This isn't good," Sam groaned. "If that catches on anything, it could flip us."

"Just keep going. Don't stop, no matter what." Kane slung his rifle over a chest rig loaded with eight rifle magazines and a few fragmentation grenades. He climbed up the ladder outside the cab and onto the roof of the train just in time to see a bunch of vehicles spinning their tires on the dirt as they approached the train from the rear. Kane conducted a quick assessment.

"Twelve vehicles. About fifty bad guys. Definitely Coyotes." Kane said to himself, as he ran across the top of the train toward the rear. He grabbed his radio, a multitude of thoughts stopping his transmission. *Is this it? Is Malak with them? Michael and Rachael?*

Kane cleared his head of distractions that would get him killed and keyed the radio.

"Ari, Courtland, and everyone else, they're going to try to board us. If they do, we're dead. They've got us outnumbered. Defend the train but identify your targets. They could have my kids or other hostages with them."

Kane ran to the edge of the car. Dropping to a knee, he took aim on the raiders as they drew alongside the chugging train, their screams wild with psychotic hate. Kane fired and saw his rounds find their marks with each pull of the trigger, his targets slumping or tumbling from the bouncing vehicles as they struggled to keep up with the train.

Pulling the pin from a frag grenade, the spoon sang as it ejected. Kane hurled it as hard as he could into the midst of the pursuing bandit vehicles. With a flash, the grenade disintegrated a vehicle's tires, causing it to roll and catch fire. The bandits inside were trapped, their screams fading as the train gained speed.

"Ari, did you copy that?" Kane yelled, bullets pinging off the railcar around him.

From the dark interior of the rearmost railcar, Ari took a deep breath and nodded to Courtland. "I copy," she replied, stone-faced. "You worry about the sides of the train. I've got the rear covered."

Courtland unbolted the double doors and flung them both open with a shout. Immediately five of the bandit vehicles came into view, their painted riders screaming as they approached to board. Ari swung the barrel of her stationary M2 .50-caliber machine gun in the direction of their pursuers and watched as rage and invincibility gave way to unchecked terror.

The heavy machine gun pounded to life, in a surge of absolute, overwhelming violence. Ari snarled with iron determination, her entire body shaking with the pounding of the weapon. The Coyotes' vehicles exploded, metal and glass shrapnel flying everywhere. The bandits, now wild with hysteria, swerved their vehicles, desperate to get clear of the devastating weapon.

Ari tracked them with controlled bursts, the thin metal husks of the vehicles proving insufficient cover from the large, devastating rounds fired by the heavy machine gun. The highwaymen screamed as buckets of hot lead ripped them apart, tossing torn limbs into the air and showering the bodies of their comrades in bloody pulp.

The remaining six cars approached from either side of the train, trying to get close enough for the psychos to board. Shana approached up the right side of the train with two beat-up, full-size trucks and an old flatbed tow truck loaded with goons. She screamed, swinging her arms and shouting for her men to board the train.

"Now!" Jenna yelled. The locomotive came alive with the sound of gunfire, the shooters in Kane's group opening up on the bandits from the length of the train. Jenna took aim, choosing her targets and pulling the trigger as her rifle recoiled again and again against her.

Kane watched the Coyotes' vehicles approaching, his people striking good hits on the bandits and thinning their numbers as they tried to close the gap. He continued to fire, his weapon running dry. He extracted a fresh magazine from his carrier, inserted it in the mag well, and slapped the bolt catch. From the corner of his eyes, he saw Courtland leap from the left side of the train. The Coyotes never saw the giant coming.

Dropping in with a roar, Courtland landed with a titanic boom against the engine block of the lead vehicle, an old Chevy S-10, causing it to flip. Bellowing, surging with heavenly strength,

Courtland caught the vehicle by its roof as it flipped upside down in the air. Taking two lunging strides, he pivoted and slammed its tailgate down like a giant sledgehammer into the top of the second vehicle. Spinning, he flung the crushed vehicle from his hands sending it flipping end over end, launching mangled bodies from the windows.

"Hit that big bastard!" a thug in the third vehicle shouted, encouraging the driver to floor it at the now-stationary giant. Posting up and digging in as the train continued past, Courtland balled his enormous bowling-ball-size fists and prepared for the vehicle to hit him.

"Strike me down if you can!" the giant shouted in defiance.

In one deft movement, just as the bandit's vehicle prepared to make contact with him, Courtland dropped low and assumed his old Crushball lineman stance. The giant bristled with inhuman power as the vehicle collided with him. From atop the train, Kane watched in amazement. There was no doubt that the opponents of Courtland "the Sledge" Thompson had faced a similarly unstoppable force in the famed Crushball arenas of the old world. The bandit occupants of the vehicle might as well have hit a bridge support at eighty miles per hour, their broken bodies melding with the twisting metal of the truck, their screams cut short.

Atop the train, Kane cheered as Courtland stood free of the mangled vehicle. But his elation was short-lived as bullets zipped past his own head, causing him to duck. Kane turned and watched as the last two cars made their move for the driver's cab.

"Sam!" Kane shouted and began to run back to the front of the train. Just as he arrived, he slung his rifle and jumped, forgoing the ladder. Grabbing a crossbar as he fell, Kane swung his legs toward the opening of the cab just as a thug scrambled up the ladder from one of the vehicles. With the full force of his body weight, Kane planted both feet in the chest of the man, launching him from the opening with a howl, his body disappearing beneath the wheels of the closest vehicle.

The second man was up the ladder fast, as Kane dropped from the crossbar and chanced a look at Sam, who was still trying to control the train. The painted man, wild with fury, rose into the cabin and leveled his handgun. Kane had no time to unsling his rifle. Dodging to the left as the bandit fired twice, Kane intercepted the man's gun hand at the wrist. Torquing the barrel, Kane disarmed the thug, kicking him in the pelvic bowl and firing a round point-blank into the dead man's face.

Stepping to the opening, Kane pulled his last frag grenade, tossing it through the open window of one of the closest trucks. He emptied the thug's handgun into several bandits who had latched onto the train, knocking them from the side of the cab. He dropped the bandit's weapon at his feet, and transitioning to his rifle, he tabbed the selector switch into the full-auto position. The rifle blazed a white-hot stream of lead into the final two vehicles, just as the frag grenade exploded inside the truck, turning its driver into a loose pile of meat. Out of control, the truck slammed into the side of the train with the sound of metal tearing.

Kane ran dry, made his weapon ready, and fired again into the last vehicle; the M16's rounds cutting through the sidewall like a hot knife through butter. Slowing, the vehicle drifted away from the train, inert.

"Sam, stop the train," Kane shouted, lungs heaving with exertion. He turned to see old Sam clutching at a bad chest wound. The blood had already spread across his shirt and was beginning to soak the front of his pants. He had been hit by one of the two rounds Kane had dodged.

Reaching past the downed man, Kane disengaged the throttle and engaged the brake lever himself, bringing the train squealing to a stop. "Come on, Sam, don't do this to me." Kane broke open a military trauma pack and pulled a chest seal from the pouch. Sam stopped him.

"Forget about it. I've about exhausted my usefulness anyway," he said, wheezing.

"Dammit, Sam, that bullet was meant for me." Kane frowned, still putting pressure on the old man's wound.

"It's alright. I showed you everything I knew about this old thing. You drive the train now. You don't need me."

"Not true. You've been with us since we took refuge at the radio station. You're an asset and a good man."

"Well, between you and me, you are needed much more than I am. Go and save your kids."

Kane nodded. "I will."

"That's good. Don't lose hope," the old man said in a whisper, his body going limp.

Kane ducked his head, mourning the loss of another one of his people. Swearing, his anger building, he picked up his rifle, exited the cab, and started back toward the ruined bandit vehicles. Approaching the truck that had veered away, he saw a figure crawl from the passenger side, mortally wounded.

The rest of Kane's group was exiting the train, everyone weary with the stress of battle. Kane scanned the wounded female bandit for weapons but came up empty.

He turned and saw Ari hop down from the train, alongside several others. Everyone else was cheering and hugging and giving high-fives over their victory. Behind them Courtland approached, just now catching up with the now-stationary train.

Kane turned back to the female bandit, a flare of recognition in his face.

"Shana?"

"Yeah," Shana sputtered. She had more holes in her than he could count.

"Where's Malak? Too scared to fight his own battles?"

Shana smirked. "My lord is above fucking with you people any longer. He has his sights set on greater glories."

"Then what the hell is this about?"

"It's about murdering you and everyone associated with you."

"How's that working out for ya?" Kane quipped.

"Pretty good till this," she said, smiling with evil in her eyes. "Your friend...that kid, Jacob? That obnoxious little shit was my kill."

Kane's face hardened.

"Yeah, brought the whole fuckin' roof down on you, didn't we? Did your wife. Enslaved your kids—"

Kane placed the barrel of his rifle against her head, a remorseless look of disgust hanging on his face. "You should think real hard how you want to spend your last few moments, because you aren't going to mention my wife and children again."

"Heh." Shana spat blood. "Don't you wanna know?"

"Know what?"

"How we knew where you would be. How we knew where to set this little ambush?"

"Seems irrelevant now that we've won."

"Oh, but it is relevant," Shana said, gurgling, crimson bubbles foaming on her lips as she choked back her own blood. "There's a traitor in your midst."

Behind them Winston began to back away, shaking his head, his face a mask of horror.

"Yeah, that's right, Winston. You're in trouble now," Shana gloated.

Kane turned to look at Winston. "What's she talking about?"

Winston continued to back away, unable to speak.

"Winston, what's going on?" Jenna said, approaching.

"Yeah, Winston, what's going on?" Shana mocked, initiating a bout of coughing. "Tell them," she resumed. "Tell them how you dimed them out to save your own skin. Tell them…" Shana coughed, gasping and gurgling as she grabbed at her wounded body and slumped over dead.

Kane turned toward Winston, who drew a blue snub-nosed revolver from his waistband and pointed it back at him. Kane didn't bother raising his hands. "You sold us out, and now Sam is dead for it."

"Sam?" Jenna questioned Kane with loss in her eyes.

Kane nodded but didn't take his eyes off Winston.

"I didn't have a choice—you don't understand!" Winston shrieked.

"Winston, just put the gun down. Let's talk about this," Jenna said.

Kane shook his head.

"I didn't have a choice!" Winston shouted. "They made me do it!"

"Winston, please," Jenna pleaded.

Winston turned the gun on himself, pushing it to his temple. "I can't live with myself. I wasn't strong enough. I know. Kane was right. I *am* a coward."

Kane took a deep breath and let it out, checking his own anger. He couldn't figure out how the Coyotes could have gotten to Winston—much less swayed him against them. The man had been with them the entire time. "Winston put the gun down. You don't want to hurt yourself."

Courtland, Ari, and a few others approached with caution. "Come on, Winston," Courtland began. "It's never too late to come back. You're one of us. We'll work it out."

Tears of shame dribbled down Winston's cheeks. "No. It *is* too late. You don't understand. They put something inside me—*something evil*. I wasn't strong enough to fight it, and now I've gone too far. I can't come back, not now."

"That's not true, Winston," Jenna said. "You can always come back to us. You've done a lot of good—you saved all those children at the station. Don't end your life over a mistake you made. We understand why you had to do it."

"Come on, Winston," Ari whispered.

Kane's face softened. "Winston, seriously, don't do this. You are still one of us. Sam was enough. We don't need to lose you too. Don't do this. We'll work it out."

"Please, brother, put the gun down. It's going to be Okay," Courtland pleaded.

"No…it's not. It can't ever be okay now. I can feel it moving under my skin. I want to get it out. Help me get it out!"

Kane and Courtland exchanged a worried glance as Winston continued.

"I don't want to live in this world anymore. I'm all used up. I'm a traitor, and traitors deserve to die."

"Winston, look at me. Look at me," Kane started.

Winston seemed to calm considerably, his eyes distant, a confirmation of some terrible decision. "It's alright, guys. I won't bother you with this. I can get the darkness out. I know how. I don't want it *inside me* anymore."

"Don't do it, Winston!" Jenna cried.

Kane, Jenna, Courtland, Ari, and several others all shouted, pleading in unison for him to stop. Winston pinched his eyes shut and pulled the trigger. In an instant, the revolver's hammer slammed down, concussively exclaiming the final moments of Winston's life. His friends were unable to do anything but look on in shock and horror, as the poor man blasted the contents of his skull into the air.

24

IN THE FADING light of the day, Dagen brought the desert-tan military Humvee rolling to a stop. He was close enough, for now. He sat in the silence of the vehicle and watched the Glen Canyon Dam facility through a pair of military issue binoculars. No sign of Malak on the top of the dam or on the adjacent bridge that crossed the canyon. The place was a fortress—armed to the teeth. There was plenty going on as well. Men hustled back and forth, setting barricades, positioning weapon systems, and generally making preparations for the assault they knew Kane would be bringing. Kane and his people were walking into a death trap.

Dagen set the binoculars next to him on the seat and leaned his head back against the headrest. Was he really going to try to make contact with the Coyotes? Did he really want to see Malak again? The endless questions tumbled through his mind and threatened to drive him mad. He looked at the unopened bottle of Blistered Pig whiskey on the seat next to him. He'd found it by accident at the army base and decided to save it for a day like today. Just one sip… Dagen pulled his eyes from the bottle and pinched them shut, screwing his face together at the war inside.

Jenna.

He loved her for what she'd done for him. He loved her for who she was. But he never should have allowed himself to pretend he was worthy of such love. How foolish he had been to think he deserved to love or be loved by a woman like that. He could never repay her the debt he owed. Not in one hundred billion lifetimes. He had done unspeakable things throughout the course of his life but what he had done to her had been the worst. It was his curse, and there was nothing he could do to lift the weight of it from his shoulders. There was nothing God could do for him now. He was a monster. Why was he trying so hard to not be one? Better for him to accept the nature of what he was than to try to pretend he was something he clearly wasn't.

Dagen looked at the station again. He couldn't just drive up empty-handed. They would murder him without so much as a question. He had to first do something to ingratiate himself to their cause. The only way for him to do that was for him to turn on Kane's people. To show Malak that he didn't belong with them and never had. It wouldn't be easy, but if he shut himself down inside and remembered the old him, if he refused to remember that he knew these people on a personal level, he felt he could do it.

Dagen allowed a blanket of vengeful anger to smother his spirit. He *knew* he could do it. Kane and most of the other survivors loathed him, avoided him, and ridiculed him. Why should he have any loyalty toward them? He looked over his shoulder at the massive .338 Lapua long-range bolt-action rifle in the back of the Humvee. The killing would be done from a distance, as was his skill set. He would set up his hide and wait for the festivities to start. Then he would pull the trigger on each of them, Jenna included, with Kane and Courtland the first to go. After all this, after all their talk of Jesus and redemption, they were really just like him—just like everyone else out there. Broken. Ruined. Floundering in an unsavable world.

If he could do this one thing, Malak would take him back. He was sure of it. Then he could finally return to what he was good at. He'd shrug off all this useless fear and emotional garbage for the mantle of power he deserved.

Dagen licked his lips and looked at the bottle filled with beautiful, caramel-colored liquid next to him. Before he did any of that, he would just take one sip. Just one. He unscrewed the cap and with trembling hands pressed the bottle to his lips. Gulping deep, the whiskey slipped down his throat and burned its way into his belly. Soon Dagen was lost in the hypnotic combination of sloshing whiskey and crystal glass, his anxiety and traitorous shame disappearing into it with each upward tilt.

▲ ▲ ▲

Saxon didn't know much, but he did know the end was near. He could sense the electricity of it in the air like an approaching tempest. An end to everything they understood. Maybe even an end to all things.

"Bah," Saxon spat, turning to see Malak pacing, restless like a caged lion, up and down the dam road. The men before him were bringing up the Machine, as he had called it. Saxon watched as the man carried a locked case that looked impenetrable. Malak stared holes through the thing, pacing on and on. To say their leader had ever been stable would be laughable, but Malak was growing crazier by the hour. His obsession with this Machine was nothing short of sheer insanity.

Maybe the thing was what Malak said it was. If that was the case, he had the sneaking suspicion that they all were going to be in for a few surprises. If it wasn't, well, then shit hadn't changed. Regardless, it was not something he was going to worry about now.

He turned back and saw as the nerdy electrical engineer who called himself Nick worked diligently on the roof of one of the towers that jutted straight up from the sloping upper wall of the dam. This one was the tallest structure on the dam itself, and it had been Saxon's idea that the experimental high-powered-microwave device be set up and made ready on the roof of the tower.

HPMs were a concept that the US military tried to develop for years. Essentially an HPM was a nonnuclear radio-frequency energy field. It had the ability to be used as a weapon when a powerful chemical detonation was transformed by a special coil device, a flux compression generator, into a strong electromagnetic field of microwave energy.

The idea behind HPMs was the strategic use of a device that affected electronics in a very similar fashion as an electromagnetic pulse, or EMP, could. Where EMPs affected entire areas or regions depending on the altitude at which the pulse was initiated, an HPM was a constantly generated field with a conical antenna for precise, focused delivery of the microwaves into electronic systems, causing catastrophic destruction.

As far as the general public was concerned, this device never successfully did what it was created for or passed the numerous safety inspections required for such a device. What researchers did discover during the creation of this particular device was that the focused microwaves were so powerful they inflicted injury on humans caught in the radiation cone. Furthermore, it continued to prove lethal to the "gunner," who had to operate the aiming of the antenna. This forced the weapon to be controlled by remote and added to the already enormous cost.

Since a weapon that caused people's skin to blister and slough off while delivering a lethal dose of radiation would never make it onto the civilized battlefield, the prototype was abandoned, and another was developed on a much lower power scale for civilian crowd control. It too was quickly abandoned when the radiation levels ranged from no effect at all to cancer-causing lethal. In the end, anyone who ever tried to weaponize an HPM came to the same abrupt conclusion: it was too risky of a device to use in any capacity.

Saxon watched Nick work for another moment and wondered if the poor bastard had figured out yet what was going to happen to him. Climbing the exterior ladder, Saxon stepped onto the roof of the tower to inspect the device. Before stepping closer he shouted over to the engineer. "Hey, is this thing on yet?"

"No, no, of course not; I'm still working on it." Nick looked around. "Why?"

"Just making sure," Saxon smirked.

"So, uh, I'll just finish up here, connect the power source, and then we just need the remote—"

"There is no remote," Saxon said, the blue-painted designs across his face twisting into an ugly smile.

Nick wasn't getting it. "So if I can just make sure it's working, then I can go?"

Saxon shook his head but said nothing. Nick looked on bewildered.

"I don't see what you need me for up here…"

"There's no remote," Saxon said again.

Suddenly the notion dawned on Nick Corvaleski in a wash of disbelief. "Oh, you mean you want me to… No, wait, I can't aim it. We don't have the protective equipment."

"You're the low man on the proverbial totem pole, my friend."

"It'll kill me." Nick gulped.

"Maybe so, but if you displease Malak, you'll face a fate worse than death," Saxon said matter-of-factly.

"What is all this for?" Nick whimpered, gesturing at all the barricades and mounted weapons.

Saxon checked himself before answering and took a breath. "Look, some people want the power Malak has. They're *bad* people. They want the artifact all for themselves—so they're going to come and try to take it from us. We can't allow that, "he looked down at the man's name tag. "Right, Nick?"

"Uh, well, uh…Okay, but what am I supposed to do about that?" Nick shook when he spoke.

Saxon strode forward and grabbed the thin man's hair with a jerk.

Nick spasmed as Saxon shoved him toward the edge of the tower. Under him, the wall of the dam sloped away toward the greenish water eight hundred feet below, pushing and churning away from the massive concrete fortress.

"What you're supposed to do is kill as many of the intruders as you can before you succumb to the radiation yourself," Saxon snarled.

"I can't!" Nick struggled in Saxon's grasp, the toes of his shoes clinging to the surface of the roof as Saxon pushed him farther out into open space.

"You will! If you don't, I'll make you wish I'd tossed you over. Do you get that?"

"I get it! I get it!" Nick shrieked.

Saxon turned and drew Nick back in, setting him next to the HPM device, an overwhelming look of despair flooding the man's features as Saxon proceeded to loop leg-irons through one of the supports and clamp them onto Nick's legs. "Look, we can't have you just running around—but if you do a good job and survive? Well, that would earn you a place in Malak's army. Maybe a high place."

Nick said nothing.

"Finish working on it and have it ready by nightfall. Malak wants everything ready to go," Saxon said.

"And then what?"

"Stay here with it and be ready."

"Ready..." Nick mumbled.

"Yeah," Saxon sneered. "Ready to power this baby up and watch your skin fall off."

▲ ▲ ▲

The train loaded with Kane's group, now down old Sam and Winston, chugged into Page, Arizona, in the inky black of a moonless night. Beside Kane, Ari clicked her rifle safety off and on, off and on. As the train slowed, the grinding of steel shrieked in the silent night. Kane begged for it to stop. At this hour and just over two miles away from the dam, Kane might as well have been knocking on the front door.

Locking the brake lever down, Kane motioned for the two men helping him to shut down the furnace. Kane turned to Ari and motioned with his chin to the door. "Come on, let's get this stuff unloaded."

Ari nodded and set to work directing a few of the others.

Kane hopped down from the train and stopped as a familiar, shadowy form toward him from out of the silent dark. Ari was nowhere near as comfortable or curious as she shouldered her rifle and aimed it at the large shadow. "Identify yourself!"

"I see you've made some new friends." The voice said, still encased in shadow.

Kane smiled. "But we never forgot the old ones."

The large shadow before them separated into two parts as Tynuk and Azolja stepped forward from the gloom. Ari immediately stiffened at the sight of Azolja, her rifle still up, her finger moving to the trigger. Kane stayed her, pressing the barrel of her rifle toward the dirt.

"They're friends, Ari. Don't worry. Everyone has the same reaction the first time they see Az."

Ari muttered something in Hebrew. "What is it?" She said.

Kane stepped forward and extended his hand to the boy. "If you can figure it out, you let me know," he said to Ari. "How you been, Tynuk? You guys are a sight for sore eyes."

Tynuk took the offered hand. "A lot has happened since."

Kane nodded. "Yeah."

Out of nowhere, Courtland grabbed Tynuk in a giant bear hug. "My friend! It's so good to see you!"

Azolja flinched at the surprise, but upon seeing him cocked its head and nuzzled it against the big man's side in an open display of affection. Courtland laughed, rubbing deep into the creature's jet-black mane. "So good to see you both!"

Jenna and the others had gathered around now, most wearing big, tired smiles at the return of a few familiar faces.

The strangeness of the reunion was now sinking in with Kane. He raised his hands, shrugging his shoulders. "What is going on? I mean, how are you guys here? What are the chances?"

"There are no chances. Like I told you before, it is fate, our paths are intertwined."

"Of course they are!" Courtland beamed, his hands still upon his friends.

"The visions I had directed us. We knew to go toward the dam, and on the way, we saw the train. So we followed a hunch and found you here," Tynuk said, opening his hands.

"You knew to come?"

Tynuk bobbed his head. "The vision is for all who are in the service of the Great Spirit. We had to come—to see this finished."

"Well, you two are unmatched warriors, and we would gladly accept your help here in the battle to come," Kane added. "Will you join us?"

Tynuk beamed at the praise. "You will have our support and much more."

"More?" Courtland furrowed his brow.

"Yes, my friend," Tynuk straightened, "one hundred fifty warriors from the New Comanche Nation are at your service, battle bred and ready to fight against this evil."

"A hundred and fifty…" Kane couldn't find the words to finish.

Courtland raised his hands. "You found your people!"

"I did. Our meeting was not without its share of trials, but they are now with me and at my command."

"Yours to command?" Kane said, still reeling.

"That's correct. I am now the war chief of the New Comanche Nation," the boy said with unfiltered pride.

The entire group stared at the boy, waiting for him to crack a smile or let on it was a joke. He didn't.

"Where are they?" Courtland asked, hesitant.

"They will be here before dawn. They are traveling on horseback."

"How did you get here so fast?" Kane asked.

Tynuk glanced and tilted his head toward Azolja. "My friend here moves faster than the wind driven across the open prairie. He is my mount."

"Will you be staying? Do your men need any weapons or supplies? I know they will have traveled all night."

"We don't require much, though we may accept a few rifles if you have any to spare. My people are hardened and used to difficulty, but as a result of years of self-induced isolation, they are not the most social people—especially with outsiders."

"I see. So they will not be coming here?" Kane looked around.

"I think it is best that they don't. They will fight and die for our shared cause, but they may not be too accepting of formal relations with your group."

"The enemy of my enemy is my friend, that sort of thing?"

"Something like that." Tynuk inclined his head. "We will wait for your signal, and we will meet you in the battle. What is your plan?"

"We'll look to make our assault at first light. I'll send the bulk of our force down the plateau, where we will try to draw Malak's forces out and into the open, so you can flank them. Do you have enough men for that?"

"We are speaking of the proud people who single-handedly brought the might of the Spanish war machine to a grinding halt as it pushed into North America."

"Oh?"

"After conquering, murdering, and enslaving every group of indigenous peoples they came across in their northward push, the Spanish believed nothing could stop them. They were wrong."

"I'll take that as a yes."

Tynuk gave a wry smile. "But you do understand that no Comanche plan of attack in the course of our long history ever involved sacrificing large numbers of warriors to take a single position, don't you?"

Kane said nothing.

"Historically, it was also our great weakness, an inability to press our advantage. It is of no consequence. My people will ride with me against our foes."

Kane paused. "Well, I can't say how humbled I am that you would devote your people to this fight. You must have gone through the wringer to have already earned their unwavering trust," Kane said in astonishment, noting Tynuk's bandages.

Now it was Tynuk's turn to smile, as he stepped forward and put his hand on Kane's arm. "We have all been through one ordeal or another. It is the ordeal that forges us into the person that the Great

Spirit intends us to be. It would be my honor to finish this fight the way that I started it, alongside my friends."

Kane placed his hand on the warrior boy's muscled shoulder. "I can't think of any way I'd rather do it."

25

*U*NDER A MOONLESS sky, the hulking warlord checked the last of the dam's fortifications. Carefully monitored by Corvaleski, all of the dam's systems were now up and running. At full capacity, it produced more than enough power for his purposes. He noted each weapon placement, including the experimental electrically powered rail guns that had been found in the deepest levels of the dam's research facilities, along with the HPM device. Everything was in position. If Kane were to come in search of his children or to fulfill some greater oath of vengeance, his forces would be ready.

The glow twinkled across his plane of vision, a remnant of his previous dose of Z that was still working to calm his nerves. Shana had never returned, just as he expected. He could only hope that she had somehow injured or demoralized Kane's team by going out to meet them head-on. She was no real loss, as long as her life had bought them some more time to prepare for the coming assault.

Malak strode across the top of the dam, purposeful but unrushed, as he made his final assessments, passing without a word through groups of bloodthirsty Coyotes, who eyed their leader while mashed into clumps around small fires in the cool evening. Z smoke hovered like smog in the air around them, formless, refusing to dissipate. Bandits high on drugs or some found stash of alcohol lay about on bedrolls or propped back in half-broken chairs, waiting for the end to begin. Coarse, pitiless laughter mixed with curses and boasted deeds as the men spoke of how they would slaughter Kane's people in the coming battle. A young woman cried nearby, a poor, hopeless slave of the vile men. Taking notice of her again, the men whooped with psychotic pleasure, slapping and choking her against the ground where the ragged bits of clothes she wore were torn from her body yet again. Some men stumbled about looking for somewhere to relieve themselves, as others, men with absolute darkness inside them, the worst of their kind, lay just beyond the fire, their black eyes telling no lies of the evil hiding in their hearts.

Malak relished the darkness found here. Something about the evil in these men soothed a nagging restlessness deep inside him. They were the worst humanity had to offer. They would serve him well.

Making his way back to the stairwell, Saxon emerged from it and bowed his head, acknowledging his master. "Lord Malak, as I'm sure you have seen for yourself, the fortifications are in place, and all preparations have been made."

Malak did not reply, instead, he scanned the area once more in the light of the fire and noticed the barricaded canyon bridge his men manned that ran parallel to the dam. The two rail guns mounted there were capable of massive destruction. They would hold the bridge and have a second angle of fire on the only entrance to the dam this side of the canyon.

Malak cut his eyes at his lieutenant. "Yes. I see we are ready."

"Good," Saxon said, pleased that Malak wasn't in a rage for once. "Is there anything else you need, my lord?"

"The children. It is time," Malak intoned.

Saxon nodded, considering a thought. "Lord Malak, forgive my asking, but if this Machine is so powerful, why haven't we used it already?"

"The Machine was created long ago. Its power is not meant for the hands of men."

"So if I touched it—"

"It would kill you instantly," Malak said.

"But you?"

Malak grinned. "I am not a man. Not anymore."

"If you can control it, then why keep the children and their purity?" Saxon spat the words, clearly unsatisfied with the fact that the little ones had been kept from him.

Now Malak appeared to become irritated, the question hinting that he alone wasn't powerful enough to control the Machine. "You're like a gibbering woman. The children are my insurance plan. Their souls will help to stabilize me when I take up the device."

What Malak did not say, and what no man would ever hear him say, was that the Machine was created by the hand of God and was meant for no one else. Though he was confident that the Voice within him could possess it for a time, he was not sure how long a time that was. The Voice instructed him to use the children, their pure souls, to help sustain him, like sweet little batteries, as he held the cosmic device.

"Very good, my lord." Saxon dared not to press further. "Your men will be ready to fight at your command."

"Make it happen, and ensure that you are among them. I expect you to pick them apart in minutes."

"You got it, boss."

Malak pushed the back of a heavy hand across his jaw. "Bring the children up. Keep them shackled and close to the device—but don't you dare forget to gag those little brats this time."

Saxon smiled wickedly. "It would be my genuine pleasure."

Rolling his Humvee to a stop along the low ridge, Kane stepped from the vehicle to survey the Glen Canyon Dam for the first time. Behind him, the horizon glowed with the rising of the sun, still nestled in its ashen shade. It was as beautiful as it was foreboding, threads of light piercing through the darkness, unfiltered, unrestrained.

"The light shines through the darkness," Kane whispered.

"And may it forevermore." Courtland lumbered up beside him.

Kane smiled his acknowledgment but said nothing further. The others of his party were now gathered around, peering from the low ridge toward the dam. The startling crystal-clear shimmer of the morning light against the surface of Lake Powell along the horizon gave cause for hope and, even if for just a moment, dulled the pang of fear that sat heavily in each of their chests. Until this moment, it was likely none of them fully realized the insurmountable obstacle they now faced. But now, as they viewed the scope of their target, the sheer magnitude of the fortress they were about to assault made it all too clear. Hundreds of armed sociopaths—secure within this fortress of concrete and steel, using children as bait and leverage, and led by a demon-possessed tyrant—awaited them. It was an obstacle that seemed insurmountable.

Upon rising they had found Tynuk and Azolja gone, as expected, likely to meet Tynuk's warriors. That whole bit was still being digested. There was no communication between the two groups. Tynuk had just said that upon Kane's signal he and his forces would ride. Kane indicated that he would fire a flare into the air. Tynuk had agreed upon the signal. That was it. Nothing was guaranteed, but from experience, Kane knew he could trust the boy's word.

Deep in thought, Kane raised his head, and seeing the rising of the sun along the horizon, he realized everyone was looking for him to say something. Maybe for the first time, Kane realized that these people needed his confidence in their purpose. They needed to see his strength and that he was ready to trust everything to God in this final stand. They all seemed so weary yet still willing to lay down their lives alongside him, to save his children, to save everything. He put his fist to his mouth, paused, considered his words, and then spoke.

"Here is where it ends. By now Malak will be attempting to access the power of the Machine. We have to stop him. We cannot fail. Much more than our own vendettas, more than the lives of my children…we must not allow him to unmake what the Creator in his ultimate wisdom has made. Everything happens for a reason. I know that now. God needed each of us to be where we are in our lives for this single moment in time. Who you are right now, all the sorrow and pain and fear, but also the hope and the strength and the purpose—the conviction to fight against the failing of the light. That is not by mistake. God is here with us, his hand guides us, his purpose holds us fast, and even if our eyes stray from him, he will not fail us."

"I'm scared," Jenna said, her voice wavering.

Kane smiled. "I am too, but our trust must be greater than our fear. What can we do, where can we go, that is beyond the reach of the God of the universe? Beyond the redemptive power of Jesus?"

"Amen, brother," Courtland confirmed.

"Fight to the death, because you do not fear your own death! That question has already been answered for us. Our place in our father's house is assured. He will honor our sacrifice, and he will send his angels to fight by our side. There is nothing for us to fear. They may have superior numbers, but we will defeat them."

"Our God stands with us," Ari stated boldly.

"That's right. Stay calm, aim true, and keep pulling the trigger until each threat is no longer a threat. These Coyotes are just men.

They bleed like men, and they die like men. We have all seen it. They are not special or superior or smarter or braver than us. We must out-fight them! If you are shot, if you are wounded, get up and continue to fight. Let nothing stop you. You have the living God on your side. What have you to fear?"

"And what about Malak? Your kids?" Courtland asked.

"We fight to the mouth of the dam first, using our initial plan. Once we get there, you and I will focus on Malak and go from there. Planning beyond that may be futile."

Courtland nodded.

"I never thought I'd say this," Kane said and looked to Jenna, "but I wish Dagen was here with us. We could use his rifle today."

Jenna said nothing, nodding stoically.

Courtland placed his arms around Kane and Jenna and bowed his head. "Let us pray together, brothers and sisters."

The small band of heroes lowered their heads. Together, each in his or her own way, they begged for their God to preserve them, to honor their resolve, and to win this darkest day in the name of all that was good, true, and just. Though none said it to the other, they all felt the bond of their common purpose and the closeness of God in the midst of their fear. And together, with the light of hope growing inside them, they steeled themselves for the coming storm.

▲ ▲ ▲

Malak looked out at the low ridge to the east, where the light of the sun was beginning to show. He could just make out the vehicles and bodies lined along the ridge. It was such a pitiful force to bring against him. He brimmed with unquenchable hatred for his enemies.

"Behold!" Malak raised his arms from where he stood on an elevated platform, the Machine visible in its container before him, Kane's gagged, tear-streaked children chained behind him. "Behold the mighty armies of God!"

The hundreds of Coyotes waiting on foot and packed into vehicles along the dam erupted into wild, hysterical laughter. Their enemy now seemed so desperate to try to go against them with such an insufficient force.

"Embrace the darkness," Malak continued. "These fools hold no power over us! We are God, and we will do what we please!"

Crazy cheering and jeering filled the air from the scores of bandit warriors as they foamed at the anticipation of bloodshed.

"Ready your guns and your blades! Seek a terrible lust for blood you have never known until this day! Today we will mercilessly crush the warriors of God beneath the heel of the Master. They will not have the device! This is our world now! Our world!"

Gazing with lust, Malak lowered his eyes to the Machine. His hands hovered over it, feeling its warmth and the smallest tremor it emitted. Without warning, powerful, dark tentacles emerged from the flesh of his back. The children screamed at the sight, recoiling against their bonds. Lashing back, the dark smokey snakes coiled around the small bodies and necks of the children as their little voices screamed. Malak, now connected with the children, thrust his hands down and seized the Machine, lifting it in the air over his head as he spoke in unearthly tongues. Below him, the churning masses of Coyotes screamed with madness, as a dark light filled their eyes.

26

KANE STOPPED TALKING strategy to Courtland in midsentence as something he couldn't quite put his finger on caught his attention. Everyone else turned toward the dam as something began to happen, an eerie grinding hum in the earth, the sky turning dark as night. The screams of war rang in their ears as the bandit army flew from the dam in vehicles and on foot, swarming up onto the plateau, coming for them.

"He's using the Machine. This is it! Stick to the plan!" Kane jumped into the open-top military Hummer and felt the shocks absorb Courtland's weight as the giant stepped into the back of the vehicle behind him. Stomping his foot on the gas, Kane launched the vehicle forward and descended the hill toward the open plateau below.

"Are you ready for this?" Kane called to his friend as they bumped and jostled down the hill, the others right behind.

"I was born for this, brother. I'm with you until the end!" the giant shouted back.

"God, stand with us! Show us your power and stand with us in this place!" Kane shouted.

Pointed down the hill, gaining speed as they went, they shot forward, leading their people like the point of a spear, striking at the heart of the dark enemy rising against them.

The sound of gunfire startled Dagen awake. He shook his head and tossed the empty liquor bottle to the floor of the Humvee with a curse. More gunfire. He froze. It was starting. He had almost slept in a drunken stupor through the start of the battle. Cursing again, he grabbed his rifle, leaving it in its drag bag and throwing the harness over his shoulders. Pushing the door open, he forwent the crutches and flopped to the ground, crawling the short distance to the top of the rise, dragging his equipment behind him.

It took him only a moment to reach his shooting position and ready his equipment. Looking through the scope of the powerful .338 Lapua, Dagen slowed his breathing and watched the battle unfold. With a sharp forward snap, Dagen drove a round into the chamber and locked the bolt down, making his final calculations and adjustments to his scope. Looking through the glass, he watched Kane's meager group fling themselves headlong toward the bandit army. It was the stupidest and bravest thing he'd ever seen.

Come on, Dagen! Shoot!

He licked his lips and took aim on Kane. Terrible angle. No shot. He adjusted, aiming at Courtland, a man who had genuinely befriended him—a man who had taken the time to talk with him and then actually listened to what he had to say in return.

Shit, Dagen. Do it! Shoot him!

Dagen felt a prickle on the back of his neck and slowly touched the trigger. Then, just beyond the giant, he saw it just off to the right. He released his finger. There in his glass, a thin arm hung on to one of the rear supports of a Hummer as it bumped and careened across the red-rock plateau. And then she stood into view. Jenna. Her body so thin, her face twisted with fear and anxiety—the look of someone

going to their death. She stood, adjusted her rifle, and vomited, clinging to the Hummer for dear life.

Shoot her, you worthless idiot. Shoot her and free yourself.

In an instant Dagen lost where he was, his mind recalling some
repressed passed event. He was lying on the ground, his legs shattered
by a nasty fall. Jenna was there, and though his pain was excruciating,
she was helping him. After all he'd done to her, she was there. Even
after he'd wounded her, murdered those she loved, and cursed her
faith, she'd saved him. He remembered Kane approaching amid the
smoke and debris and telling her to clear away from him—that he was
no better than a maimed dog in need of a bullet. Jenna refused, covering Dagen's body with her own. When Kane, in complete confusion, asked why she told him that Dagen was not beyond redemption.
Kane balked, but she was as serious as a heart attack. She actually
believed it and, in turn, lived it.

Dagen raised his eyes from the scope, blinked a drop of sweat
from them, and shook his head, an internal battle raging within.
What she'd said to him in the barracks—it was emotion, fear, and
exhaustion. It was human. But that wasn't how she really felt; she had
shown him the truth by the way she lived her life. A life lived in the
service of her savior and the people around her—a life of sacrifice.

Dagen swore again. Enough. He swung the barrel of the large
rifle around, acquiring his first target and firing without the opportunity to reconsider. The blast of the rifle was deafening, the jolt shuddering through his entire body. Through his scope, Dagen saw the
head of the lead bandit captain explode, his body tumbling forward as
it spewed blood across the windshield and flipped beneath the wheels
of his mechanical chariot.

"Not today, Jenna," Dagen whispered. Working the bolt, he
ejected the spent cartridge, racked in a new round, took aim, and
fired again. "You won't die today."

Kane's vehicle slid to a stop, followed by all the others, except one. A Hummer with a mounted .50-caliber heavy machine gun zipped past them in a widening trail of dust. Ari was in the turret. Snatching the charging handle back, she let it drop back into place with a snap. How she'd allowed them to use her as bait was anybody's guess, but the reality was she was most suited for the direct action.

She watched as the massive bandit army approached with unnerving speed. Ari aimed and readied to fire, and just when it seemed that her vehicle would collide with the front lines of the bandit ranks, the Hummer swerved hard to the right, making a loop and heading back toward her people. Ari pivoted the armored turret and opened fire, the heavy machine gun banging to life once again in a storm of lead. Bullets pinged and zinged off the armored vehicle all around her, but her resolve held as she continued to fire, leading the large bandit force away from the security of the dam.

"Get ready, Jenna!" Kane called into his radio.

"*Ready.*"

Kane watched as Ari tore the front ranks of the bandit vehicles to pieces with the pounding of her weapon. Though she was dealing heavy damage, still they came, wild and furious. They were closing fast, now inside of one hundred yards. Courtland stepped from the back of Kane's vehicle, hefting his huge, black scimitar-shaped blades in his hands. Kane leaned out the window. "You sure about this, boss?"

"I've never been more sure of anything in my life." Courtland glowed with the power of heaven. "Go."

Kane turned his attention back to the front, waited a moment, and then shouted into the radio, "Now!"

Jenna raised her arm high in the air and fired a single red flare that traced across the early morning sky in a fiery trail of smoke. At the same moment, Kane's group cleaved in two, pulling in separate directions as though fleeing. Courtland was left, alone, in the center of the plateau. Each group of vehicles, all armored, military-grade Hummers, peeled off to the outside, flanking the bandit army, which was now drawn out from the fortress. Kane led the group that flanked to the right, with Ari and Jenna leading a charge down the left side, their vehicles now taking heavy small-arms fire but also returning heavy-machine-gun fire into the flanks of the bandit army as it continued to bear down on the mighty Courtland.

"Come, you devils! Come and witness the justice of the Lord!" Courtland shouted, holding his blades before him. Bending his knees deep, Courtland launched himself into the air and over the first line of bandit vehicles as they spun their tires on the dirt, chasing Kane and the others. Landing square in the midst of the Coyotes' ranks, he extended his massive arms and swung his blades in wide cutting arcs. With inhuman strength and speed, the giant moved with the grace of a dancer. Turning and shifting with power and precision, he cut his foes into ribbons, tossing their dismembered parts into the air before slashing down again and again.

▲ ▲ ▲

Amid the din of battle, gunfire, and human screams, Saxon saw a dark-haired woman shouting with fury as she fired her heavy machine gun into their midst, tearing them to pieces. It only took him a moment to recognize the fearless Israeli woman in the turret of the passing Hummer.

"How is that Jew bitch still alive?" Saxon shook with rage. "Get me over there, and I'll finish what Shank couldn't!"

Swerving hard to the right, Saxon's vehicle crashed into another, knocking bandits from it, who screamed as they fell. Pulling free of the gaggle, Saxon slapped his driver and pointed to Ari's vehicle. The driver jammed down on the gas pedal with a yell.

▲ ▲ ▲

Tynuk watched the bright red flare streak into the sky, hovering for a moment before dropping out of sight.

"It is the signal," he called out, already mounted atop Azolja. The beast, seeming to know what was coming, shook his great head and chuffed, stamping a massive, taloned paw against the ground.

"It will be my honor to ride with you this day, war chief," Queenashano said, from atop his mustang.

"And it will be my honor to ride with you and lead these noble people into the battle."

"Then what are we waiting for?"

Tynuk smiled, his round face swiped with red and black war paint. He hoisted his strong, handcrafted Osage orange bow into the air. "Ride with me, brothers! Ride with me and let this filth witness the power of our people!"

A howl arose in the red-rock canyon as Tynuk and Azolja shot forth, followed by Queenashano and the rest of the battle-clad warriors, their mounts winding through the narrow gulch toward the battle.

It only took moments for them to clear the walls that surrounded them and burst forth onto the short plain before the dam. The forces of the New Comanche Nation opened up and unfolded as they charged with reckless abandon toward the bandit horde.

Stunned, the bandits watched as 150 Native American warriors, streaked in war paint, flood from the canyon to their right. Still stalled, trying to turn and chase Kane's split forces, they had lost their forward momentum when Tynuk's forces slammed into their ranks.

Arrows filled the sky, flying in all directions as the bandits fired at targets that were there one second and gone the next. Many of them floundered, having no understanding that to stand on open ground in a battle with mounted Comanche was a death sentence.

Queenashano hung his hide shield on his left leg and slung himself down to the right, under his horse's neck, firing twelve arrows from his bow in the time it took his enemy to reload one magazine. The stunned bandit toppled to the ground, no longer anything more than a human pincushion. Fearless, Tynuk rode ahead, yelping and dashing one thug in the face with his war club. He drew his bow and struck multiple hits on another who had just pulled the pin on a grenade. The man and the grenade fell into the bed of the truck and, in a flash of smoke, obliterated the entire truckload.

The larger bandit force was overwhelmed, reeling from the piercing ambush on their right flank, as Tynuk's hardened warriors cut through their ranks on horseback. Riding hard, Tynuk made straight for Courtland, who he could see bellowing and tossing bandits into the air as they surged around him, firing their weapons at the giant.

"Az, Courtland is in trouble. We will honor our promise!" Azolja roared in response as they crashed headlong into the seething throng of bandit scum. When Tynuk launched from the back of the beast, it was already sinking its fangs into its first victim. Tynuk landed and rolled, coming up back-to-back with the giant. Slamming his war club into the jaw of an approaching thug. "Courtland," Tynuk called, "I'm coming up!"

"Come on, then," Courtland said between the passing swipes of his deadly blades. Moving with unparalleled agility, Tynuk launched himself up the giant's back and onto his shoulders, the boy's feet easily finding purchase. With a movement practiced a thousand times, he swung his bow from his shoulder and into the grip of his left hand. Now working in tandem, the very visage of unstoppable force, Courtland belted scripture while slashing his enemies apart. At the same time, the warrior boy turned war chief fired arrows from the shoulders of the giant, launching them with strict precision into each long-range threat that appeared.

Tynuk fired arrow after arrow, the last piercing a bandit through the eye. Below him, Azolja leaped, slashing two bandits open with a swipe of his paw and grabbing a third, sinking his fangs into the man's neck, shaking him, and tossing him off to the side.

Tynuk twisted his body to better see the dam and the strange darkness that spread out above it. Inside it, if for only a moment, he thought he could make out indiscernible dark shapes moving and dancing.

"I don't like that business over at the dam," Tynuk said, drawing another arrow.

"It is a door to another world." Courtland swung down again, dicing men apart like the blades of a blender. "Malak is trying to merge the spirit world with ours. Let us pray that we are not too late to stop it!"

▲ ▲ ▲

"Tynuk and Courtland have them preoccupied." Ari's radio crackled with the sound of Kane's voice. *"We make our move for the dam now."* Ari picked up her radio and keyed it.

"Copy."

She opened her machine gun and prepared to load another belt of ammunition when a blast tore through the driver's compartment of her vehicle. Rolling with the shock of the blast, the vehicle groaned, and Ari fell to the floor of the turret, knocking her head against a steel support pole. A wash of nausea passed over her, everything inverted, and all went dark.

▲ ▲ ▲

From the cliff above, Dagen saw Ari's vehicle flip. Then he watched as Jenna's vehicle swerved to take cover in the hills below. Across the field, Kane's vehicle took a hit, tearing the back end away and sending the vehicle spinning. Kane fell from the burning passenger's compartment of the ruined vehicle and crawled for cover. In a matter of seconds, the thunderous pounding of the electromagnetic rail guns brought the entire advance to a grinding halt. The massive kinetic cannons had incredible reach and near-pinpoint accuracy, powered by the abundant energy of the dam. With kinetic projectiles tearing holes in the earth around them, Kane's people were now hopelessly pinned down.

Dagen reloaded his .338 Lapua and turned to look at Jenna's vehicle, close to where Ari had wrecked. Two cars of bandits drew near, sliding to a stop on the dirt. Raiders stormed from the vehicles, salivating at the thought that their next victims would be women. This group included one of Malak's new lieutenants, a dark-headed man with blue face paint.

Dagen took one last look at the distant rail guns, pounding away on Kane's people from the safety of the parallel bridge. Kane and his people were never going to make it to the dam as long as those guns were functional. He had no way of shooting the operators since the cannons were controlled by remote.

He shifted his eyes. Below him, the Coyotes closed on Jenna as she fired from behind the cover of her vehicle, her face full of fear and doubt.

"Not this time, Jenna. I've got you." Dagen huffed his breath mostly out and allowed his body to become still as he took aim on his next target.

28

*A*RI CAME TO in the smoky interior of the flipped Hummer, the mixture of smoke, fumes, and dust threatening to put her back out again. Crawling, she dragged herself through the ruined vehicle, her head pounding, aching to the cadence of gunfire. She stopped long enough to note that the driver was gone—vaporized by the blast that tore open the driver's compartment and flipped the truck.

"Cannon fire." She grunted. "Maybe twenty millimeter."

Kicking a door open, Ari wiggled her body out of the burning cab and into the open. She gasped, coughing and inhaling cleaner air. Her head was swimming with dizziness and pain. The battle was still well involved, the Comanche warriors howling like lost souls. She watched as one warrior folded as he took a round in the chest, rose to his feet like the undead, and was shot twice more before delivering his spear into the chest of the bandit.

She looked to her right and saw Jenna crouched behind her vehicle, firing blind at a group of approaching bandits. She was doing just enough to keep them on their toes. Ari watched as two groups of bandits moved on her and Jenna. Then she saw him, the man from her nightmares with the blue face paint—the one who had cut her brother's throat and left them both to rot.

Ari tested her legs and arms and tried to stand but was overcome once again with dizziness. She watched, helpless, as the savage men moved on Jenna.

The unmistakable crack of a rifle, followed by another and another. The bandits fell, clutching mortal wounds, struck down by some invisible protector. The rifle cracked, and the bandits fell, until the only one left cowering behind a vehicle, was Saxon. Ari was struck with the irrational fear that the painted man too would be shot and she would lose her opportunity for vengeance. She waited, the air around them filling with silent tension.

Saxon stood cautiously looking up and around for the sniper's nest. "Someone's looking out for you two," he called out.

Jenna caught Ari's attention and gestured with an empty rifle. It was just as well. Ari motioned for her to remain where she was. Ari tested her body again and found that this time she could stand.

"Lion of Judah, be my strength," she prayed. As she stood, still partially behind the cover of the burning wreckage of her vehicle, Saxon came into sight on the other side of his vehicle.

"Well, well! You're a tough little Jew, aren't you?" Saxon said.

"You're about to find out how tough."

Saxon laughed. "Sure thing, Princess. I'll let you show me all your best moves."

Ari snarled, drawing the Beretta from her waist and firing as she began to run at a forty-five-degree angle to Saxon's position. Saxon drew a big-bore revolver and flanked in the opposite direction. Both circled each other in a counterclockwise movement as they fired at each other. Closing the distance, she felt a round burn through the cloth of her shirt, searing her arm. She continued to fire, furious, a scream on her lips—the sound of an untamed creature. The final round found its mark, staggering Saxon but not felling him with a hit to the upper chest.

Dropping their handguns, they collided with each other. Saxon, much stronger than she anticipated, struck her in the face and sent her reeling. Ari shrugged off the blow and stayed in the fight, ducking another and rising to his outside, where she landed four hard blows, the last of which struck his gunshot wound. Saxon screamed, blood foaming on his lips.

Saxon lunged for her again, and she kicked low to his knee and then hard into his groin, dodging to the outside again with a hail of palm-heel strikes to the side of his head and jaw. He recovered fast, and she failed to deflect the uppercut that landed in her gut, pitching her forward. Before she could draw air, he was upon her, grabbing her by the neck and forcing her to the ground, where he mounted her back and forced her face into the dirt.

Ari struggled and received a series of punishing blows to her head and face.

"You look the fuck away from me, Jew bitch," Saxon groaned, pressing himself against her. "I'm gonna do you just like I did your little brother!"

Spinning onto her back beneath him, Ari cried out, pulling her hidden karambit knife from her waistband and slashing like a trapped lioness. Jumping back, knife already in hand, Saxon swiped at her, a blow that would have removed her head had she not anticipated it. Flicking her knife forward, she split the fingers of his hand and caused him to drop his blade.

Fighting now with an unbridled fury, her heart burned with singular purpose. She delivered a crushing round kick to the side of his leg and then another, spinning the opposite direction to connect the heel of her boot against his face. Saxon spun with the force of the strike and dropped to his knees. Ari closed the gap, delivering strikes of her curved blade to his torso before she planted her foot in his back and kicked him to the dirt. Jumping down on him, she dropped her knife and grabbed his chin, along with a handful of his long, braided ponytail.

"You don't have it in you..."

"Listen to me now, you filthy dog. My brother's name was Aviel! This is for him!" Ari violently twisted Saxon's head and felt the spine separate under the force. With tears forming in her eyes, she gasped and shoved Saxon's lifeless body to the ground. It was finished.

▲ ▲ ▲

With a piercing crack, the high-powered rifle echoed, resounding against the red rock canyon walls. It took a few shots for Kane to locate the shooter and determine that he was shooting at Malak's forces. But who was it? Ari and Jenna were pinned down like him. Courtland, Tynuk, and the Comanche were in the thick of it behind him. No one else in the group would be familiar with a long-range bolt gun like that—no one except Dagen.

Kane watched as the next few shots from the sharpshooter struck true. This wasn't just some guy with a rifle. It was an expert with a rifle. Kane screwed his face up. They weren't going anywhere until those guns on the bridge were disabled. He had to swallow his pride and take the chance. He pulled his radio from his belt and keyed it.

"Kane to Dagen, do you copy on this channel?"

Radio silence.

Kane tried again, deciding this time to pad the man's ego. "Dagen, do you copy? I know that's you up there. No one else out here has skill with a long gun like that."

"*Gald you're willing to admit that,*" Dagen replied in a wash of static.

"Dagen, we need your help. We're pinned down by the cannons on the bridge."

"*I can see that.*"

Kane took a breath. *Why does this guy always have to be so difficult?* "Is there anything you can do to help? These guns are going to pound us into the dirt."

Again, radio silence.

"*I'm working on it,*" came the sharpshooter's reply, cold and distant.

▲ ▲ ▲

Dagen pivoted his rifle to look again at the bridge guns, which were blasting over and over again at both Kane's and Jenna's positions. He looked for any way to disable them with a perfectly placed shot. He came up with nothing. They were armored and positioned in such a way that there was nothing he could do.

Dagen stared long and hard for a moment, his whole being quiet. Kane's voice came over the radio again. "*Dagen, maybe you care about what happens to us down here, or maybe you don't, but we are going to be dead as soon as one of these rounds finds its mark. We need your help, now!*"

Dagen, lost in thought, didn't reply. He watched the massive rounds blowing craters in the dirt below as Jenna and Ari crouched together, pinned helplessly behind an overturned Hummer.

Pulling the bolt of his rifle open, he removed it altogether and flung it away to his right, disabling the weapon. Leaving the rest of his equipment in place, Dagen crawled on his belly, dragging himself down the short rise to his vehicle. He opened the door and pulled himself into the cab of the Hummer. Cranking the vehicle, he grabbed the steering wheel and looked up the road the way he had come. He could leave right now. Go off and leave these unfortunate people to their war. Live the rest of his days and never think of all this madness again.

But that wasn't what he was going to do. Dropping the Hummer into gear, he shoved his hip forward, pushing his crippled foot down on the gas pedal. Tires spinning, Dagen careened down the embankment and crashed onto the highway, the shocks jumping beneath him.

"Come on, Dagen," he said, a look of hardened resolve forming across his face. "For once in your miserable life, do something right. Do something that matters." Gaining speed, Dagen flew toward the bridge, abandoning all hope for any other course. "Semper fi."

⅄⅄⅄

Jenna heard the transmissions between Kane and Dagen. She knew now that he had been the sniper shooting over them, killing the men that came for her. Always trying to watch out for her.

Crouched behind cover, she watched a Hummer bump down the hill and hit the road with a bark of rubber on asphalt. There was no question it was Dagen and that he was about to do something really stupid.

Cautiously she keyed her radio. She had to say it. "Dagen, I know you can hear me." She waited but received no response. "I need to tell you how sorry I am for what I said. I know that's not who you are anymore." Jenna wiped the tears from her face. "Please tell me you can hear me. Please respond to me."

⅄⅄⅄

Dagen looked down at his radio, his vehicle gaining speed as it approached the elevated arch bridge. The highwaymen on the bridge fired their weapons in his direction, the bullets striking up the hood and cracking the windshield as he gained speed.

He reached down and picked up his radio. "I hear you, Jenna. Don't worry about it, I'm going to be alright. All I ever wanted was to repay you the kindness you showed me. Please, let this be enough."

"Dagen, don't—"

With a twist, Dagen turned his radio off and tossed it on the floorboard. He reached into the passenger seat, revealing several bricks of C-4 explosive. Shoving the detonators into them, he took the dead man's switch he'd rigged in hand, pulled the bricks into his lap, and depressed the button with his thumb.

One of the rail guns pivoted in his direction and, with a flash, tore his vehicle apart, shredding his right side with shrapnel. He screamed as high-powered rifle rounds ripped through the cab of the Hummer and into his flesh, and he and his ruined vehicle slid across the bridge toward the rail guns.

"Jesus, forgive me. I want to see you—"

Bullets slammed through Dagen's body, his Hummer crashing and spinning to a stop in the middle of the bridge, amid the wild bandits, who continued to dump hundreds of rounds into his vehicle.

Dagen coughed blood, a thick string of it hanging from his mouth. Though mortally wounded, he still managed to smile with an odd sort of peacefulness. Looking down at his hand, his breathing slowed, his thumb releasing from the pressure switch.

▲ ▲ ▲

Kane watched in sheer amazement as, a brilliant flash and a deafening concussion, tore the bridge apart. Steel, concrete fragments, and human bodies launched into the air in a ball of fire, causing the massive rail guns to plummet into the depths of Glen Canyon below.

Kane would have cheered if he wasn't so busy swallowing his shame. Dagen had just saved them all by sacrificing himself. With a pang of guilt, Kane realized he had never, not once, thanked the man for anything he had done that was worthy of praise. He watched the rest of the bridge crumble into the canyon, destroyed. It was the miracle they needed. Their path to the dam was open.

"I was wrong about you, Dagen." Kane lowered his head. "I was wrong, brother."

▲ ▲ ▲

Ari watched the last of the highway bridge crumble into the deep canyon and patted Jenna, who was now sobbing. "Come on, Jenna, we're still exposed here. We need to move."

Ari looked back at the battle again, which was now waning, the dead lay by the hundreds, scattered across the plateau. The Comanche, though fewer in number, had crushed the bulk of the bandit army with their mounted tactics, fighting spirit, and sheer skill. Only a small number of the bandit force that met them on the plateau remained, many of them running for their lives as the Comanche, led by Queenashano and Penateka, hunted them down on horseback. The deceased bandits lay gutted, their heads removed or scalped or their severed genitals stuffed into their mouths. The Comanche long-standing reputation of ruthlessness existed for a reason.

Ari saw Courtland and Tynuk move to Kane's position. Her radio came to life with Kane's voice. *"Ari, are you guys okay?"*

"Yes. Saxon came after us. I killed him." She said.

"Best news I've heard all day."

"The bridge?" Ari said.

"It was Dagen. He went out a hero."

Jenna shook her head, mumbling. "He didn't have to do that... Why'd he do that?"

"He did it for us, Jenna. He did it for *you*. That's what friends do." Ari patted Jenna again and keyed her radio. "Kane, we've lost almost everyone. It's just us. How do we do this?"

"*We trust in our God to deliver us.*"

Ari shook her head, understanding but also uncertain. She exhaled. "What do you need from us?"

"*I need you and Jenna to cover us while we move onto the dam. Don't go down there; just cover us from the rise on the edge of the canyon.*"

"We can do that." Ari turned to Jenna. "Alright, Jenna, we are still in the thick of it. Kane and the others need our help. We will mourn Dagen's sacrifice later."

"Alright, I just...okay, I'm moving," Jenna said, standing with Ari's help. Ari retrieved their rifles and as many spare magazines as they could find, and together they moved as fast as they could to the overlook, where they'd watch Kane, Courtland, and Tynuk's movement across the dam.

29

MALAK HELD THE Machine high, the darkening sky, black as pitch, stretching open above. Behind him, the children moaned, unable to move as Malak held them imprisoned, his dark tentacles in heavy coils around their fragile necks, drinking in their precious life force.

"Yes!" Malak called, flinging his hands high in the air. "Come, my brothers! It is time for us to reclaim what belongs to us. We will merge our planes of existance, and when we have enslaved this world, we will overthrow the kingdom of heaven!" The second wave of Coyotes along the dam screamed, thrusting their arms in the air, their eyes dancing with dark light.

"Now murder these slaves of God!"

Kane, Courtland, and Tynuk approached the entrance to the dam and saw the reserve forces the Coyotes were prepared to send against them—at least two hundred in number. Kane's heart sank, doubt creeping into the edges of his mind.

Trust. The armies of heaven stand with you.

Kane looked to the evil forces that waited to destroy them. "We have to trust. Our God will not abandon us. Not now. Not after all this."

"We are with you, my friend," Courtland said.

"And we will not back down," Tynuk added.

"Then we will finish this the way we started it—together," Kane said.

Beside Tynuk, the black beast tossed its head and huffed, stroking a wet tongue across its fangs.

"Jenna, Ari, are you guys all set?" Kane called into his radio and looked to the low edge of the canyon just above.

"*Yes*," said Ari.

"We're moving. Cover us."

Kane swung his leg forward—a towering step of faith in his God, whom he prayed had not yet abandoned them. As his foot connected with the ground, something unexplainable happened. There was a rumble like thunder, the clanking of armor, the sound of a massive army. Before his eyes, a veil was lifted, and for the first time, he could see what truly lay beyond the world he knew.

Ahead of them, upon the dam, was the most chilling sight he had ever seen. Creatures filled in the ranks of the bandits. Black as night with eyes of blue fire and wings like leather, they stood in silent formation—their dark, savage-looking blades and claws poised to strike. Behind the dark ones were two behemoths, built like gorillas, huge and shaggy. They had tusklike teeth the length of a man's arm, and their massive frames were larger than a two-story building. Kane froze in fear at the demonic force assembled before him, at all of this evil now gathered on the dam, ready to devour his pitiful resistance.

Then he turned his head and caught sight of something else. The beast, Azolja, was standing on his haunches, except that now they were no longer haunches but legs, powerful and bare. Covering the man down his back, the skin of the beast engulfed him, like a great cloak. The head of the creature adorned the man's head, its jaws open in a fierce snarl, the visage of a great barbarian warrior.

The warrior simply turned to him, gesturing at the hills beyond as he boldly stood his ground. "I am Raziel. My brothers and I are here to aid you. You will have what you need for the battle."

Kane couldn't speak, his mouth locked open.

"My faith is so small," Courtland said in disbelief.

Before them, behind them, and across the hills surrounding them stood the most majestic army Kane had ever seen. The figures were larger than normal men by several feet, with distinct, inhuman facial features. Upon their bodies they wore gleaming, mirrorlike helmets with purple plumes and armor with robes of a near-purple crimson, which barely concealed the great golden eagle's wings that lay tucked beneath. Carried in their hands were the most majestic weapons of war he had ever seen: almost-translucent swords adorned with gold and silver; massive war hammers lined with spikes; ornate, shimmering longbows; and brilliant, teardrop-shaped shields. There were thousands of the imposing newcomers, their armor flashing in the piercing rays of the early morning sun. They far outnumbered the dark creatures upon the dam that now screamed and shook at the sight of the shining warriors.

There was little doubt now in any of their minds as to what sort of armies these were. And suddenly, as quickly as the vision had appeared, it was gone again. Nothing of it remained; it was just them, the Coyotes, and the dam—all as it was before.

"What is happening?" Kane turned in disbelief to his friends, looking for the beast, which was now gone. "Az is… an angel?" Kane stammered.

"Our worlds are merging. We are running out of time," Courtland said.

Tynuk, still in awe, looked for his shaggy friend. "It was you who led me from the canyon and guided me through the desert. Do not leave me now, my friend."

"I have a feeling he hasn't left us yet," Kane said.

"Azolja—this Raziel—fights with us from the spirit realm," Courtland said.

Tynuk grinned, "Then what have we to fear?"

▲ ▲ ▲

Jenna supported her rifle against the low ridge. It wasn't real. It couldn't have been. She pulled her eyes from the dam long enough to chance a look behind her to see that the Comanche warriors had routed the last of the bandits along the plateau.

She turned back to what was unfolding before her—Kane, Courtland, and Tynuk now moving on the dam. Even though she had just seen the unthinkable, armies of angels and demons surrounding them, her thoughts still returned to Dagen, the reality of what he had done for them all now sinking like a cinder block in her chest.

Stop it, Jenna. Ari is right. Now is not the time.

Jenna chanced a look at her stoic Israeli friend beside her, still in awe over what they all had seen. If only she could be as tough and resolute as this amazing woman.

"Ari, Jenna, do you read?" Kane said over the radio.

Ari nodded to Jenna, and Jenna raised her radio. "Go ahead, Kane."

"Tell me you just saw that."

"Yes." Jenna looked at Ari, who nodded, wide eyed. "We both did."

"Then you know heaven is with us! Listen to me. Courtland, Tynuk, and I are going in. When we do, open fire on the front ranks of those bandits. Take as many down as you can."

"We'll do it. You guys be safe."

"You too."

"This is crazy. This can't be happening," Ari mumbled, taking aim with her rifle. "Get ready to fire, Jenna."

"Yeah."

"Now."

Their rifles cracked in unison, the bullets flying over the heads of their people. Ari landed a perfect head shot, while Jenna drilled another bandit in the chest. The mass of bandits screamed and surged forward toward Kane and the others.

"Dear God, make our aim true." Jenna said.

"Keep firing!" Ari shouted back as they each took aim on new targets and fired again.

▲ ▲ ▲

Rushing forward onto the dam, Kane kept moving and raised his rifle, firing as fast as he could acquire targets. Onward the Coyotes rushed as Courtland raised his voice and his blades to them, Tynuk steadily pulling arrows and launching them from his bow.

From behind his forces, Malak laughed. "Come, O warriors of heaven! Come to the death feast I have prepared for you! You are in *my* world now!"

As the Coyotes closed in on them, Courtland shouted, "You have no idea the power you contest! We are the army of the Lord!"

With a sonic boom, a huge swath of the enemy forces exploded into the air, launched by some invisible heavenly presence. Twisting, powerless, they fell by the tens over the wall of the dam. Another shuddering boom rippled across the dam; more bandits were sent flipping over the walls of the dam.

Kane and the others shouted in triumph as they ran forward into the fray. Kane fired, scoring multiple vital hits with his rifle. Beside him Courtland charged into the midst of a group of bandits and began furiously swinging his blades, shredding them to bits. Stooping low, Tynuk launched into the air, landing on a goon's shoulders, clubbing him in the skull. With the grace of a bird, the boy ran across the shoulders of the men, who fired their weapons in all directions. With each new shoulder beneath his foot, his club also found the top of a bandit's head.

It was working. The Coyotes were confused, demoralized, killing even their own people without thought. But just when Kane and the others thought they had broken through, a wall of invisible energy slammed into them. With a burning pain, it scorched its way into their bones.

Kane held his hand up and watched the blood from his nose pool in it. He felt dizzy, nauseated. Scanning, he vomited and saw the dish on the tower above. Humming with radioactive power, the device was locked on their position.

"Tynuk…" Kane gasped.

The boy, whose nose and ears were bleeding as well, snapped his attention to Kane.

Kane pointed weakly at the tower; then with all the energy he could muster, he fired his rifle at two approaching Coyotes, dropping them where they stood. He yelled, "The dish on the tower!"

Running at full speed, the boy vaulted up the tower wall and snagged the ladder, climbing as fast as he could. Reaching the top, he did not hesitate to fire an arrow through the operator's chest, slinging his bow across his back. Raising his war club high over his head, he faltered as the HPM hummed, radiating lethal energy. With a scream, blood dripping from his nose and ears, Tynuk slammed his war club down upon the control panel, sending a shower of sparks into the air. In seconds, the humming of the dish clunked to a stop.

Below him, the battle raged. Tynuk took a deep breath and wiped the blood from his face. The nausea was passing. For the first time, he noticed the dish's operator, a man with no shielding or protection. The man's ruined features were revolting; his blood-covered skin, gray and loose, dripped off his arms in long strings. The overexposure to radiation had ruined the man's physical form beyond measure. Then Tynuk noticed something else that changed his perspective—the man's feet were chained to the device. He still wore an ID badge that read *Nick Corveleski*.

"I'm sorry." the man managed to gurgle as his head lolled back, dead.

Tynuk screwed up his face. He turned back to consider the chaos of the battle below him.

In a flash it was different, like moving panels of distorted glass before his face, the image of the battle was shifting. One second all was as it had been, the next, a war of unfathomable scope raged all around him. The forces of heaven, shining like mirrors, slammed into the oily black demonic lines. Beautiful, translucent swords clashed against blades dark as night.

Immersed in this otherworldly battle, he reached for his quiver and touched his last two arrows. He drew an arrow, eyeing a bandit from his elevated position. As the arrow moved, it passed in front of the boy's face. He stopped. Though it felt like a regular wooden arrow and held the same balance, the sight of it was not of this world. Light streamed from the thing, it was like holding a ray of sunlight. Tynuk hesitated only a moment. He notched the light arrow, drew back, and let it fly, this time straight toward a howling demon. As the bolt neared its target, it broke into three. The arrows struck the target demon and two others beside it. In a flash of holy flame, the monsters disintegrated, reduced to screaming ash. He reached for the final arrow and, oddly, still felt two. Drawing another light arrow, he grinned and let it fly.

Below, Kane felt himself pass through the shifting worlds. He shuddered at the bawling maw he suddenly found himself engaged in—stuck right in the middle of a war between demons and angels fighting to the death.

A demon, moving fast, came at him head-on, its blade slashing down to finish him. A clang was followed by a shower of sparks as something invisible stepped in front of him and deflected the demon's blow with a mighty shield. A fraction of a second later, a sword of fire cut through the air, turning the demon to crippled ash. For just an instant, he could see the flicker of a barbarian warrior's form shielding him.

Keep moving. Find the warlord. I am with you.

"I'm moving," Kane said, struggling to steady his nerves.

Gasping for breath, Kane ran, ducking and dodging his way through the chaos. "Courtland!" Kane called to the giant, whose blades now glowed white in this strange place. Courtland crossed blades with the hideous demons that came for him. One by one he turned them to ash.

"Courtland, I'm going after Malak!"

"I will keep them distracted. Go!"

Stumbling over a body, Kane scrambled to all fours, righted himself again, and continued to run. Ahead of him, the two behemoths lumbered forward. With earthquake-inducing strikes, they crushed the angelic armies at their feet. The heavenly warriors seemed powerless against the brutes, as winged archers launched volley after volley of light arrows into them. Kane stopped, huddled behind a pile of debris, searching for a path through the madness.

An angelic horn trumpeted three times, and the clouds above them churned with fire. Several stunning blasts of lightning snapped through the ashen ceiling, striking down on and disintegrating waves of the fallen. Another bolt gave a direct hit on one of the behemoths, slowing it but not stopping it. In the wake of this air support, a huge bolt of white light struck down with an earsplitting crack on the dam in front of Kane and the remaining angels.

Light swelled and encased the goliath that now began to rise from its huddled landing position. With a hiss, it came to life in a whirring of mechanical light. Neither living nor dead, towering like a titanic suit of autonomous magical armor, it stood to its full height, stories tall. The seraphim had arrived. The armies of heaven rallied, cheering in triumph for their champion.

The earth shook as the single light-filled seraphim collided with the ugly behemoths along the top of the dam, two on one. Buzzing with magical power, the seraphim grabbed one behemoth by the neck and, rising high, slammed down into the other monster's skull with an armored fist the size of a truck. Battering into each other with blows that could level buildings, the two behemoths clamored around the vital seraphim, as the titans brutalized each other again and again in a display that might well have belonged before the backdrop of a ruined Tokyo.

The earth shuddered again, and in the blink of an eye, Kane returned to the world he knew. The screams of men rang in his ears, his nostrils full of smoke and dust. He felt like he was losing his mind. One minute he was fighting for his life among droves of bandits, the next he was fighting for his life among hordes of demons. Gunfire rang out all around him, and he ducked lower. He checked his rifle and found that it was jammed—a double feed. Kane stripped the magazine and tried to free the bolt, but the thing was frozen in place. He was still in the fight, and he had to move. Slinging the jammed AR-15, Kane drew his Glock 17 and tucked it to his chest, clasped in both hands. He could just make out the path he would take toward Malak. He would have to navigate a few bad spots, but it was the most direct route.

Double-checking the round count in his Glock, he could just see Malak ahead of him, screaming at his forces from an elevated platform. Behind the monster of a man, he saw, for the first time since they'd been taken from him, his dear Michael and Rachael. He had to move. The worlds were shifting into each other faster now. Time was running out.

Through her scope, Ari watched Kane crouching behind the debris pile. She made a sucking sound through her teeth. "I don't like it."

"You don't like what?" Jenna looked exhausted as she peered down her rifle sights.

"Why is Kane going after Malak alone?"

"He's not alone."

"Yes, Courtland, the Indian kid, and an army of angels are with him. But right now I'm watching him, and he's alone."

Jenna rubbed her face, the stress cracking her resolve. "I don't know how much more of this I can take. I hope it doesn't change back anymore. I've seen enough warfare to last ten lifetimes. I think I'm losing my marbles."

"Jenna, focus!"

"Yeah, Kane's alone. So?"

"We should be down there with them."

"Are you *crazy*? Kane told us to stay here. We should."

"Why?" Ari's tone gained an edge. "Because we're women? Screw that. Let's go."

"Ari, I don't think I can!" Jenna cried. "I'm not like you. I'm not a warrior."

"You are today, sister!" Ari pulled Jenna to her feet and shoved her toward the last intact Hummer. "We're not going to sit here and watch our friends die."

"Lord God, be my shield against this evil! Only you can save us from this!" Kane chanted to himself as he ran farther into the sprawling madness. He stopped, his legs spread in a stable platform, his arms punching out into a combat shooting stance. The Glock recoiled in his hands as he fired and acquired a new target again and again. The bandits were unable to get a shot off as Kane leveled each one with critical hits to the chest and head.

In an instant, he was running again, his legs driving him forward in a desperate attempt to reach Malak and his children before it was too late. But he could now see that the way was blocked. He had taken the best route he could, but now the bandits had shifted, and a large group was blocking his path. Kane gnashed his teeth in desperation. He would have to fight his way through them. There was no time. He had no other choice.

Kane spun at the noise of tires screeching against the pavement behind him. The beaten Hummer slid to a stop. Ari jumped from the driver's door and ran at a full sprint toward the thugs ahead of him. She slowed, chopping her feet against the ground to stop herself while drawing the Beretta from her waist. Flaring her elbows high in the Israeli point-shoot method, she punched her weapon forward and began firing into the bandits with astonishing accuracy. Behind her, Jenna's head was just visible in the heavy-machine-gun turret. Clenching the weapon in fear and desperation, Jenna began to fire into the surging mass of bandits on their right flank, the .50-caliber machine gun flashing and barking as it tore their ranks apart. These two amazing women had come to his aid, carving a bloody path to his destination.

Kane didn't wait another instant. He ran for the platform, now closing within fifty feet. Just as he reached the platform, the two dimensions collided again, everything blurring and twisting against each other. A titanic boom made the world around him shudder.

He turned and saw one of the behemoths shaking, a gaping wound through its chest. The monstrous beast flashed into flames, screaming as it dropped to its knees and fell over the side of the dam. The massive Seraphim now wielded an unbelievably large sword, a weapon of unsurpassed size and power; the second behemoth raged and collided with the armored titan again as the dam came apart under them. Around him, the armies of heaven and hell screamed and threw themselves against each other as the forces of light began to overwhelm the forces of darkness. But Kane could no longer worry about them, his focus fell like a laser beam on the ugly warlord who held his children hostage.

As he flew up the stairs onto the platform, he heard the frail voices of his children call his name, and for a moment, he feared he might shatter inside. His babies looked so used, not at all the way young children should look. A deep and consuming fury bloomed within his chest as he prepared to confront the demonic warlord.

"You just won't stop! I should have killed you *myself!*" Malak shouted. "You and your merry band of idiots have been a thorn in my flesh from the beginning, but you're too late. You can't stop it now. All you can do is watch as I suck the life from your precious children!"

Another tremor shook the dam as the seraphim slammed into the behemoth with the magical sword, dealing a fatal blow. The beast bellowed and fell toward them, crashing against the dam behind the platform. Everything crumbled, and Kane, Malak, and the children fell through the floor as it disintegrated beneath them.

An instant later Kane was struggling to his feet in a darkened room swirling with smoke and dust. The spartan, gray walls of the interior of the dam surrounded them. The floor had collapsed under the weight of the behemoth, and they had all fallen down to the next level. Kane's weapons were now lost in the rubble at his feet. He looked up, coughing, and could just see the dim light from the sky above through the occluded room.

From across the room, the vile, chortling laughter of the demon rippled toward him. As the air began to clear, he could now make them out. There Malak stood, next to Kane's dust-covered children, who now whimpered quietly. Kane made a motion to move, and Malak held up his hand.

"Ah, ah, ah, hold on there, tough guy. One more step and I shatter their little necks easier than I would a handful of baby birds."

Kane froze, the sickening feeling of helplessness before this demonic tyrant filling him once again. He watched the dark tentacles twist around the necks of his children, causing them to gag and struggle for breath. It was the worst sort of déjà vu he could imagine. Kane turned his eyes back to Malak, whose human appearance was beginning to fray at the edges. Dark mist seeped from his black eyes, his massive musculature bulging with inhuman power.

Kane, save our children. Promise me.

"Why not just face me? If you're so powerful, killing me shouldn't be this difficult."

"Why so eager to die, Kane Lorusso?" Malak said, as two of the fallen army, black blades poised to strike, appeared beside him.

"You need them? What are you so afraid of?"

"Afraid? Who said I was afraid? Maybe I'm just stalling for time." Malak motioned, and Kane noticed the Machine, still clutched in Malak's viselike grip.

"So all I can do is stand here and watch you suck the life out of my children?"

"Yes, but don't worry, Kane. I'll let you tell them that it's going to be okay one last time before I turn them inside out—for old time's sake!"

"You've taken enough from me!" Kane shook with the words.

"I haven't even begun to take from you!" Malak snarled. "I will make your pain and misery last forever when I enslave this pitiful world and topple the kingdom of heaven!"

"You're a powerless child, bitter and discarded. All you know is destroying what others cherish. Stop your talking and finish me!"

"Yes! I believe I will!" Malak intoned. "But first, the children!"

Kane grabbed two pieces of heavy chain from the debris at his feet and coiled them around his hands and forearms. He prepared himself as his children squirmed and the oily black demons flanked him, their black blades ready to strike him down.

"Holy God, spare them. *Please...*"

With a flash of light and the squall of thunder, Courtland fell through the hole in the roof, slamming his boots into Malak and launching the warlord across the room. Crackling with power, he stood between the children and their foes, an impenetrable fortress of righteousness. The demons immediately turned on the giant, screaming. Above them, more began to drop through the ceiling.

"Destroy him, Kane! I will stand for your children!"

Kane launched himself forward, his body moving faster and feeling stronger than it ever had before in his life. His eyes took in his chain-wrapped hands that now glowed white hot with an unmistakable holy power. A demon came for him, slashing down as Kane deflecting the blow with a chained gauntlet and punched through the creature with a flash of holy fire. Kane charged across the room, striking the demons in his way, turning each one into a pile of smoldering carbon.

Behind him, Courtland cried in desperation, "You shall not have them!" He swung his white-hot blades, obliterating the demons that swarmed around him and the children.

Kane strode across the room with unparalleled purpose. At the far side, Malak raised himself up, his form distorting hideously as the demon inside took over.

Malak launched himself at Kane, but this time Kane was moving just as fast. The two collided in a flash of energy as Kane groaned, striking Malak again and again with his chain-covered fists. The tyrant swung at Kane with a balled fist, but Kane ducked and delivered an uppercut to Malak's ribs and then followed up with several hard strikes to his head and neck from behind.

They went back and forth, blow for blow, Kane deflecting with his gauntlets, Malak absorbing an unbelievable amount of punishment. Malak struck with his coiling tentacles, wrapping around Kane and slamming him into the ceiling. For a moment everything dimmed, the room now white and hazy, bells ringing, Malak laughing. Swinging his arm in a downward arc, Kane severed Malak's grasp on him. He fell to the floor, disoriented, everything spinning. Kane struggled to his feet as Malak came again.

Dodging another swipe of the dark, smoky tentacles, Kane slammed into the warlord with what felt like the force of an entire army. He was fighting harder than the mind could comprehend, faster than should be humanly possible, fueled by an everlasting holy power and an unquenchable thirst for justice. Again and again, he slammed his fists into the brute, crushing him, defeating him. Whirling with dark power, Malak crashed into Kane, knocking him off his feet and into the far wall.

Kane was empowered, now too much for Malak to defeat. The demonic man launched himself across the room, desperate to kill all that Kane loved. Courtland saw him coming and stepped in front of Michael and Rachael, his body a human shield, just as Malak lashed out with a dark tentacle that severed the giant's right arm from his body. A second tentacle whipped across low, striking at the giant's legs. Falling back and clutching the ragged stump at his shoulder, Courtland looked at where his arm used to be. Blood pumped through his fingers as he tried to stop the flow of life from him and protect the terrified children at the same time.

"No," Courtland gasped, "you will not have these children. You'll have to kill me first!"

"Of course!" Malak said. He stooped, grabbing Courtland by the neck. "When you see your God, tell him I'm coming for him next!"

Without warning, Kane flew onto Malak's back with a scream, locking him in a brutal choke with his chained-wrapped arms. Malak gagged, choking and sputtering, and released Courtland, who slumped to the ground, still shielding the children with his body. Across the room, Kane and Malak flailed, crashing back and forth into walls and groaning in the darkness of the room.

"Now it's your turn to fail!" Kane groaned.

"You can't! This can't be!" Malak gurgled, falling to his knees and grasping at the chained arms that now choked the life out of him, arms that were suddenly so impossibly strong for a mortal man.

With a wrenching movement, Kane pulled hard and felt Malak's trachea crush beneath the force.

"Agggh!" Malak groaned in terror as he suffocated, unable to stop what was to come. Kane rode the savage man to the floor and immediately began to pummel the warlord's head against the ground with his chained fists. "You murdered my wife! You murdered my friends! You enslaved my children!"

"Kane, it's done," Courtland said.

Kane struck again and again until nothing remained of Malak's deformed skull. Kane sat back gasping, rising from the warlord's corpse as his hands dripped blood and bone.

"Now it's done. I had to be sure."

For a moment all went still. Nothing moved in the room around them, save for the soft humming of the Machine—still clutched in Malak's cold, dead hand.

Kane was just stepping away, gasping for breath, when Malak's torso lurched against the ground. Kane jumped back, watching in horror as the warlord's body animated unnaturally, twisting in the dimness of the room.

"No," Kane said with a moan, "I knew that was too easy."

"Kane," Courtland moaned in terrible pain from behind him, "you have to get your kids out of here while you have the chance."

Kane stepped backward, hearing his friend but unable to pull his eyes from the writhing form on the ground. "How bad are you hurt?"

"Pretty bad."

"Hang in there, Court. I don't think we're out of the woods yet."

The flesh of Malak's back split open, the white disks of the spine pushing to the side as something black began to emerge from Malak's body, leaving the deformed carcass crumpled on the floor like a used suit.

The black form laughed with evil intent. As it stood free of Malak's body, the huge, dark, bestial form of a creature came into view: Abaddon, the destroyer. It bent and pulled the Machine from the frozen clutches of Malak's hand, glowering. "You should know by now, human. I can't be destroyed by mortal men!"

Kane swallowed, terrified. "I don't care. I stand in the name of God!"

"But you won't have to," another voice said, as the form of Raziel stepped forward and stood between Kane and the archdemon. "This fight is not for you." With a singing sound, the Blaze slid from its sheath and hung burning in the air. "Kane Lorusso, take your people and get as far from this place as possible."

Abaddon laughed and produced his own terrible blade. "Raziel, my old friend, it's been too long."

"Not long enough," Raziel spoke with an edge.

Abaddon laughed. "You cannot stop the turning of the Machine. The gateway is now open, and the Machine cannot be destroyed. You all have failed."

"There is still time to stop this, and such is my duty."

"You are such a fool, Keeper. You think you can stand against me? Even with your holy sword, you are outmatched. You always have been."

Raziel shifted and raised the Blaze. "I once was, but that was eons ago, and since, while you have been consumed with selfish greed, I have set myself to mastering this holy blade. It alone has the power to destroy the Machine."

Abaddon sneered. "You must be joking."

"I am not. I stand ready for you this time."

Abaddon laughed again. "Yes? Alright, I'll entertain your delusions, Raziel. Show me what you can do!"

With a terrible snarl, Abaddon flew forward, but Raziel was ready, parrying the dark blade and stepping past gracefully, the Blaze leaving a streak of flame across the thick, black hair on Abaddon's ribs as it sliced through him. Abaddon faltered, astonished, and with a scream of rage flew at Raziel again, slamming into him and knocking them both through one of the walls and into an adjoining room.

Kane shook the chains from his arms and searched frantically through the rubble of the ruined room.

"What are you doing?" Courtland murmured.

"I have to help."

"Kane, this is a feud that has lasted for millions of years. It's not your fight."

"Forgive me if I disagree." Kane tossed a chunk of concrete aside and pulled his Glock from the pile. Holding it in his hand, it began to glow as all their weapons had in this strange place, trapped between dimensions. "Stay with the children!" he yelled as he ran through the hole, following the sound of commotion in the next room.

"What are you going to do?"

"Something really stupid!" Kane's voice echoed back.

▲ ▲ ▲

Courtland stroked the children's hollow faces, their eyes reflecting the horror they had endured. Courtland held his huge, blood-covered hand to their tiny cheeks, as a radiating light flowed from him into them. "Children have no business looking so used. Maybe this will help."

Above them, Ari and Jenna, along with Tynuk, poked their heads over the edge of the hole.

"Guys?" Jenna called. "Is everyone okay?"

"Jenna, get these children out of here," Courtland said.

"What are you doing?"

"Sharing what I have to give them. They need it more than I do."

Courtland pulled the children close, whispering a few sage words and rocking them gently. Jenna and Ari watched in astonishment as their little gray faces filled once again with color and life. The children were returning, but their eyes remained far away, still in shock.

"Courtland, your arm!" Jenna called.

"It's okay, dear. My healing ability has slowed the bleeding. I'm just a little weak," he said.

"We need to get you out of there," Ari called.

"The children—get them out. I will stay with Kane."

"But—"

"There is no but. I am staying. Take the children to safety."

With supreme care Courtland raised each child with his good arm. Ari and Jenna pulled them out of the hole while Tynuk watched for threats.

"Take them and go. I don't know how this battle will end, and I won't leave Kane to fight it alone."

Tynuk looked into the hole toward his wounded friend, his bow and quiver glowing with holy light. "I too will fight with you."

"I would welcome that, my friend."

Tynuk dropped into the hole and readied his bow, scanning.

Ari cradled the children close to her, Jenna looking down to Courtland one last time. "You guys finish this, and then you come to meet up with us. You understand that?" She wiped a tear from her face. "We will be expecting you—all of you."

"I understand, my dear Jenna. We will see you soon." Courtland smiled with effort, knowing full well, it would be a difficult promise to keep.

▲ ▲ ▲

Striding through the jagged hole in the wall, Kane followed the sounds of the melee as Raziel and Abaddon clashed in an immeasurable display of violence.

"What are you doing, Kane?" he said to himself, pushing through the dust and crouching low to get a better look. He looked at the Glock glowing in his hands once more. He was either going to be able to help, or he was going to piss off an archdemon and sign his own death warrant. Only one way to find out.

Kane moved to where he could see the two forms locked in immortal combat. Raziel moved like a master swordsman, his black wolfskin cloak swishing as he moved, the Blaze leaving a tail of magical flame as it sliced through the air over and over. Abaddon filled with a mighty rage, bloodred eyes glowing in the dimness of the room. He shrieked and struck at Raziel with his blade, pushing the angel back with the sheer force of each strike. Clashing, they continued on, bits of white flame illuminating the darkness with each clang of their weapons.

Kane drew down on Abaddon, taking the demon in his sights. The Glock recoiled in his hand as a light-filled round fired like a tracer from the barrel. Abaddon howled as the glowing projectile pierced his side.

"Kane, do not interfere!" Raziel yelled.

Shoving Raziel back, Abaddon took advantage of the opening as his dark blade found its mark, and Raziel staggered back and fell to the ground, wounded. Abaddon turned and flew across the room toward Kane. With a pull of the trigger, another round fired, streaking across the darkened room, as Kane tracked the demon. Round after round struck the creature, causing it to howl with rage as it came for him. He had nowhere to go.

As Kane continued to fire, he felt a presence come alongside him, though he dared not pull his eyes from the enraged demon as it charged.

"We are with you, Kane!" Courtland shouted as he came along one side of him and Tynuk pushed forward on the other.

"Go, Courtland," Tynuk called. "Draw it away!"

But Courtland was already running off to the right. On the left, Tynuk broke into a sprint, firing light arrows from his bow as fast as he could draw them.

Screaming with rage as the light arrows lodged in his flesh, Abaddon turned, swinging his dark blade at Tynuk. The agile boy dodged back and forth, jumping, ducking, and bounding off the wall. Abaddon swung, again and again, tearing the wall apart in a flurry of blows. Faking one direction and moving in the opposite at a speed that was incomprehensible, the demon outmaneuvered Tynuk, grabbing the boy's body and flinging him against the wall. Unconscious, the warrior boy fell to the ground in a pile of concrete rubble.

With a roar, Courtland hit the demon with the hardest tackle he could muster, knocking the demon's sword from his clawed hand. Wrapping the demon with his good arm, he groaned as Abaddon struck him again and again with deep, savage blows from his claws.

Courtland slumped to his knees, his energy fading. From across the room, Kane dropped an empty magazine from his Glock and slapped a fresh one. Stomping forward with righteous fury, he fired as fast as his finger could slap at the trigger.

"Why don't you just die!"

Abaddon, now in a wild, frothing lust for death, focused on Kane and smiled maliciously.

"Yeah, that's it!" Kane shouted and charged. "Come on! Kill me if you can!"

Kane continued to fire, Abaddon flinching as each glowing round struck his flesh, searing into him. He was injuring the terrible beast, but it wasn't enough, as it closed the gap and struck the weapon from his hand, grabbing him by the throat.

"Human worm! You dare to challenge *me*?" Abaddon snarled. "I could destroy you a hundred times over with a twitch of my finger. But since you have been such a terrible irritation, I believe I will have some fun pulling you apart." Abaddon raised the Machine between them and began speaking in tongues that Kane could not understand. The Machine hummed, buzzing and vibrating in the archdemon's clawed hand. "With this, I can remake anything I desire in the image of the Master. What is it you fear most, human?"

Kane gasped in the clutches of the demon as a pall of despair began to cover him.

"I know because I can see it in your fragile soul. You fear failure. You fear your inability to hold to your insignificant faith. You fear that this all has been for nothing!"

Behind the demon, Raziel stirred upon the ground. Kane's eyes grew wide in the presence of such pure evil. "No. You are not greater than the one true God."

"But do you really believe that? What happens when the faith of a worm dies out? When it is replaced by nothing but loss and despair and hopelessness?"

Kane struggled in the viselike grip, the hope that he would hold his children in his arms again fading, the faith that he could succeed at his mission, dying. "I've been there already. My God has gone before me!" Kane cried as the Machine whirred, and he felt himself begin to change, darkness filling him from the inside.

Abaddon laughed with glee. "Release yourself unto it. There is no fighting the power of the Master!"

Kane faded, slipping into an eternal hellish darkness. It was then that he saw the movement behind the hellish beast.

"Gotcha distracted, didn't I?" Kane murmured with a smirk.

With a flash of fire, Kane fell to the ground and scrambled backward to see a look of absolute shock and terror on Abaddon's face. The archdemon looked down to see the Blaze protruding from his chest, the Machine severed by the thrust.

"Die, foul traitor!" Raziel shouted from behind the demon, twisting his flaming sword in the creature's chest. The Machine, cut in two by the holy sword, fell to the ground in pieces and began to shake.

"No!" Abaddon shrieked. "I am too powerful to be destroyed!"

Without a word Raziel snatched the Blaze from Abaddon's chest and pivoted, cleaving the demon's head from its shoulders in a magical flash of white fire. Abaddon screamed a sound that made Kane cringe, as the archdemon caught fire and flared into ashes, whipping away into the wind.

Kane got to his feet and ran to Courtland's side. "Come on, brother, we gotta go!"

Courtland tried to raise himself, his whole body quaking.

"Come on, Court, I've got you." Kane slipped under the massive arm and heaved with all his might to help the giant stand. He turned to Tynuk, who was now stirring. "Tynuk, we've gotta go! Now!"

"Hurry," Raziel urged. "There is little time! The Machine has been shattered. Our worlds will not hold together much longer. If you want to survive, you must go now! I will try to contain it and buy you some time!"

They pushed through the smoke and dust, as the earth began to shake like a great sleeping titan beneath them. Stumbling in a panic back into the room they had first fallen into, Kane let Courtland rest below the gaping hole in the roof. Behind them came the warrior boy, coughing.

"We did it," Courtland said and smiled. "We stopped Abaddon."

"We sure did, brother." Kane panted for air.

"It's going to be alright. I can feel it, in my bones. A good omen."

"Okay, Court." Kane looked around for a way out. "I think the Machine is going to blow. How do we get out of here?"

"We can't, but you and Tynuk can." Courtland held a blood soaked hand against the stump at his shoulder.

"No. Stop with that. Come on. I'll help you out."

Courtland shook his head. "No, brother. I am hurt bad. That last bout finished what strength I had left. This is the end for me."

"Stop screwing around and get up through that hole! I know you can!" Kane yelled.

"I can't, and both of you together couldn't get me out of here in time. You'll die trying. Go. Live. Enjoy the time you have left. I am proud to have given my life at your side and in the service of my God."

Tears of loss and frustration filled Kane's eyes. "You stubborn old man! You're my magnetic north. I'm not going to leave you."

"You're not leaving me, my friend. I'm asking you to go. Don't worry about me. I'll be around to keep an eye on you," the giant said with a weak smile and a wink. "Now get out of here. Get the others to safety. Take care of them for me."

The typically stoic Tynuk swallowed hard, fighting to check his emotions. "You are a true friend, Mr. Courtland. We will see each other again."

"I know we will, Tynuk. I'm sure of it."

The three comrades stared at each other for a long moment as each remembered the depth of history between them.

Courtland nodded to Tynuk and, grabbing him, pressed him up through the hole.

Kane wiped the tears from his face and shook his head. "After all this, to say good-bye…" He paused, struggling to master himself. He looked deep into the eyes of his friend. "I'll earn this, Court. I won't forget you. I won't waste this gift."

"I know you will, my brother. I know you will." He grasped Kane by the arm. "Don't you ever stop believing in a God who loves to do the impossible!" Courtland grabbed Kane, groaning and pressing him upward with a single arm, struggling with the task after losing his heavenly power.

Kane grabbed the concrete slab, pulling himself up and onto the surface of the dam as Tynuk grabbed his shirt and pulled from above. Smoke wafted through the air and passed over the orgy of blood, body, and bone. Ari and Jenna had left the Hummer for them. Kane stood and gave one last look to his old friend, who now sat calmly in the rubble below, pulling the tattered picture of his daughter from his shirt pocket.

"I'm ready to come home, Mar," Courtland whispered. "I'm ready to come home to my Jesus."

With a wrenching of his heart, Kane turned from his friend. He and Tynuk made for the Hummer, the ground shuddering beneath them. Entering, Kane cranked the heavy vehicle, saw Tynuk holding on, and slammed on the gas. The Hummer rocketed forward, jumping and jostling over bodies and debris as it picked up speed. There was a thump below him and a dull flash of blue light that seemed to radiate from the center of the dam. Without warning, a concussion launched the Hummer forward, almost off the edge of the dam, as the surface began to crumble apart and fall away beneath its tires.

"Step on it!" Tynuk yelled.

"Hold on!" Kane stomped the accelerator.

Bucking, breaking contact with the ground, the Hummer soared from the dam and onto the desert highway as a second flash, much brighter than the first, leveled the dam and sent the entire thing imploding in on itself. Water from the lake launched into the air as millions of gallons of Lake Powell dumped into the Glen Canyon basin along with the final remnants of the Glen Canyon Dam.

Sliding to a stop, Kane jumped from the Hummer, his eyes locked on the crumbling fortress of concrete and steel. Jenna ran from around the vehicle, seeing Tynuk clinging to the side of it. "Courtland? Kane, where's Courtland?"

"I couldn't get him out, Jenna. I tried…I just couldn't. He's gone."

"No!" Jenna collapsed to the ground, weeping.

Kane shook his head, gasping for breath. "He stayed with me till the very end, just like he said he would."

As the dam crumbled and the water gushed, Kane thought he saw Raziel standing against the background of destruction. The barbarian figure gave a definite inclination of his head, a gesture that seemed to say, *Well done.* Kane returned the nod, as Raziel turned and disappeared along with several other majestic angelic warriors.

Tynuk, seeing it as well, spoke to the fading image. "Farewell, my friend. I was glad to have you by my side for a time."

"Daddy!" Michael and Rachael cried as they rounded the vehicle with Ari.

Kane turned and dropped to his knees as his dear children plowed into him, their little arms encircling him in a smothering vise of love. Kane cracked, as tears of love and loss and relief and sadness streamed down his face. He shuddered, sobbing and clutching his sweet babies against him, their little faces now full of warmth and life. Courtland's final gift had made the difference.

"It's over! We did it! God stood with us, and we did it." Kane pinched his eyes and clutched at his children as the others gathered around. "I got 'em, Suz." Kane wept, shaking with emotion. "I got 'em, and I won't ever let them go."

Epilogue

IN THE DARKNESS, nothing stirred, save a faint whisper of some lost soul wandering amid the nothingness. Beyond the black was more of the same, an endless horizon of emptiness, like ink sloshing against the walls of its occluded bottle.

"Where am I?" Abaddon spoke, his voice oddly frail in this place. He twisted his limbs, reaching out, and felt nothing but the dark of this prison. Looking down, he could see nothing of himself—no body, no existence inside this place.

"What has happened to me! I cannot be destroyed!"

"And you have not been." The familiar voice spoke back to him.

"Raziel! What sort of sorcery is this?"

Raziel continued unamused, "To say you cannot be destroyed is a fallacy. The Blaze, a weapon unlike any other, created by the hands of the high king, has the power to destroy you. And as much as I wish it had, it did not."

"What are you saying? Where am I?" Abaddon fumed.

"As I said, the Blaze was created by our father, and he saw fit to imbue it with certain magical properties. One might even say this weapon has a mind of its own, since it can choose the fate of its victims."

"Stop your driveling and tell me what has happened."

"I really shouldn't. I should leave you in this place, with only your own voice to comfort you. The perfect retreat for a self-absorbed creature such as yourself, don't you think?"

Abaddon did not reply.

"But alas, I will tell you," Raziel continued, "since I find it amusing." He paused. "You see, instead of destroying you, our king had the foresight to *use* you instead."

"What is it you are saying to me?"

"I'm saying that your essence, your consciousness, was captured and imprisoned within the Blaze."

"*What?*"

"Yes, naturally, after all you have done, you could not be allowed to continue to roam at large, so instead, the high king in his ultimate wisdom imprisoned you within this weapon."

"I am *inside* your sword?"

"Yes, indeed," Raziel replied. "Right now our brothers probably think that I am crazy, talking to my weapon like this."

"Where is my body?" Abaddon whimpered, and for the first time, Raziel sensed fear within his voice.

"It has been destroyed, and you have been repurposed. You will now be the engine behind my holy weapon as it uses your life force to generate even more power."

"What am I supposed to do in here?" Abaddon thrashed about within the unending blackness of his prison.

Raziel laughed. "Nothing, of course. You desired a world ruled by darkness, and now you shall have it. Farewell, my old foe; we will not speak again."

"Don't leave me in here, Raziel! *You can't—*"

Raziel slid the Blaze into its sheath, silencing the voice within, and turned to see Michael, Jophiel, and Zadkiel approaching, royal-purple robes swishing beneath mirrorlike armor. They stopped short as Michael gave a nod to Raziel, and Zadkiel and Jophiel followed with slight bows.

"Commander," Raziel said, nodding and bowing. He then looked to his standards and added, "Gentlemen."

"Keeper," the standards replied.

"It's good to see you, Raziel; welcome home." Michael spoke with formal sincerity.

"Thank you, Commander. It's been a long time."

"Too long," Michael said. "So long, in fact, that much has changed."

"Yes, I see. Little is how I remembered it." Raziel scanned the celestial fortress with a sigh.

"Is there anything I can do for the former keeper of secrets?"

"Former?" Raziel bowed low. "Commander, if I have failed in my station, let me be disciplined, but please leave me my position."

"Stand, old friend. You are not being stripped of your title or status. If anything, you are to be honored for your bravery and dedication in this most recent conflict involving the humans and that fiend Abaddon." Michael nodded to the Blaze at Raziel's side. "I trust he is enjoying his new accommodations?"

Raziel smirked. "He is not, Commander."

"Excellent." Michael smiled. "So, as I was saying, after your prolonged absence, we had to establish a new keeper in your stead."

"I see."

"But I have something else in mind for you, my friend, an assignment that the high king has already approved."

"Oh?"

"I'm putting together a small unit, specifically for dealing with direct threats to our interests. After your recent heroism in the earthly realm and with that particular weapon at your side, I believe you are the one to lead this group."

"I am not a leader."

"Untrue, my old friend. You may have some room for growth there, but you are one of the most noble and courageous angels I have had the pleasure of knowing, and your skill with that weapon is unmatched."

"I don't know what to say. What sort of unit is this?"

Michael smiled and placed his hand upon Raziel's shoulder. "Small, a bit of a motley crew, very clandestine. But we can talk about all that later. For now, just say yes."

"Yes, of course, Commander." Raziel nodded.

"Perfect." Michael smiled, urging Raziel forward. "Now, let's get you fitted with some new wings. You will need them where you're going."

▲ ▲ ▲

Warm, unfiltered sunlight poured across the base at Camp Navajo in the late-afternoon hours of the day. The spring months had brought the first prolonged sunlight they'd had in years, the air warming under the gaze of a heavy sun. It had been most welcome after so long without it.

With the clearing of the sky, the earth began to recover, growing once again even after all it had been through. Even though still scarred and barren, some areas had grown back up with wild grasses and weeds and even a few young trees. Those at the base had even been able to cultivate the soil, and although the first yield of crops had been meager, it had been something. Promise lingered in the air—the start of a brand-new day.

Kane and Ari made their way across the base, holding hands. Ari was pregnant with their second child. The first, a son they named Joshua, nuzzled closer, napping against the chest of his mother. Never far behind, Michael and Rachael teased each other as they followed the steps of their father. The twins had recovered and had grown inseparable from each other and their father.

As the community at the base also grew, protected within the fortified walls of Camp Navajo, many approached Kane, asking him to lead the group again. He declined, while still offering to help in any way he could. He said he just wanted to try living and raising his family for a change and that the people were able to lead themselves. This was all fine and good, but everyone knew that if they needed him, if some terrible evil were to rise against them once again, he would be there. Though much in him had changed since the beginning, he never stopped believing in a God who relished the business of working miracles.

Ari kept herself busy helping to look after Michael and Rachael, as well as the new addition, but woe to the man who constrained her to "womanly duties." She would always be a lioness, bred for war. As such, she kept herself sharp, volunteering to keep watch or training others in how to fight or shoot. Though two pregnancies had slowed her down a bit, her fiery spirit and her desire to protect those whom she loved remained undiminished.

Jenna continued ministering to the people who now made Camp Navajo their permanent home. She did this in her typical way, using a life of service to others as the example of her savior. Everyone loved her, and though her heart still ached sometimes for those she had lost, she never again fell into despair about it. She volunteered with the medical clinic, delivering several babies, including young Joshua. But what she loved the most was teaching and playing with the children. She believed in cultivating the future and those who would live in it. And she never let go of the belief that no one, not even the worst of us, was beyond the saving grace of Christ.

They all still saw Tynuk once in a while. Though he had gone through puberty and was a little stockier than they all remembered, he was still the same wild warrior boy they'd known back then. Valiantly leading his people, the New Comanche Nation, Tynuk saw that they grew and flourished, finding their way back to the oldest ways, just as the prophecy foretold. Queenashano remained close to the boy, mentoring and developing him into a wise and fair leader, and over the years, the old war chief became a father figure of sorts to him.

From time to time, the war chief Tynuk and a few of his warriors would stop by Camp Navajo to trade goods they had scavenged and to reminisce over old stories. Though Tynuk would never admit it, he missed his companion, Azolja—or Raziel, or whatever name he wore—as well as his old friend, Courtland. And as time went on, though they were sure they would never completely lose touch, Kane and the others began to see less and less of their mysterious friend and his reclusive people.

Smack-dab in the center of the base, near the flagpole that still flew Old Glory, was a monument with the words: "A few gave some and some gave all." Listed below were the names of those lost since the beginning. Among them were Molly Stevens, Susan Lorusso, Courtland Thompson, Dagen, Jacob, Aviel, Sam, and Winston. Beside the pillar was a second stone with a few simple words carved into it: "Greater love has none than this, that a man lay down his life for his friends. Thank you, Dagen and Courtland. We are forever grateful. Rest in peace."

It had been two years and three months since the Battle for the Glen Canyon Dam, as it was now known. It was a story that would be told over and over again in legend, remembering when a handful of faithful people took on an entire army of evil and stood against the fading of the light. Miraculously, they had won. Some would tell the story by saying that the armies of heaven had fought beside our heroes, that they had won a victory that no one had anticipated and that future generations would fail to understand the significance of. Others would scoff and say that, like most legends, none of it ever happened at all. But Kane and the others knew. They had seen it, struggled through it, and survived it. It would leave scars that they each would live with for the rest of their days.

Malak and his Coyotes were dead and gone. Kane's children had been rescued and the Machine destroyed. As far as they knew, they never saw Raziel or any of his kind again. And though it was a wild, frontier sort of life, for the first time since the missiles fell from the sky, people could live in relative peace again.

Kane and Ari stopped for a moment before the pillar of names and the stone marking Dagen and Courtland's sacrifice. They stood for a lingering moment, the weight of old memories prevailing as Kane touched his fingers to the grooves of the stone. "The light shines in the darkness..." he whispered.

Ari squeezed his hand and touched her cheek to his shoulder, her deep brown eyes gazing at him. "You okay?"

"You know what?" Kane said, patting her hand and catching her eyes with a wink. "I am." A worn smile crested Kane's lips as he heard a group of the children singing with Jenna from across the way, their little voices drifting and riding the breeze like a heavenly chorus.

"By his grace, we have come, in his grace, we now go, wrapped in the love and goodness of Jesus our Lord, to whom all glory and honor, power, and praise be forever and ever. Amen."

Acknowledgments

THE *ACTION OF Purpose* series was a labor of love: love for my God, love for my fellow man, and love for the art of creation. I set out to write this particular series in a way that I felt it had not been done before—mixing the indelible truth of the gospel with the harsh truth of this depraved world. I wanted to tell the story that God wanted told—one that mirrored his own book, a story of desperate faith and true purpose. I hope that in the reader's eyes I have met that mark.

There are just a few people I feel compelled to thank for their support and assistance in bringing this final chapter of the *AOP* trilogy to life.

To Kara, your constant gentleness, selflessness, and patience are indispensable commodities in my life. None of these stories would be written without your unfailing love and support.

My proofreaders, David Jones and Gareth Worthington (author of the excellent *Children of the Fifth Sun* series)—your thoughtful yet harsh constructive criticism has enhanced this novel beyond measure.

To Tzviel "BK" Blankchtien, my very good friend, whose personal experience as an Israeli soldier helped greatly in the core formation of Ari. Thank you, brother (she turned out awesome!).

The editing team at CreateSpace who handled my manuscript and did a wonderfully professional job tightening the narrative and removing all the small inconsistencies that plague any creative effort.

I also owe a great many thanks to any and all who contributed to this work in ways large and small. It is because of you and your support and/or feedback that this project is a reality.

Finally, I thank you, the reader. The sheer fact that you hold this book means you had the heart to take up this journey in the first place. By purchasing this book, you are also an instrumental asset in the war on human trafficking. Thank you for your support.

Taking a Stand against Human Trafficking

We cannot simply bandage the wounds of victims
beneath the wheels of injustice.
We must drive a spoke into the wheel itself.

—Dietrich Bonhoeffer

ONE HUNDRED PERCENT of the profits from every physical and digital book sold in the Action of Purpose series will go toward combating the epidemic of sex trafficking in the United States.

Buy a copy of *Through the Fury to the Dawn, Into the Dark of the Day,* or *Against the Fading of the Light,* and an equal contribution will be made to Blanket Fort Hope and/or The Wellhouse, two faith-based nonprofit organizations dedicated to stopping the sex trafficking of women and children and assisting in the recovery of those affected by this evil practice.

Please also consider leaving a review of this book online on Amazon, Goodreads, or social media. Reviews increase exposure, and help generate more profits for these incredible charities.

For more information about other books in this series or future projects in the works, visit the series website at www.actionofpurpose.com or the author's website www.stujonesfiction.com.

Made in the USA
Columbia, SC
01 March 2021